The
Penalty

NIKKI JEWELL

This one goes out to my ever growing indie author family. You are my inspiration, my support system, and my knowledge base. You help me celebrate the wins, and survive the self doubts. I couldn't do it without you.

CW & TW

CONTENT WARNINGS

Thanks for choosing The Penalty. Here's a few things you should know going in. There may be some spoilers, so feel free to skip if you've got no triggers.

This is a steamy romance novel and contains explicit open door sexual situations, as well as alcohol consumption. The hockey boys are a little crude and use a fair bit of adult language, so if this offends you, this isn't the book for you. This is intended for a mature over eighteen audience.

Some events or situations may be triggering for some including talk of past childhood neglect, food insecurity, foster care and alcohol and drug abuse by a parent. The death of a parent is mentioned. Although there is nothing too graphic on page, I would read with caution if this is a trigger of yours.

I care about my readers well being and mental health.

1. Go Big or Go Home – American Authors
2. Bad Habits – The Federal Empire
3. I Feel Good About This – The Mowgli's
4. Turn – The Wombats
5. Trampoline – The Unlikely Candidates
6. Carry On – Young Rising Sons
7. Ready Set Let's Go – Sam Tinnesz
8. Born Ready – Zayde Wolf
9. Mustang Kids – Zella Day, Baby E
10. New Best Friend – Neon Trees
11. Poison – Rita Ora
12. Church – Aly & AJ
13. Honest – Song House, Kyndal Inskeep
14. Do I Wanna Know? (triple j Like A Version) – CHVRCHES
15. River – Mily Cyrus
16. Believer – American Authors
17. Sinner – Andy Grammer
18. The Walker – Fitz and The Tantrums
19. Live A Little – Chaz Cardigan
20. Radio – Lana Del Ray
21. Sparks Fly (Taylor's Version) – Taylor Swift
22. sick of myself – Whethan, Nessa Barrett
23. Slow Hands – Niall Horan
24. You – The Pretty Reckless
25. Hey Heartbreaker – Dream Wife

CHAPTER ONE

RUNAWAY TRAIN

CECE

Waking up in jail was not how I planned to end my junior year at Cornell. But here I am with a demolition crew jackhammering my skull from the inside. The hot tingle at the back of my throat warns me I'm about to make a bad situation worse by hurling on the cold, concrete floor.

I roll over to at least avoiding puking on myself. Although, judging from the crustiness of my hair, I may have already achieved this at least once. My body hits the unforgiving floor with a painful thump that's going to leave bruises. My hand is shaky when I reach up to brush away the tangled mess of my hair, swallowing hard to keep the remaining contents of my stomach down.

What the fuck happened last night? My memories have that hazy, faraway quality of a drunken night. The last thing I remember is being surrounded by people. My house full of all my friends, and acquaintances. Not to mention the hundred or so strangers who were more than happy to take advantage of everything proximity to the Whitaker heir offers. The party was thumping as we celebrated the end of another school year.

After that? I search my memory like a CSI agent, trying to find any strand of evidence to help me solve the problem of how I ended up here. Darkness, darkness, and then a single patch of gray.

My best friend, Pen, has her talons in my arm as she drags me out my front door. Bella is with us, and I can hear the shadow of Trent's pretentious laugh. Wait? Why exactly was he with us? Our on-again, off-again relationship is definitely in a permanent off position. Who knows with him, though. He was probably trying to creep his way into Bella's pants. She's the only one of my friends he hasn't slept with at some point or another. Our little inner circle tends toward the incestuous.

But that's all I've got. No matter how hard I try, there's nothing after that but a dark void. What is wrong with me? I learned my lesson the last time I got blackout drunk. Callie's New Year's Eve party, the year I turned eighteen. Or at least I thought I had, but apparently not. A few years later, I'm right back where I started.

Why did I let myself get to that point? Maybe it was the message from my mother that they wouldn't be able to make it to my art show. Maybe it was catching Trent getting a blow job from my econ tutor in the library. At ten thirty in the morning. Who does that? It might be easier to deal with if I passed economics, but nope. One more thing to add to the Cece Whitaker list of fuck ups. My father is going to disown me when he finds out.

Fuck. This isn't me. Why have I let this year fly off the rails like a bullet train with a missing section of track?

I groan, then whimper when my head smacks into the concrete wall. Well, that's it. My life is over. My father is going to kill me, or maybe he'll lock me up in my room for the rest of my life, like Rapunzel. Not sure which is the worse option.

"Cecelia Whitaker. Come with me."

The sound of keys jingling and the groaning clank of a barred door sliding open forces me to peel open my crusty eyelids. It's as if it's reluctant to let anyone out. I've gotten myself into some shitty situations, but this is a first, and hopefully a last.

A gray-uniformed guard looks down at me, disgust pinching his mouth into a thin line as he roughly grabs my arm, but I hold the yelp inside. Never let them see when they hurt you. I know exactly what he's thinking. Spoiled princess thinks she can do whatever she wants. And maybe he's right. Maybe it's time I take a look at myself and try to do better.

The churning in my stomach kicks up a notch at the man here to bail me out. "Holmes?" My father didn't take the time to come for me himself. It's no surprise a five-and-a-half-hour drive would be too much of an inconvenience for his only daughter. But I think I'd prefer the judgment on his face to the sympathy on the face of my family's long-time driver.

"Miss Whitaker." He dips his silver head in a respectful nod I one hundred percent do not deserve.

I'm shuffled over to a desk to sign some papers, before accepting the large yellow envelope the officer hands me. He looks almost as tired as I am, with deep grooves etched beside faded blue eyes. My cell phone in its glittery silver wallet case slides out, along with a few items of jewelry. They're comically out of place under the fluorescent lights of the grim place. I blink, but the stabbing pain at the back of my eyeballs doesn't dissipate.

Each step to the car feels like I'm fighting through quicksand, and if I thought the artificial light inside was bad, I was mistaken. The sun is out in full force, and my stomach revolts against the increased throbbing in my head.

I bend over next to the shiny black sedan, retching the bile that is all that's left in me.

Holmes pats my back, handing me a bottle of water.

"You're being too nice to me, Holmes." My voice is a croaky rasp.

"Someone has to be," he says, swinging my door open and helping me inside.

Instinctively, I fling up an arm to shield my face from the familiar click of a camera. Fuck. That's all I need. To be exposed once again as an object of derision. If my twin brother Beau is the golden boy of the Whitaker family, I guess I'm the tarnished brass penny.

I curl up against the buttery soft leather seat and shut my eyes, taking small sips from the water bottle. It's clutched in my hand as if it can save me from the wrath

I'm awaiting at home. The chilled water flows down my parched throat like a glacial waterfall, soothing the ache.

"Miss Whitaker. We're home." Holmes's gentle call drags me back to reality, and I blink groggily awake.

As we pull up to the tall iron gates at the end of the long driveway, I'm regretting consuming multiple bottles of water as a tsunami crashes around my guts.

It's all fun and games until you pull up to the family estate. At least it's a long ass driveway. I drag my fingers through the snarled mess of my white-blonde hair and smooth a hand down the glittery skirt that matches my phone case. My phone flicks on when I snatch it up, studying the screen. Notifications are popping up at an alarming rate. Nope. Not even going to look. I do not have the energy to deal with that right now.

I'm out the door before Holmes comes around to open it for me. He'll be disappointed, but I think I need to get this over with as soon as possible. Face my punishment and move on. The rhythm of my heels clacking on the cobblestoned walk matches the thump of my heartbeat echoing in my head.

The heavy wood door gives under my trembly push and I'm here. Home bitter home. Goody. All traces of sleep are chased away by the anxious dread chilling my body.

Eddings takes a step back as I'm charging in. At least he looks annoyed with me, or maybe it's the fact that his stiff white collar is too tight. He pretty much always looks annoyed. Not like Holmes.

I give him a nod and the friendliest smile I can muster up. He returns the nod, but his frown only deepens as he takes in what I can only assume is a wild appearance. Definitely not suitable for the Whitaker family.

"Your father is expecting you in his study," he says to me in a voice as stiff as his collar.

The big window catches my eye as I'm passing through the large sitting room to get to my father's study. I could bust out and try to run for it. The manicured back lawn disappears into a wooded park I could hide in for days. But I'm not much of a hunter-gatherer, so I'd be pretty hungry at the end of a day or two. Not to mention the unsuitability of my club-worthy attire for backwoods survival.

Instead, I take a deep breath, pull my shoulders back and reactivate the steel rod in my spine years of debutante training have formed. My father is not one to accept weakness or any kind of defeat. It'll only make it worse if I show him the fear that's been swirling around inside since my unpleasant wake-up call this morning.

My three sharp knocks on the door are greeted with... a big fat nothing. Is he even here? Eddings doesn't lie. I don't think he's been programmed for deceit, so he has to be in there. Must be ignoring his wayward daughter.

Finally, he issues an impatient. "Come in."

I push open the door. If I was uncomfortable before, stepping into my father's inner sanctum ratchets up the feeling tenfold. This room is all him. Pure wealth and male energy. From the fuck-you heavy antique desk to the shelf of pretentious books behind him that rarely get read. Clothbound classics and rare first editions are the general vibe. Although there are a few shelves dedicated to newer business books, and I know he's read those.

He doesn't rise as I step inside, not that I expected him to. Just nods to the chair across from him. It's shorter than his, so he looms over you. In case his perfectly tailored custom suit and stern expression aren't intimidating enough.

"Cecelia."

I dig my teeth into my lower lip to avoid correcting him. I usually tell him to call me Cece like everyone else, but correcting him is not a wise idea at this particular moment in time. "Father."

"What do you have to say for yourself?" Straight to the point.

I've always thought this was the stupidest of questions. What exactly is he expecting me to say? I fucked up. I was possessed by a demon. Is there any answer that's going to make a difference to him? No. Why even try?

"It was just a party." Since I'm still in the dark about what happened after I left my party and the events that led to me ending up in a cell, I'm going with that.

The lines between his eyes deepen. "Cecelia. A party did not get you arrested and splashed across the Internet."

The cold sweat starts back up again. "Splashed all over the Internet?" That could mean anything. It could be the pictures that got taken earlier this morning while I puked outside the car. Or maybe it was whatever happened during the gaping black hole in my memory of last night. But since I'm still unaware of my crime, I'm quite concerned.

"Don't tell me you haven't seen the pictures."

Suffocating heat presses in on me, leaving me light-headed. Pictures posted online never cast you in a positive light when your family is as high profile as mine. At least not the ones of me.

I shake my head, struggling to swallow around the lump at the back of my throat.

He swings around the open laptop on his desk to reveal a picture of me. Am I??? Attempting to scale the statue of Ezra Cornell? I flip to the next picture, closing my eyes when I catch a flash of bright pink panties and... oh no... my tits. Holy fuck. My tits are on display on the Internet. And I'm the one lifting my shirt to show them to the world. I have nice tits, I'm not going to deny that, but I don't exactly want them on display for everyone with access to the world wide web. Especially not while I'm disgracing the statue of my school's illustrious founder.

My neck goes weak, head falling to my hands.

"Anything to say now?"

"I don't remember."

His long pause is designed to make me squirm, and it works.

"You don't remember." He enunciates each word like a laser-targeted weapon. "Cecelia. I thought you were over this nonsense. You had your wild spell, but when we sent you off to Cornell, we trusted you to uphold the family name like you have been raised to do since birth."

"I have been." Mostly. I haven't done anything of this magnitude, that's for sure. Nothing you would hear about if you weren't on the campus of Cornell. But I guess I let the stress of exams and unrealistic expectations take over. The Ivy League school filled with students who share the same blue blood as I do. Other people who would like nothing more than to bring people like me down. It's not fair, to be honest. Beau is the golden boy, the favorite twin, but he's allowed to party and drink, sleep around. Boys will be boys and all that misogynistic nonsense. But not their angel girl child. No, I'm supposed to keep quiet, smile demurely and drink my bottle of wine without a single wobble on my heels.

"No, you haven't been. Because if you had, this wouldn't have happened. If you were in control of yourself. Aware of your pedigree and the expectations of someone with our name, you would never have embarrassed us like this."

Of course. It's all about control with him. His control of us, and our control of ourselves. As if we're not college students with our own minds attached to underdeveloped prefrontal cortexes.

"I'm sorry."

"Sorry won't make this go away. I'm pulling you from Cornell."

That gets my attention. "What? I only have one year left. You can't pull me."

"You'll be transferring to Lakeview, where your brother can keep an eye on you."

I shake my head, gripping the desk until my knuckles ache. "No. All my friends are there. I know the professors."

"And look where your friends have gotten you? Disgracing our family name, failing economics. You're not going back."

"But..." The nausea is back again, twisting my insides into knots.

"There are no buts. It's already done. I've arranged for Lewis to send all the paperwork."

And there it is. My future settled with a few words to his lawyer. My years at Cornell wiped away like they meant nothing. I was finally going to be able to take the animation elective I've been aiming for my entire time at the school. What a waste.

"You'll take an online course this summer. I've hired you a tutor to make up that economics credit you failed, and you'll still graduate on time."

He turns his laptop back around, dropping his eyes to his keyboard, fingers punching the keyboard with harsh, staccato clicks. And just like that, I've been dismissed.

"Dad, please."

He doesn't look up from his screen, so I stand up, trudging out. My stomach growls at me and I look up, glancing toward the kitchen. Nope. I can't face our chef Shelley right now. She'd be so disappointed if she saw me in those articles.

I sigh, swiping a hand through my hair and making my slow way up the back stairwell. I don't want to run into anyone else, especially not my mother. If she's even here. I doubt she wanted any part in my disgrace. Leave father to deal with it and move on with her life. Gloss it over next time I see her or save it for later to send a targeted dig at me during a future argument.

Maybe Beau is home. He might drive me crazy sometimes. He might be overprotective and the standard I can never live up to, but I still love my twin. It's not his fault our fucked-up world has such gross double standards.

I guess there is one bright spot in this disaster. I'll get to see him more often now that we'll be going to the same school. Hell, maybe I can live with him. That has both pluses and minuses. Pluses, hot hockey boys, minuses my brother monitoring my love life. Definitely no hockey boys. Bad idea all around.

Chapter Two

Unwanted Visitors

Dev

"Lakeview, Lakeview, Lakeview!!!" The entire team is chanting as we crash through the front door of the hockey house. I'm going to miss these guys so fucking much. Saying goodbye to Woodsy, Seb, and Jacks hurts. I've been playing with them since my freshman year, and they fought their way into my life, getting closer to me than anyone else. At least I've still got Beau.

"Dev, man." Beau is slurring his words as he slings an arm around my shoulder. His blue eyes are glassy, hair slipping out of its usual smooth style. I guess getting drunk might make it easier. Numb the sense of loss as our closest friends head off to live their dreams. But that's not my thing. Not after the things I saw growing up.

"What?"

"It's just you and me now."

It's true. We're like a band breaking up after years together, but instead of making kickass music, we've been playing stellar hockey. Our tightly meshed team could almost read each other's minds.

"Yeah."

"That's all you have to say?"

I shrug. What else is there to say? There's nothing we can do to change the facts. Their lives are moving forward.

Everyone is reluctant for the night to end, but at least it's only the team tonight. Usually there would be a gaggle of random college students hanging out in this place, wrecking Beau's house. Girls trying to sleep with us. Not in the mood for that.

"What are you up to this summer, Lucy?" Our sophomore goalie, Jenson, comes bouncing up to me. Apparently, he thinks he thinks he's going to slide right into the spot Jacks is leaving behind. Intrusively friendly. Entitled to personal details I don't share easily with anyone.

My right eyebrow heads straight for my hairline, and I cross my arms over my chest, leaning back in my seat.

Beau laughs. "JJ, my man. If you're looking for a conversation, you're nattering at the wrong defender. You have not earned the right to more than single word responses from Lucy. Take it easy on him. He's shy."

I roll my eyes at him. It took a while, but he earned one of the limited places of trust in my life.

"Tell the man what you're up to this summer, Devlin." He's going to leave a handprint with how hard he slaps me on the back.

I roll my eyes at my best friend. "Working."

"That's cool. I've got a job lined up with my dad's company. Only a couple of days a week, so I'll have plenty of time for practice. He hired me a new goalie coach for the summer. Blake Thompson. You've probably heard of him. He's trained some of the best. You know..."

"We're done here." I cut him off. That's way more information than I needed from the young punk, but he can't seem to keep his words contained.

JJ pulls back for a second, brushing a hand through the shoulder-length mess of brown hair hanging in his face.

Beau's shoulders are shaking beside me as JJ takes off to spout nonsense at a more receptive audience.

"Do we have to let those two move in with us next year?" I ask Beau, eyeing JJ and Grant, who are now competing to get their voices heard. I guess I survived living with Jackson, though, so I can eventually handle these two. Yeah, maybe by this time next year when I'm on my way out.

"We don't have to, but I think the place would be lonely with only you and that broody fucker to keep me company." He nods at the corner where Cole is sitting with Jacks. He was all by himself until Jacks descended on him, and now it looks like they're actually engaged in a conversation.

"Sounds good to me."

"Awww, Lucy, you would be lonely too. I know you'd never admit it, but you like the company."

I stare at him through narrowed eyes. "Do I?"

He nods. "Yes. You do. You're going to miss us over summer break, all alone in this huge house. Are you sure you don't want to come home with me? My family wouldn't mind. If they even noticed you were there. They're away so much we'd have the place to ourselves more often than not. Other than Sissy, but she's got her own packed social schedule. It would make the summer break so much better."

I shake my head. "Can't. Got my jobs lined up."

"You could get a job or three in Pittsburgh."

He's persistent. That's for sure. But I'm already taking enough of his charity living in this place. Rent here is way cheaper than anything else in the college town, but that's the benefit of his parents owning the house. I wonder if they'll sell it after he graduates or keep it as an investment. Sounds like something rich people do. Not anything within the scope of my life experience.

"I'm good. Thanks for letting me stay here."

"It wouldn't be the same without you, man." A warm smile full of perfect teeth flashes across his face. "And maybe try to take it easy on the new guys. They mean well. They're just like little puppies that aren't quite housebroken yet." Beau can come across as a cocky asshole sometimes, but he cares so much about the team.

"I'm not potty training anyone. Sounds like a job for you, captain."

He shakes his head at me. "Shoot me a message if you want to come for a visit. You're always welcome."

I know he means it, but I've been burned before by people who claimed they cared about me. This can't last.

We'll get through this year and move on with our lives. The only bright spot is the pro contract I'm going to sign with Vancouver. As long as nothing goes wrong, I'll set myself up for the rest of my life. After graduation, I never want to rely on anyone else or worry about how I'm going to pay for my groceries.

Beau is great, but he lives in a very different world than I do. He'd never understand how important it is for me to earn as much as possible over the summer. I need to be able to afford the bills not covered by my scholarship, plus save whatever I can.

"Sure."

"I know you don't mean it, but I'm still putting it out there. I've gotta go make Woodsy and Seb do some shots before they try to sneak out of here with their girls."

He pushes up, swaggering over to the other guys. Might be time for me to call it a night. Slip out of here before things get too emotional. Yes, I'll miss the members of our team who are graduating this year, but I'm not shedding tears over it. Too many people have come and gone from my life. Plus, they're moving on to better things. The life I want and will do everything I can to get.

I'm the first one up. A major advantage to not drinking alcohol is no hangovers. I head down to the gym space in the basement to work out. My headphones are blaring a pounding rock beat in my ears, and who knows how much time has passed when Beau steps through the door.

I grab my towel, swiping it down my soaked face. It's been longer than I thought.

"What are you punishing yourself for?" Beau asks, tilting his head so a chunk of his dark blond hair falls in his eyes. It's unusual to see him before he's perfectly put together.

"I'm not punishing myself. Just working out. Isn't that what we're supposed to do, captain?" I ask my friend. He's been given the captain spot next year with Aspen leaving, and I'm proud of him. He deserves it. He was raised to be a leader. Me, I was born to be just what I am. A bruiser. An enforcer. We're a perfect defensive duo.

"Yes, but not right this second. You can take a day off, Dev."

I can't. Not one day of this summer will be wasted. I'll be at work, at the gym, or on the ice when I can snag some time there. My job helping at the local rink at least guarantees me some ice time.

"Nope."

"Fine. Are you at least going to come up to say goodbye?"

I shake my head. "Going to work." I've got my landscaping job starting today. The source of the bulk of my income. It's a decent paying job with the city. And I get to be outside in the sun all day. I prefer that to being cooped up in an office or a store. I'll take the freedom and fresh air every day. Enclosed spaces make my skin crawl. As a bonus, it's a solid workout. I'll be even more jacked when the guys move back at the end of the summer.

He pulls me in for a bro hug, which I tolerate only from him.

"Have a good summer," I say.

"I'll see you later, man. You know I'm not leaving until this evening."

I dip my head in a nod but refrain from correcting him. I'm working at the rink after the landscaping gig, so I won't be home until the rest of them have cleared out. It's for the best.

I fucking hate goodbyes.

Hockey keeps me in amazing shape, but I'm still exhausted when I hop off at the bus stop down the street from our house. A long, hot shower and an easy dinner are in my immediate future. My mouth is already watering at the thought of the leftover pizza in the fridge.

Beau ordered a pie of every flavor for last night's blow out. Detroit style. The best. And now, with the rest of the horde cleared out, all the leftovers are mine. It'll feed me for a week. Maybe a few days. All this manual labor is making me exceptionally hungry.

A rusty old silver Civic looks out of place parked down the street from our house. Probably from one of the other student houses. Maybe a summer subletter. Not my concern.

I devour all four steps up to our front porch in one leap, letting myself in and taking a moment to breathe in the peace and quiet. It's strange though. Walking in and not getting pounced on by Jacks with a million questions or having Seb drag me off to play Mario Kart. I'm not sure what to do with myself.

Shower or food first? My stomach growls as I roll my aching shoulders. Food first. Even though I know it's still going to be there when I get out of the shower, it's hard to break the habit of scarfing down every bite as soon as it's in front of me. I'm shoveling a cold slice of Hawaiian into my mouth when something dark flashes past the corner of my eye. I cautiously set the rest of the slightly gross concoction of pineapple and ham on the counter, swiveling to track the movement.

A tiny fuzzy thing darts out, ripping a scream from my chest that a banshee wouldn't be ashamed of. Unfortunately, the creature is not phased. Instead of fleeing, the thing runs at me, and I bolt.

Fuck the pizza. Fuck the shower. Fuck the house. My skin is tingling all over and the heavy thud of my heart pounds in my ears as I make it out the front door, slamming it behind me. The frame is still shuddering as I slide down the smooth surface until my ass hits the porch.

Stupid. It's a stupid, harmless mouse. I try to catch my breath, dropping my head into my hands. As I'm starting to get my shit together and calm my breathing, a shadow falls over me.

At least none of the guys witnessed that stunning episode. They'd never let me live it down. The Devil is afraid of rodents.

But when I look up, something far worse than a mouse is standing over me, worn hands clasped in front of worn Levi's.

"The fuck are you doing here?" I snarl at him. If I could back up, I would, but I'm trapped between him and the rodent-infested house. No escape. I glance beside me at the empty street. The streetlamps cast eerie shadows, and there's no sign of a bus. I sigh. Even if there was, what would I do? Go stand there and wait for the bus while the man who contributed to half my DNA follows me. *Get your head on straight.*

"Are you okay?" His wrinkled brow and muddy brown eyes give him the appearance of a concerned parent. The resentment simmering inside since he showed up is precariously close to boiling over.

"Fine until I saw you." Not exactly true, but I'd take a mouse over this man any day.

The hard lines of his face stand out against the spider-web of tiny red veins spreading across his nose. His eyes look clear, though.

"Devlin. I understand you're mad at me, but I've been getting help. I've been clean and sober for over a year now and I wanted to come see you. Apologize. See if there's any way..."

"There's not." No way in this life or any other is he getting any semblance of forgiveness from me.

"I get it. But is there something wrong? You came tearing out of the house like it was on fire... Should I call the police?"

My laugh is flat and empty. "No. Just a fucking mouse." What do I care if he thinks I'm a wuss for my fear of mice? It's his own damn fault. No five-year-old should have to wake up, shivering under their thin blanket because the heat got shut off again, only to find a rat crawling across their arm. Fuck him.

"I can help you get rid of it." He offers, looking hopeful.

I want to stomp on his hope and crush it under my heel. "Not a chance you're coming in there with me." He'd probably steal the artwork hanging from the walls. At least the guys have moved most of their stuff out for the summer, but I'm sure the Whitakers don't buy cheap prints from the discount store at the mall.

"We could go out. I could buy you a drink."

"Didn't you say you were sober?"

"I am. I can get myself a soda or something. Coffee." I shake my head at him to back off as he takes a step closer to me.

"I don't drink."

"Good, good." He's nodding. "Dinner. We could get something to eat. Pizza? That used to be your favorite, right?"

I unfold my body, rising to my feet, uncomfortable with staring up at him. It makes me feel like I'm five again.

I gain a sense of control over the situation, staring down at him, and he takes a step back when I move in closer. That's also a satisfying feeling. "You know nothing about me, and you never will. Why did you really come here, Dad?" I put as much scorn into the word as I can. He's no father to me. "I don't have any money. I'm a student, barely paying my bills." The scholarships only cover so much.

His lips are turned down at the corners, eyes sad, but I'm not falling for his show. "I'm not looking for anything. I told you. I'm sober. I've got a job. I got my mechanic's license." He reaches up to rub at his scalp and I hate that how familiar the gesture is. "I'm doing better. In fact. If you need help with anything. Extra money for school. I can give you some."

Rage and anger, sadness and fear are all swirling around in me, competing to take over, but I let the rage win out. That's the easiest. The best. The one I'm most familiar with. I lift a shaky hand to poke him in the chest. "I don't need or want anything from you. Except for you to leave and never come back here. I don't want to see you again."

He backs up. Arms in the air. "I understand you're not ready. I won't come back here, but I'm going to leave my phone number and email address here. Please call me when you're ready to talk."

He holds a shaky hand out, offering me a crumpled piece of paper. I snatch it away, jamming it into my back pocket. "I won't." It's not like I even want the paper, but I also don't want him standing here any longer than necessary.

"I hope you do, Devlin. It looks like you're doing well, and I'd like a chance to get to know my son. I've missed so much, and life is too short to not make amends."

"I'm not your son. Forget about me and lose this address." How did he even get it?

I turn to go back into the house.

"Good luck with the hockey season next year, and congratulations on winning the championship."

I push through the front door. He doesn't deserve an answer, but at least that solves one conundrum. He must have seen an article about the team. That's how he found me. He's hoping to ride my coattails when I become a pro hockey player. All the making amends stuff is bullshit. It has to be.

The house rattles, shaking the expensive paintings as I slam the door on him. I slip to the floor, knees weak, trembling all over as I hug myself. It's like I'm a kid again, left at home by myself for three days with no food while he's off drunk somewhere.

The emptiness of the house is less friendly now, like it's about to swallow me whole and drown me.

I take deep rhythmic breaths to keep the fear at a reasonable level when the little mouse pokes its snout out of the kitchen doorway, blinking jet-black eyes at me. There's no more room in me for fear, so I glare at the creature until it scuttles away. Tomorrow, I can buy some traps. I'll never sleep knowing that thing is sharing the space with me.

I drag my exhausted body up. The only thing on my mind now is a hot shower. Even talking to him left me feeling dirty, small, and helpless, and I hate that feeling. I want to wash it away in a stream of scorching heat.

Not the way I wanted to start my summer.

CHAPTER THREE

GOOD BEHAVIOR

CECE - 3 MONTHS LATER

S ometimes good behavior pays off. I couldn't convince my father to let me keep my car for the semester. But he oh so graciously granted me an early release to attend the Great Lakes Fan Con I've been waiting for all year. He kept me so busy with community service, and doing grunt work at his office, I only hung out with my friends at home a handful of times over the summer. Turns out I wasn't as upset about it as I thought I'd be. After what went down at Cornell, all the pieces have been falling into place. I'm realizing the toxic friends who share my privileged background are not the ones who are going to stand by me in a crisis.

But other than looking down his nose at my online "nerd friends," my father doesn't consider them a threat.

Hilarious. If he knew the things I've done at comic conventions, he might reconsider. But I'm not telling.

And now I'm free. The convention is in Detroit, not far from my new school, so I told him I wanted to settle into the house before my roommates show up. The roommates I've only met on a video call, by the way. I'm sure it'll be fine. If not, I'll hang out at Beau's house. I'm not so into hockey after being dragged to chilly arenas a million or so times during my childhood, but the hockey players? I can get behind those smoking hot athletes. Not that Beau will let them go anywhere near his precious twin sister, but he can't stop me from looking.

The closer I get to the hotel, the taller I'm sitting, and I'm staring out the window, watching each tree pass by, bringing me closer to the con. The bus was a no go. Dad wouldn't even let me take the train. So, I'm watching the world go by from the passenger seat of a sedan driven by Holmes. Poor guy.

"Sorry Dad made you drive me, Holmes."

"Oh, I don't mind, Cecelia. I don't get on the open road as often as I like, anyway. City driving is not the same." Having known me since I was a baby, he's one of the few people I haven't been able to convince to use my full name.

"I still appreciate it. Thank you."

"My pleasure."

"Too bad Colin couldn't come with us." Holme's son is only two years older than me, and he's a major comic book fan. I've always gotten along with him.

"Yes. He would have enjoyed that."

"Right? How's his new job going?" After graduation, he got a job with a new tech start up in Boston. He's my go to fixer for all computer related problems. I'm out of options if turning it off and back on again doesn't work.

A smile spreads across his face, and his brown eyes gleam. I'm one hundred percent sure I've never seen that much pride on my father's face. "He's loving it. I don't understand a word when he tells me about all the computer stuff, but it's going great."

My smile is a little tight, but I nod. I'm so happy for Colin, but I can't stop a twinge of jealousy from creeping up. If only my dad and mom were as accepting as Holmes. But it's fine. After I graduate, the world is wide open. I can do the artist thing. Just have to get through this last year of college without getting into any trouble.

We pull around the curved driveway, stopping at the drop-off zone in front of the convention hotel. As soon as the tickets went on sale, I locked in a room. Since I wasn't expecting to bring a chaperone, the hotel predictably filled up fast. Holmes is staying somewhere on the outskirts of the city. He'll make the trek back to Pittsburgh tomorrow. At least my father didn't make him stay to babysit me at the con.

I drop a hand on the older man's jacketed forearm as he rises to help me with my luggage.

"It's okay. I got this Holmes."

His eyes crinkle at the corners, and he tips his hat at me. "Embarrassed to be seen with this old man?"

"Obviously." I laugh, but yes, I am. Not because of him, specifically. He's fantastic. Although I try not to let people's opinions of me cut too deep, the little scars I've accumulated over the years often break open under scrutiny. And showing up with my family's chauffeur at a comic book convention is a little too direct a target. Not that anyone will even notice me yet. Hopefully.

"Well then. You enjoy yourself and have a great school year."

"I will. Thanks again for the ride. I'll see you at Christmas, if not before." Probably not. There's not much reason to go home before then. I can beg off Thanksgiving. Fingers crossed. Schoolwork is always a solid excuse. And with the only family member I care to see on the regular at the same school, I'm good. Although Beau will probably drive me up the wall within a week if he gets all protective brother on me.

I tug the brim of my black baseball hat down lower, adjusting the white-blonde ponytail sticking out the back. I'm not usually a ball cap kind of girl, but there's been a media target on my back since the "incident" and my hair is like a beacon. The flurry has died down, but I'm still on constant high alert. The spotlight on my family is always there, but when it's focused on me, the unflattering light they cast me in is oppressive. Those are the times I envy my brother. He gets caught coming out of a club looking a little disheveled with a girl on his arm and he's a hero. If I'm caught in a miniskirt with smeared lipstick, I'm a drunk hot mess whose thighs are looking thicker than usual after putting on the frosh fifteen. Assholes and their double standards.

All the negative thoughts dissipate as I pass through the slowly revolving front door into the bustling hotel lobby. It's not the usual crowd of hotel guests. The business people in their tailored suits and crisply ironed blouses look out of place surrounded by the fans in jeans and graphic tees. It must feel like an invasion of their natural habitat. A colorful array of unnatural but gorgeous hair colors is represented. Maybe I should have dyed my hair before I got here. That would be a surefire way to disguise my signature locks, but I've got to be on my best behavior. And that one time I experimented with royal blue hair had me in tech jail for an entire semester of high school. I'm hoping to earn my car back by the new year.

I join the lineup of people shuffling around as they wait to check in, avoiding the VIP desk. That would shine a glaring spotlight on me, and I'd probably get identified. Not the way to start off the weekend.

The small group waiting in front of me is debating the merits of the newest Game of Thrones spinoff series. One of the girls has shimmery metallic pointed ear cuffs that are giving me jewelry envy. If it wouldn't draw attention to me, I'd ask her where she got them, but that kind of conversation can wait until tomorrow when I can melt into the crowd and hide under a wig. Thank goodness for cosplay.

My knuckles are aching from clenching my huge rolling bag, and I force myself to relax my grip. The next desk agent flashes me a smile that puts every inch of his bright white teeth on display as he calls me over.

Excited jitters are twisting my insides as I step forward, sliding my credit card across the desk.

"Cece Whitaker," I whisper, eyes darting left and right.

I hate the way his smile falters for a second before he composes himself, turning his eyes down to stare at the screen in front of him as he taps away on his keyboard. His dark brows draw together.

"Miss Whitaker, you're a VIP member of our rewards program. There was no need to wait in this line." He turns to look at the lonely-looking agent manning the VIP desk.

I sigh, leaning forward to drop my elbows on the smooth surface of the desk. "Listen. I'm trying to keep a low profile here. I would appreciate it if you would keep it to yourself that I'm staying here. Please." I lean in a little closer, pleading with my eyes. I'm not afraid to beg.

His shoulders straighten as his professional smile snaps back into place.

"Of course, Miss Whitaker. I would never give out guest information. Privacy is our policy here at the Four Winds."

"Thank you."

I sign my scratchy signature on the paper he slides over and slip him a hundred after he hands me the little envelope with my room keys.

He doesn't flinch, dropping a casual hand over the bill. His cuff slips up to reveal a mid range gold watch.

I duck my head down again as I pad along the shiny lobby floor to reach the bank of elevators. Twenty-third floor. I keep my head lowered the entire ride up as people come and go, shooting through the doors as soon as they slide open.

My shoulders don't relax until I tap my key on the door pad and the green light flashes.

My first move is to hang the do not disturb sign on the door before I slide the bolt and latch home. I spin around, letting out a squeal as I spot the huge white bed. Finally. I'm free.

I make a run for it, jumping onto the bed with a soft bounce and a giggle.

Spending the summer on my best behavior left me drained. I'm going to enjoy the fuck out of myself anonymously this weekend before I head off to my new school. Beau will do his best to keep his eye out for me. The way he acts, you'd think he was born two years earlier not two minutes. Nope. But he's so busy with school and hockey, and we're living in different houses, so it shouldn't cramp my style too much.

If I thought the hotel lobby was a fun place yesterday, today it's like an explosion of beautiful chaos. Zombies are mingling with vampire hunters. Anime characters huddle in a group around a full-blown transformer with working mechanical parts built into the suit. The colors, sound, and energy are electric. I'm with my people for the first time all summer.

The energy of all these passionate, creative types fills me up, replenishing my soul. My fingers are twitching to work on my own graphic novel. I brought the usual assortment of notebooks, sketchbooks, and my tablet, but I don't expect to use them much over the weekend. I'll be too busy absorbing all the sights and sounds, maybe making a new friend or two.

I follow the crush of people down the tunnel to join the registration line. The wait is going to fly by. I stretch my neck out, standing on my tiptoes, searching for my friend Tess. She said she'd meet me in line at nine, and I know she's planning on dressing up as Storm. There are a handful of heads with long white hair, but not hers.

It is hard to see over the massive guy standing in front of me. He makes a better wall than the temporary panels dividing the conference area into sections. His black tee clings to unreal back muscles, and I'm tempted to reach out to trace a finger around the ridges of his delicious, muscled arms. But that would be rude, so I resist the urge. An assortment of tattoos sneaks out below the short sleeves, and a shiver clenches my gut at the same time my phone has the audacity to ring in my pocket. Should have muted it.

At least I sewed pockets into the tight bodysuit of my costume, so it's accessible. I drop my eyes to the black boots as I answer the call.

"Cece. I'm glad you answered. I'm so sorry, but I have to cancel. I'm in the hospital. It's a nightmare. I'm so pissed I'm going to miss this weekend."

My stomach flips over. "Tess, are you okay? What's wrong?"

"Oh, I'm fine. You know I was at the regional finals this week?"

"Yes."

"Welp. I landed badly, and my leg is a mess. Now I've got to have surgery. Ugh, I'm so mad I'm going to miss the con."

"What? I'm so sorry." Tess is a gymnast. She competes at a high level, but she sounds more upset she's missing the expo than the fact her season is likely over.

"It's fine. Hurt like a beast, but I'll recover. It doesn't really matter."

Disappointment eats away at the high of excitement I've been riding. She was one of the first people I met when I started dabbling in online fan groups and we've been tight ever since. But we've only gotten to meet in person a few times since she lives on the other side of the country. "You look after yourself."

Her voice is way too chipper for someone with a broken leg. "I'll be fine. But I'm going to need you to do something for me."

"What's that?"

"Have twice as much fun. And send me pics. Maybe bang a hot dude. Just make sure he takes his mask off first. Remember Iron Man? Ugh."

I laugh. I do. She met up with some guy dressed as Iron Man two years ago. It was an unpleasant surprise when she brought him back to our hotel room and he took off his mask to reveal a sweaty, bald dude twenty years older than us.

"Will do. And don't worry. I'll never forget. He's imprinted on my brain for all eternity, thanks to you."

There's a beeping sound and a voice in the background. "Kay. I gotta go. My doctor's here. Talk soon."

"Bye." I click off the phone. While it's disappointing Tess won't be here, I'm going to enjoy every second of this weekend.

Someone shoves me from behind as I'm sliding my phone back in my pocket. I stumble forward, clipping the brick wall of a guy waiting in front of me. I step past him, trying to regain my balance.

Two warm, calloused hands close around my biceps as I'm heading toward a treacherous sea of feet.

"I'm so sorry," I apologize, looking up at the guy who's gotta be a full foot taller than me.

"Not your fault."

His brow is pinched with anger, and I'm about to shy away from his glare when I realize it's not directed at me. He's focused on the pair of guys behind me still goofing around and body checking each other, but they freeze mid headlock, heads tilting up to take him in.

"Watch it."

"Sorry, man." The shorter one drops his gaze, shuffling his feet.

"Just be careful." He nods at them, turning back to me.

"You okay?" His voice is deep and rough, as if he doesn't use it often, and his eyes are a rich brown color I could melt into. His jaw is so sharp you could chop wood with it and there are hard muscles packed across his massive chest and arms as well. Like a sexy lumberjack. He can chop my wood any day. Yum. This is not an Iron Man situation. Tess would totally approve.

I take a hot minute to drag my eyes away from the ridged muscles visible under the black tee. It's hanging on to his chest for dear life. When I do, a white skull symbol snags my attention.

"Punisher!" The excitement has me bouncing up and clapping my hands. I scan the handful of guys jostling each other in front of him and the assortment of anime characters behind me, but it doesn't look like he's with anyone. "I think this was fate. Me standing behind you in line today. We were meant to be friends."

He raises one brow, tilting his head to look down at me, and a barely audible grunt comes from his mouth.

He doesn't look hostile, just confused by my random burst of enthusiasm, so I keep going. "I mean. Obviously, I'm Black Widow. You're the Punisher. We should team up. Are you here all weekend? Or have you got a single-day pass?"

His lips twist the slightest bit at the corners. Pretty sure he's trying to hold in a laugh, but he finally gets a couple of words out. "All weekend."

"Amazing. Are your friends here yet, or are you meeting them inside? My con bestie bailed on me, so I'm in the market for some hang buddies."

"No friends. I'm here alone." The smile is visible now. He couldn't keep it in.

"You don't have any friends? I'm so sorry. I bet you're glad you've got me now."

He shakes his head, but then his eyes trail down the skintight latex encasing my body. The heat in his gaze is another sign I've got him. A buddy for the weekend. What kind of buddy is still to be determined.

If he turns out to be a complete weirdo, I can ditch him. But if not... well, maybe I can make use of the solo room I've got now and really enjoy my last weekend of freedom before it's back to school.

The mass of people shifts in restless anticipation as the doors swing open and the line inches forward as people step up to the registration table. It's on.

My new friend doesn't seem to notice the shift of excitement in the air, his eyes still glued to me in bemusement.

"The line's moving. Come on. We've got to get ready."

"To move three inches at a time?" he asks.

"Yup. Limber up." I reach over my head, but my attempt at a stretch fails as the tight fabric groans. I shrug, flicking the red wig over my shoulders.

A short bark rips from his chest, and his shoulders shake. I broke him already.

"I thought that was going to be way more of a challenge."

"What?"

"Making you laugh."

His shoulders put extra strain on the shirt when he shrugs.

"Since we're going to be spending the weekend together, I should at least know your name. I can't call you Punisher all weekend. Although I will in company if you're a purist about staying in character."

His mouth opens, closes, and opens again as if he's reluctant to give me his name.

"I promise not to steal your identity." I tell him.

"Dev. My name's Dev. And you?"

"Cece." There's no hesitation for me. Sometimes I'm more cautious about giving out my real name. Especially after my most recent spectacular escapade. But there was not an ounce of recognition in his eyes, and he scanned me so intently it was almost like he could read my thoughts.

I hold out a hand to shake on it. His warm palm closes over mine, swallowing it up, and a tingle of excitement shoots through me at the contact. This is going to be an epic weekend. Maybe even life changing. I can feel it.

CHAPTER FOUR

CHERRY ON TOP

DEV

I'm not sure why I sought out the bubbly girl who claimed me as her con buddy in line. Normally, I'm more than happy to attend these rare events by myself. Between school, hockey, and jobs, I don't often get the opportunity, so I'm thrilled to be here. After we split up to join the alphabetical registration lines, I was planning on grabbing my lanyard and losing myself in the horde. It wouldn't be too hard with the mass of people who have already spilled into the sprawling conference center. And when I got through, I didn't spot her bright red Black Widow wig. Disappearing in this crowd would be easy. I'd be just another nerd, but I didn't. Instead, I leaned against a big square pillar, waiting until she came bouncing out the doors.

"Castle! You waited." The smile she gives me spreads across half her round face, and her blue eyes are sparkling when they land on me. Her use of my character's real name has my lips twitching for the second time since I met her.

"Looks like it, Romanoff."

Maybe I need to get laid. It's been a long summer working three jobs. Without the guys around to drag me to bars and social gatherings, it's been a few months since I enjoyed the company of a woman. That must be it. Those luscious curves encased in all that tight black latex are mesmerizing.

"Where to first?" She joins me at the little oasis by the pillar I found off to the side of the room. She's rooting through the black leather crossbody bag slung over her chest.

It's a nice touch. She brought a bag, but it blends in with her costume. My worn backpack might be out of place with the bad ass Punisher look, but I never leave home without it. Force of habit I haven't been able to shake despite my few years of security at Lakeview.

"It's got to be in here somewhere." She's got a wad of folded up papers in her hand, and she's still digging in her bag like a crazed squirrel.

Something gold catches the light as it clatters to the floor, and I duck down to pick it up at the same time as her. A musical laugh bubbles out as she looks up at me, and a pang of need punches me in the gut. She's even more gorgeous up close. Full lips painted into a defined bow, the shadow of a dimple in her chin, and round cheeks.

Her soft hand brushes mine as I pass her the tube of lipstick.

"Thanks." Her voice has gone a little husky and my eyes zero in on the line of her pale neck as she swallows hard.

"Of course. What are you looking for?" I ask her, straightening up and leaning back to put some distance between us. I refold my arms over my chest. My dick came to life at the sight of those lips, but now is not the time. If I'm lucky, maybe I'll get to taste them later.

"My schedule. I had the entire day planned out, but I don't know..." She trails off, holding up the wad of papers in front of me.

"I printed a schedule. Let me grab it."

Her eyes fall on the faded red backpack, and I hug it to my chest, eyes narrowing.

But the expected judgment never comes. Instead, she goes back to digging through the mess of her own bag. My shoulders relax and I drop a hand on hers to still the constant motion.

"I got this."

I pull a blue plastic folder out of the backpack, carefully fastening the snap before she can take a peek. It's got a printed copy of my hostel booking information, my bus tickets, con registration, and the schedule for the weekend. I've highlighted the events I want to attend and made some notes on the papers about tables to visit.

Her eyes widen, and she looks down at the mess in her hands sheepishly. "Impressive."

I shrug, a little embarrassed, but I need things to be organized. There was so much unpredictability in my childhood I can't help planning things out in detail. Make sure everything is in order, so I don't end up disappointed, or lost. Missing out on the thing I've saved up all year to attend. "Sorry."

"What? That's amazing. I only wish I were as organized as you."

I duck my head, fixating on the neon colors of the highlighted schedule in front of me. As I run a finger down the events, she leans in close, sneaking a look. A hit of her perfume washes over me. It's soft and bright, like clean laundry and fresh lemons.

"It's all coming back to me." She jabs at the paper. "I had my eye on most of the same panels, and I totally want to check out Heller's booth, too. I'm so into his Black Tree chronicles. So dark and dirty. I love his style."

"Really?" It's hard to keep the surprise out of my voice. His work is super gritty. I'm not sure what I expected from this woman, but it wasn't that. Figures. I should know better than to judge a person by their looks. Some of the worst people in my life hid behind veneers of generosity and kindness, but when they got you in private, you saw their true selves. Anyway, I should know better.

"Yeah, don't sound so surprised. A girl can do her makeup and wear pink and still be into dark stuff."

I check her out again. Seems like my eyes keep getting pulled back to her, trailing down her stunning body. I nod. "If we're going to hit the Women in Comics panel, we should go. Probably be busy."

"Yes. You're right. Let's go."

She jumps into action, tugging on my arm as she trots off to weave through the crowds of people milling about in excited groups. It's hard to keep up with her. My large body doesn't quite fit through the narrow holes she's punching through the attendees. I have to apologize more than once when an elbow or hand strays off the path to collide with a stranger.

There's a lineup at the door to Hall C, but it's not too bad yet. The panel doesn't start for half an hour, but it's in one of the smaller rooms, and I'm sure they've under-estimated the attendance for this one. There's still not enough female representation in the comic book world.

"I'm so glad I found you. I would have still been rifling through my papers looking for the schedule if you hadn't saved the day. And then what? I would have missed this panel. The one I've been waiting for. Hahn is my very favorite artist of any gender. The fact she's a woman is just the cherry on top."

"I'm sure you would have found someone else to be-friend. Or maybe grabbed the schedule from your pro-gram." I slip the folded stack of red paper from the swag bag I got when we checked in, waving it at her.

She actually smacks her forehead with her hand. I didn't think anybody did that outside of movies.

"Duh doi. Obviously, it's on there. I'm all flustered. Too much excitement. It's scrambled my brains."

"Why are you here by yourself?" She seems like the type of person who should be surrounded by a group of friends. Befriending random people is not my thing, but

I kind of wish it were a little easier for me. She didn't think twice before claiming the massive, frowning hockey player as her friend for the weekend. I wonder if she keeps all her new friends or leaves a trail of broken hearts behind.

"You think I can't show up at a con by myself because I'm a woman?" Her full lips push out in a pout.

"No, I didn't mean that." I'm stumbling over my words when I catch the little smile on her face. "Right, you're messing with me."

That chirpy little laugh comes out. "Yup. Not that I wouldn't come on my own if I didn't have someone to join me, but I had a con buddy. Someone from an artist's group on-line I'm tight with. She called this morning. Broke her leg and is unfortunately confined to a hospital bed for the weekend. So here I am, solo rider. I feel bad for Tess, but I might not have met you if she came along. So, there's a lighter side to the darkness. As usual."

My brows pull together and I'm yanked back to a time when there was nothing but darkness. Not even the tiniest pinprick of light or hope in the endless night.

A soft weight on my arm pulls me out of my memories. "I'm sorry. Did I say something wrong?"

I shake my head, trying not to get sucked back into the past. "No. No, sorry about that. I was just thinking about how there isn't always a bright spot in the darkness. Look at what happened to the Punisher after his family was murdered. He turned into this crazed vigilante. A great storyline, but probably not the best life for him."

"Ah, you're getting into character. I love it. But he is fictional. And these deep thoughts are for the philosophy panel. We can hit that one up later and you can get out all that angst."

Right. This is a fun and carefree weekend, and I'm here to enjoy myself. No use dwelling on the past. "You're right."

The enormous doors swing open and the anticipation of everyone around us swells to a crescendo, like the moment before the puck drops. As soon as we get to the front of the line, she grabs my hand darting through everyone on a direct track to front of the room. She miraculously snags us seats in the third row.

After settling into my seat, I turn to meet her blue eyes. "So I was your second choice?"

Confusion clouds her expression when she turns to me. "What?"

"Friend had to bail out, so I'm your second choice." Her eyes drop to my bare forearms when I cross my arms over my chest before bouncing back to my face. The slight pink tinge to her cheeks lets me know she appreciates the view.

Her mouth falls open, and her eyes widen. "But I..."

I lift an eyebrow and let one side of my mouth turn up the tiniest bit.

Realization dawns on her face that I am, in fact, fucking with her, but the smack she lands on my biceps barely registers.

"I can always make some new friends if you're going to be that way."

I shrug, but as she twists around in her seat to check out who else she might be able to hook up with, I get a little concerned. Making new friends this weekend wasn't on my agenda. It was supposed to be a solo adventure. After all, school starts in only a couple of weeks, and once the guys move back in, I'll be surrounded twenty-four-seven with chaos and intrusive teammates. Especially since Beau is letting JJ and Grant move in this semester. But I'm finding her company oddly enjoyable.

There's a very real chance of something more happening between us, and I'm hoping she'll be the one to break my dry spell. She is one of the hottest women I've ever laid eyes on, and the thought of getting a hold on those thick hips while I pound her from behind has popped into my head a few more times than I'd like. The way her eyes have been lingering on my body let me know it isn't outside the realm of possibility.

Even if it doesn't happen, the time I've spent with her has been enjoyable.

She turns back to me. "The possibilities are endless, but I guess I'll stick with you for now. You better watch yourself though, Castle."

Good. Looks like this weekend is going to be even better than I was hoping for.

The whirlwind morning didn't leave me any time to enjoy a snack or anything, and my stomach lets out an angry growl. The sharp pains of hungry are all too familiar. I try not to let myself get to that point, so I'm swinging my backpack over my shoulder to grab a protein bar when she turns away from the video game artist she was excitedly chattering with.

"Crap. You must be starving. That's a lot of muscle to maintain. What time is it, anyway?" She's glancing at her watch as she asks the question. "Two o'clock. I am so sorry. I got all caught up in the excitement. Sometimes I get so involved in things, I forget to eat." Her eyes are shining as she spins around, taking in the crowded room full of stars of the industry.

"It's fine. I've got snacks. Granola bar?" I pull a pack out of my bag to offer her one, but she shakes her head.

"No, let's go hunt down some proper food."

She's rifling through her bag, but I stop her when she pulls out the disorganized mess of papers.

"I've got it." I grab my folder flipping to the venue map. "Food this way."

She jumps up and claps her hands. "Perfect. I need something fried. Cheese would be a bonus. I've been eating way too healthy this summer."

She's off again. Sometimes she takes a hot minute to make a decision, but when she does, she's like a heat-seeking missile, determined in her course of action.

The forbidden smells of grease and dough assault my senses when we make it to the noisy hall where the food vendors are set up. Tables are packed into the space. Someone walks by with a juicy burger piled high with toppings that has my head turning to track his progress. While I'd love to grab one of those, my food budget is limited, so I brought a bunch of snacks and protein bars to survive the day. The food is always way too expensive at these things.

She passes by the big chain pizza joint selling droopy slices. "Definitely not pizza. I will be getting myself some authentic Detroit style pizza while we're here. The only question is what to choose. Nachos or fries? Mozzarella sticks? What are you going to get?" she asks.

"I brought food, I'm good."

"That's no fun. Are you on some special diet or something? My brother is so boring during the season. He's on this strict athlete diet. Nothing interesting. Is that your jam? You look like an athlete." She's eyeing me again with the same hungry look she gave a funnel cake someone walked by with.

Her thoughts seem to spill from her mouth so fast I'm having a hard time keeping up, but it's kind of perfect since I'm not much of a talker. "I am."

She's off on another tangent before I can expand on the thought, and I'm relieved. People can get a little weird when you tell them you're a hockey player with a direct line to the pros after you finish college. They're either doubtful or a little too interested in hopping on the train to ride along on your success.

"At least you can go find us somewhere to sit while I order some stuff."

I look at the mass of bodies jammed around the tables in the hall. This will require a bit of strategy. I hover around the edges, scanning the tables. A handful of people cleaning up their plates catches my eye, so I slide in to wait patiently beside them. Not too close or too far away. Another group walks up just as they're leaving, but when they catch sight of me, they nod and walk away in search of another option. Perfect.

It must have taken longer than I thought to secure the table, because I'm just pulling out my assorted snacks when I spot her. She's craning her neck at the edge of the crowd, eyes darting from table to table. Something I'm not used to. Being at this kind of event and having someone out there searching for me. I keep a low profile on campus, but I know that will probably change next year when I make it to the next level. Pro athletes have to accept a certain amount of recognition and adulation from fans. The fame is the one thing that makes me uncomfortable about going pro.

I stand up and wave until I catch her attention. She lights up, weaving through the tables until she skids to a halt beside me with an overflowing tray of delicious looking fried things.

"Wow. You went all out." My mouth waters at the smell, but I glance down at the cookie dough protein bar I brought along, tearing open the wrapper.

"Did you wait for me to start eating? That's so sweet."

I nod, trying not to be too noticeable about the fact that I'm tracking a gooey cheese covered nacho to her lips. She pops it in, moaning as she crunches down. The tip of her pink tongue darts out to catch a stray strand of cheese that's oozing out, and I have to fight the urge to offer my help.

"Amazing." The tray slides toward me at her push. "Help yourself. There's no way I'm going to eat this much food."

"It's okay. I'm set." I'm tempted, but don't want to mooch off her.

"No problem if you don't want, but if you're being polite, forget about it. What I don't eat is getting tossed, so please dig in."

The thought of good food going in the trash causes me physical pain. I give in, reaching over to snag a steaming fresh cut fry, and dunking it in the little pile of ketchup at the corner of the basket. The grease coats my tongue in a delicious rush of flavor and salt, and I'm quickly going back for seconds.

"Excellent. I'm happy you're sharing."

The chatter of the crowd around us fills in the silence as we crunch away at nachos and chomp on mozzarella sticks until she pushes herself away from the table.

"That's me defeated." She groans. "So tasty, but this costume is way too tight to eat another bite."

I'm getting pretty full too, but I can't let a bite go in the garbage. I just can't do it, so I power through.

"Do you usually come to cons alone?" she asks as I'm swallowing the last fry.

"Yup."

"Gotcha." Her hands fold together, and she leans in. "That's cool. Sometimes I do too. Or I go with an online friend. My real-life friends from my former school aren't into nerd culture like me. Are you in school or do you work?"

"College. I'm a senior."

We gather up our things to let the next group of people claim the space and start moving through the crowd to our next panel as she talks. "That's what I was hoping. I'm a senior too, but I couldn't quite judge your age. Not that there's anything wrong with dating an older man, but I was hoping you weren't secretly a fifty-year-old who aged really well."

"Fifty?"

She shrugs. "You never know. What are you taking in school?"

That's an easy one. "Business. You?"

"You are such an amazing conversationalist. I see I'm going to have my work cut out for me with you. I'll be digging for days just to find out if you had any pets when you were a kid."

Somewhere on the trip through the winding paths of the massive convention space, she picked up my hand, but I pull it away, running it along the top of my close-cropped hair.

"What? I'm sorry. I don't mean to pry. Sometimes I don't feel like sharing either. How about we make a deal? No last names, nothing too personal, and we keep it fun and easy for the weekend. I have to prepare myself for the end of summer. I'm moving to a new school, and I've got to get serious about it. Business is not my vibe, but that's what I'm taking too."

I relax a little with the attention off my life. Plus, I'm curious to learn more about her. "What do you want to be taking?"

"Animation, graphic design. I love drawing and writing stories. What I want most in the world is to become one of these people." She spins around, sweeping her arms at the room.

"A nerd?" I ask, keeping a straight face.

"He can joke! Nice. Well, I'm already one of those. No, that's not it. I want to create my own comic books and graphic novels."

Interesting. I don't have any drawing skills of my own, but there are so many amazing artists I admire. Being able to create something beautiful with your hands is such a gift. But I'm the brawn, not the artist. My hands were made for more destructive things.

"What kind? Do you have any finished work?"

"I haven't published anything, but I've been drawing and telling stories since I was a little kid. I made my first comic book when I was eight. It was about a sentient rock who made friends with a bunny rabbit and a little girl. They got soaked in a puddle of radioactive sludge and gained superpowers."

I laugh. "I'd read that."

"That's a hard no. It was terrible. No need to humor me. I was eight, but my skills have grown considerably since then. Now I'm working on a graphic novel, and I want to make comics for people like me."

"Beautiful nerds?" I ask, loving the hint of pink creeping up her neck.

"No, but thank you. Plus-sized girls. There has never been enough diverse female representation in comic books. Even the ones with over-the-top powers are hyper sexualized. Objects for the admiration of men. All thin and gorgeous, with perfect hair flowing in a smooth waterfall over their shoulders in every panel. It doesn't matter what raging battle they're in the middle of." Her hands are flying almost as fast as her words. "I've never seen myself in those books and that's what I want. A gorgeous, powerful woman with curves kicking ass and taking names. Not afraid to get a little messy."

"Sounds good. I'm in."

"You're in?"

"Yes, I want to read it. Sign me up."

"Okay. It's not ready yet..." She's curling in on herself, confident excitement waning.

"That's fine. Let me know when it is. And I'd love to see some of your art. If you're into sharing." I think I've talked to her more than anyone else over the summer and I work in a comic book store part time. At least some of the time, I'm obligated to talk to the customers. Although a lot of them are taciturn nerds like me, so it's not too bad.

"I'll think about it. See how the weekend goes. If you turn out to not be a creep, I'll consider it."

I've got nothing except a slight shake of her head. She basically claimed me on sight and now she's wondering whether I'm a creep. It worries me that her creep radar is so quiet. I'm not one, but all kinds of men out there would take advantage of her openness.

"Not a creep."

"Whatever you say, Castle. The Punisher is a pretty dark costume for a non creep." The little smirk is back.

"Okay, Black Widow." The Punisher is a complicated character. But he became the man he was because he loved his family so much it destroyed him when they were murdered. I envy him that love. That kind of utter selfless devotion can't exist in real life. Not mine, at least.

We didn't need to split up for the rest of the afternoon. She told me I could go off and do my own thing if I wanted. If there were any panels or booths or anything I wanted to see that she wasn't into. But there wasn't. Our agendas matched. We wanted to go to all the same panels. We were excited about the same speakers. It was comfortable. Familiar. A strange experience that's left me a little off balance. I'm wary of new people, guarded even around some of my teammates.

So, as we're leaving Hall A after the philosophy session, her warm hand slips into mine, and she leans in close, resting her red-wigged head on my shoulder.

"I can't wait to get this thing off," she says, reaching up to scratch at her scalp.

It's on the tip of my tongue to ask her if she wants help, but that won't work. I can't bring her back to the hostel where I'm sharing a room with seven strangers. That's the equivalent of bringing someone you met on a dating app back to your room in your parents' house.

"Any chance you could help me?"

My groin tightens thinking about helping her take it off. That would only be the beginning. Then I'd move on to peel the black leather second skin off so I can see what's underneath. Every curve, every freckle. I want to devour her.

"I should find something to eat before I head back to my room." My voice comes out in a rasp. "It's a little farther out." A twenty-minute drive, but I won't be taking a car, so the bus will take longer.

"Oh. Do you live here?"

"No." I don't elaborate.

She pulls away from me. Probably deterred by my lack of a response.

"Couldn't snag a room close by? I get it. The city is packed right now. I booked last year to make sure I would have a place to stay. I've got a room here. You could... come back with me. We could order room service. Spend the night..." All the in-your-face confidence is gone, re-placed with a vulnerability I recognize. A fear of rejection or being a bother. I don't want her to feel that way. Not because of me and my issues.

"But I guess you've left your bags at your hotel, so if it doesn't work for you, I totally get it. Don't worry about it."

We've reached the door leading down the tunnel into the lobby. I could turn away. Leave her for the night and hope she doesn't decide to enjoy an after party some-where. Meet someone else to take home. Or I could take a chance. Say yes. Savor every inch of her. It's not a fair contest. I'm in. I've got a tough year ahead of me. Might as well enjoy this weekend to the fullest.

"No."

Her face falls.

"I mean, no, I left my bag in the lockers, so it's here. I can grab it. What I should have said was yes. I'd love to spend the night with you."

Chapter Five

No Pictures Please

Cece

That conversation was a bit like being on a turbulent plane ride. I put myself out there. At first, I thought it was a lock. He's into me. I'm into him. This was bound to happen. But then he shut down. The one-word answers, the hesitation. Up and down, tossing me all around. It was a little much for my sensitive self. I don't always show it, but the hurt comes hard and fast when I think someone is rejecting me. I'm so used to being criticized or overlooked by my family, the confidence I put out there is a veneer. A fragile shield sitting on top of my insecurities, concealing them from the world, but easily shattered.

But then he said yes, and now here we are. Crushed together against the mirrored wall on the long trip to the twenty-first floor. There's nothing wrong with the hotel elevator itself, but the sweaty nerd bodies all jammed in after a day spent in too many layers are nauseating. Someone coughs, and I wince, trying to hold my breath. I'm not interested in moving into my new place with a case of con crud.

Dev slides an arm around me, pulling me in tight to his side. He's so much taller than me, I fit perfectly, and as I turn my head to face the painted on white skull on the front of his black tee, I catch a soothing whiff. Whatever he's wearing is soft and fresh smelling. Like a cool breeze on a hot day. I bury my head in it, seeking the sanctuary of him. And it works. I'm surrounded by the scent of him now. It slides around me in a hug as comforting as the physical one.

I'm so wrapped up in it, I don't notice the other people leaving the elevator in pairs and small clusters until it's only us. I don't realize it until he slides his hands up my back, up my neck in a shivery rush, stopping when he reaches my cheeks. His large hands swallow up my face as he tilts it up to meet his eyes. He bends down, lips hovering over mine. A mere fraction of an inch away.

My body is begging, pleading for him to close the distance. It's been a long summer. I've been on my best behavior. I need this. So, I take it.

I push up on my tiptoes, traveling the last inch until my lips meet his in a gentle press. But that single taste isn't enough for either of us. The world disappears with the intensity of our kiss. We've both been waiting for this all day. He pulls me in closer, crushing me in a bruising embrace. I return the gesture, nibbling on his lower lip. Grasping and seeking the heat of him. His lips are soft, but commanding. Demanding surrender. He tastes like the strawberries and cream from the funnel cake we shared.

His tongue invades my mouth, sliding along my lips, begging for entrance. I'm a panting, gasping mess already as his hand moves in a slow, tentative slide down my neck to my breast. He smooths over the slippery fabric, but it's too thick. I can't feel his touch, so I arch into him, looking for more.

A loud ding startles me out of the moment, and I hate it. Stupid elevator doing its stupid job. I've never wanted to get trapped in an elevator with someone before now.

Grabbing his hand, I hurry through the door before it's fully open, glancing at the gold plaques on the wall to get my bearings. I'm in room 2308 or 2303. I'm not even sure anymore, but they're both in the same direction, so I turn down the right hallway, fumbling in my bag for the key card. Flipping open the little grey envelope, I spot the number 2308 inked on it. That's it. Perfect.

The long hall takes longer to traverse because we keep turning toward each other, stopping to steal a kiss before we move forward again.

My father would kill me if he saw me doing this. Bringing a strange man back to my hotel room. Letting him in without a background check or a pedigree he'd approve of. If only he knew what some of those blue-blooded boys he pushes me toward have done. To me, to other girls, the world in general.

I'm not stupid. I texted Tess my room number along with a pic of Dev. Just in case.

Before tapping my key card on the sensor, I turn to him. "I sent a picture of you to Tess, just so you know. She's got my coordinates and your photo, so if you're planning on murdering me in my own hotel room, you will be caught."

The cloudy glaze in his eyes clears for a moment. "Good to know. I'll refrain from breaking out my ax."

I laugh, glancing at the threadbare canvas bag he's got slung over his broad shoulder. The only piece of luggage he brought with him. I'm almost embarrassed to let him in. He'll see the very large, and very expensive suitcases I brought for my few days away. But I'm heading directly to Lakeview after this, so I had to bring some extra clothes and supplies until the moving truck arrives next week. Beau had better help me move in. He's been cagey about it. Too busy enjoying the remnants of summer to help his sister out.

"Last chance to back out." I tell him, hand hovering a safe distance from the pad.

"I wouldn't dream of it, Romanoff. You've well and truly caught me in your snare. Should I be sending a picture of you to my friend? Just in case you're the one who's about to take my life. Was this all a smoke screen?"

"Don't take my picture!" I blurt out as he holds up his phone. Words too sharp, slashing through the heat of the moment, threatening to leave it in shreds. *Get it together, Cecelia.* "Please. I don't like my picture being taken."

It's not true.

I have no problem with friends taking my picture. I only object when the media shows up and immortalizes my worst moments in the press. But if he takes my picture now, he might post it on-line for the world's consumption. And if he has comic book friends, someone could recognize me. It's a tangled mess I don't want to get involved in. This weekend is for me. The red wig and the tight costume are an excellent shield against the world and other than the desk agent, no one has recognized me yet. Even Dev after spending the day together.

But what happens when I remove the wig? Will my pale blonde hair give me away? Is this a bad idea? Or can I get away with leaving it on? A little superhero play in bed could be fun. But I can't leave it on all night if he stays.

He lowers his phone to his side, slipping it into his pocket as I'm frozen in the act of pushing the door open. Then he lifts his other arm, reaching over me to grasp the top of the door frame. The move brings his body closer to mine, infringing on my space in a way that chases the intrusive thoughts out of my head.

One hand reaches up to cup my cheek, tilting my face up to his. "I won't take your picture if you don't want me to. I know what it's like to have someone intrude on your privacy. But just so you know. I wouldn't have posted it on-line or anything if that's what you're worried about. I'm not even on social media."

What? I can't have heard that right. A college guy around my own age who is not on social media is an anomaly.

"Like any social media? At all?"

"Nope. I like my privacy."

Well, that explains a lot, and it changes everything.

I reach up, his stubbly cheeks coarse under my palms, yanking him down to my level. He seems surprised for the barest of moments before he reacts, delving between my lips to meet my demands. His hands tighten on my cheeks as he pulls me in closer and walks me backward until I'm pressed up against the half-open door.

I stumble, laughing as it gives way under my weight, but he keeps me upright and moving. Like he's been waiting all day for this, just like I have.

"What about dinner?" I ask.

His eyes go dark as he mumbles against my lips. "There's only one thing I'm hungry for right now."

I was already on the edge of reason, but that shoves me right over. A bolt of need shoots from my tingling lips to my core, and my pussy clenches.

"Fuck yes."

The door clicks shut, forcing me into the present. I reach over to snap the latch and flip the dead bolt without breaking out of his hold.

His thumbs trace shivery circles on my cheeks and then his hands travel up further and further until they're teasing the edges of the wig that's been keeping me safe from recognition all day.

I nip at his lower lip when he stills the kiss, trying to urge him on, but he pulls away, breathing a little heavier than before.

"Let me help you get this thing off." His voice is gruff.

The anxious thoughts try to kick in again, tensing my muscles and leaving me a little unsure. If I let him, he'll see me for who I am. Not the confident kick-ass persona that's easier to maintain when I'm wearing the costume. But it's okay. There's something about him that puts me at ease. A sense of protection and safety. Maybe it was the way he casually held my hand off and on all day, as if to make up for pulling away that one time. The way he let me sweep him up in the path of my hurricane first thing in the morning, or how enthusiastic he was about the women in comics panel. Whatever it is, there's something easy about being around him, so I make a conscious effort to relax my shoulders and nod.

His strong fingers slip under the edge of the wig, easing it up, but I wince as the pins holding it in pace tug at my scalp.

"Sorry. I'll just..."

I laugh. "It's fine. Just had to pin it in place. How did you think I was keeping it solid all day? It's not like we're in a movie where everyone's hair and makeup magically remain perfect in the middle of a literal war. These things take a little extra care."

I reach up to help him, placing my smaller hands over his to find the combs and pins holding it in place. He's surprisingly gentle for such a big guy, taking care to pull out the pins and untangle the strands so they don't yank on my scalp.

When all the fastenings have been dropped to the floor, he guides the piece up and off, placing it on a side table carefully so it doesn't get wrecked.

Of course, I've got a hairnet on to hide any and all strands of my own hair. He removes that next and my long pale locks are finally free, falling in a rumpled mess to my shoulders.

He pulls away from me, hands dropping to my shoulders and his eyes widen as if he's consuming every inch of me. My face, my hair. He runs his hands through it, taking care to untangle the delicate strands. A shiver runs across my scalp at his gentle touch.

"Gorgeous."

I drop my eyes. His gaze is a little too much. A little too heavy for this meeting of strangers.

"Don't look away. I want to see those gorgeous blue eyes.

I flick them back up, and he spins me around. "Can I..."

His fingers are toying with the zipper on the back of my costume.

"Please." I want to feel those hands on my skin so badly, but he takes his time, drawing the zipper down slowly inch by inch, planting soft kisses on my spine as he goes. Shivers run through me at the gentle brushes of his lips until I'm on the verge of combustion. He hits the bottom of the zipper and places one last kiss on my lower back when I don't think I can take any more of the sweet torture.

Hands smooth up my back, parting the constricting fabric as they go. They slide under the suit at my shoulders, dragging it down my arms. The material slips off and the top half falls to my waist.

He rubs up and down the ribbed sides of the corset I've got on underneath, and I'm suddenly conscious of the way my hips spill out under the tight fit of the lingerie. It makes the costume look fantastic, but I definitely don't look like a Victoria's Secret model. They strut down runways confidently in corsets that have nothing to hold in.

I spin around before he can peel the rest of my costume off, needing a little balance between us. I find the hem of his black shirt and look back at him. "Can I?"

He smiles. "Yes, please. I want to feel your beautiful skin pressed up against mine. To see if it's as soft as it looks."

Sounds good to me. I drag the shirt up and over his broad torso, and the sight of his bare skin almost takes my breath away. He belongs in some stuffy old museum. An example of the perfection of the human body. An interesting variety of tattoos covers the packed mass of muscles on his chest. His abs are unreal. I have an urge to lick the dips and curves of his stomach. My hands fly down to the roll of my stomach pushed out from under the corset, but he stops me. His hands close over mine, pulling them away and drops to his knees, kissing my softness.

"You are so beautiful."

His lips land on my right hip in a soft kiss, followed by a gentle nip. He takes his time, repeating the move across my lower stomach. I forget to be self conscious as my legs liquify while he takes his time peeling the tight suit off. I'm a little shaky on my feet by the time he finishes and rises to his feet.

"Good?" he asks, looking me in the eye.

I give him a dreamy smile and nod. "Incredible."

I'm standing before him now in nothing but the corset and a black lace thong, but his pants are still in the way. When my fingers fumble with the buckle on his belt, he takes over, sliding it out of the loops faster than I could have managed in this state. I track the movement of those skilled hands as he unzips, slipping the black cargo pants off to reveal a pair of red boxer briefs barely containing the hard length underneath.

It's way too tempting, so I reach out and stroke the length of it while it strains against the soft cotton fabric. It twitches under my touch, and he groans. His hands clasp my ass, jerking me up in his arms.

"Don't pick me up. I'm too heavy." The awareness comes back to me.

His chuckle is low and dark. "Are you kidding me? I've got equipment bags that weigh more than you. I've got this."

It feels solid. No sign of him struggling, so I wrap my legs around his waist to give myself a more secure hold, but it's hardly worth the effort. His long legs eat up the ground and he's dropping me onto the massive bed before I've latched on properly. Now it's his turn to do a little fumbling as he struggles to get his thick fingers to unlatch the hook closures of the corset.

I watch him sweat for a moment before I intervene. "My turn," I tell him, making quick work of the fastening running the length of the garment. I have more than enough experience with these sorts of contraptions. A prime example of what women are expected to wear in comics and anything in the sci-fi or fantasy genre.

My already fantastic tits look even better, though, so it can be fun sometimes. Although my superhero wears a costume that's a little more on the comfortable side of the spectrum. A little less restrictive.

The fabric parts in the front, releasing my breasts from captivity. Dev's eyes are locked on them as soon as they're free and he reaches out to cup them. They're a perfect fit for his hands. The rough pads of his thumbs create a delicious friction as he circles my nipples.

I'm arching into his touch, squeezing my thighs together, needing some sort of friction to ease the ache between my legs.

"I've been waiting to get my hands on these all day."

The need in his voice is so palpable I can almost feel it on my skin.

"Me too."

I'm not sure when my eyes fell shut, but it's a pleasant shock when the wet heat of his tongue swipes over my center. Very few guys are willing to go there for a one-night stand. Hopefully, this one will last all weekend. I could get used to this treatment.

His skilled mouth licks and sucks and nibbles until I'm nothing but sensations. Heat, tingles, and aches on every part of my body. He teases and toys with my entrance, never quite dipping in. Need is rising in my lower core. An urgent ache building stronger with each touch.

He lifts my legs, dropping them on his shoulders in a slick move that has me feeling light as a feather while he continues to lavish my clit with love.

My legs are trembling, and I don't think I can make it another second of the teasing. "Please. I need more."

"What do you need?" His lips send sharp vibrations through me to the point I'm about to lose it when he backs away.

"You. Inside me."

"Like this?"

A thick finger joins his mouth, circling my slit, slipping in a fraction of an inch, pulling away before I can clench down on it.

"Yes. Please," I moan.

"Look at me when you ask." It's a command, not a request.

"What?"

"Look at me. I want to see those gorgeous eyes on me while you're begging for it."

Why does the demand make my pussy clench even harder? Why am I getting wetter at the commanding tone of his voice? I shouldn't be. I don't let guys boss me around, but instead of making me feel like an object, he's making me feel worshiped. Like a goddess. I can't help but obey him, dragging my unwilling head up a little, dragging my eyelids open to meet his gaze through a haze of lust.

"Please touch me, fuck me with your tongue, your finger... your cock."

A slow smile stretches his lips that are wet with my juice, and he goes back to work, dipping his head down to devour me as his finger slams home. There's no resistance. I'm so wet, so open, so ready for his invasion it only takes a few plunges before the need crests. My body flies over the edge, bucking off the bed, and a shock of sensation grips me as his tongue slows to a steady rhythm. A series of mini shocks ripple through my system. I clench down on him again and again in a never-ending orgasm.

When I'm finally spent, he pulls away from me, sliding his hands under my ass to scoop me up and drag me farther up the bed until my head hits a soft pile of pillows.

"Holy shit." I think that's what I say, but my brain is so scrambled it could have been anything.

His large body slides next to mine, his hardness pressed into my hip as he curls around me. I slip my hand down, rubbing his length until he's the one arching into me.

I grip his cock through the soft cotton of his boxer briefs, and it jumps in my hand. Now he's the one begging. The shift in power drags me out of my stupor and I lean over him to study his body while I stroke him.

"Too many clothes." My hands slip under the tight waistband, tugging at it. Every inch reveals something new. There's a black lightning bolt etched into his right hip, and a lily on his right one. He shivers under my touch as I trace the ink, curious about the meaning. Or lack of meaning. Some people get tattoos for the fun of it. But he's got such an interesting array. Something about them seems purposeful. Like there's a reason behind each one, but that's not what this is about. This weekend is just for fun, so I leave it alone.

His dick springs up as a last tug brings his shorts down. I take a moment to admire the smooth skin marked with thick veins that are going to feel fantastic rubbing me from the inside. I lean down, needing a taste, licking him from base to tip in a slow swipe.

He squirms, and his eyes fly open, hand falling to the back of my head. He doesn't put any pressure on it, just rests it there to keep me close.

I kiss and lick my way up the side until I get to the sensitive head, closing my mouth over him, sucking the salty drop of precum off the tip.

"Fuck. I need you."

Triumph swells through me at how easy it was for me to bring him to the point of begging. At least for a moment. He growls, flipping me over in a quick move that has him hovering over me.

He ducks down to devour my mouth, crushing my tits to his chest, and he's right there. A small thrust of his hips and I'll get to feel him inside me. Finally.

Cold air ripples my overheated skin as he pulls back, sitting up and rubbing a hand over his head.

He's sitting back on his heels in a position that would put most people at a disadvantage. Show off their flaws. But he has none. His body is unreal in its perfection.

"What's wrong?"

CHAPTER SIX

EVERY RULE

DEV

F uck. How could I be so stupid? But then I glance down at her. Beautiful body splayed out before me. Every curve and dip waiting to be explored. Gorgeous skin and plump curves. That's how. The glaze is lifting from her stunning blue eyes and she's looking a little confused and hurt.

"Condom. I don't have a condom." I wasn't exactly planning on this hookup when I packed my bag, but I never forget to wrap it up. How incredibly careless of me. I could have... I don't even want to think about it.

Her eyes widen for a moment in an expression of shock that probably mirrors the one on my face. Then one side of her mouth curves up in a smirk. "It's all good."

She rolls over, giving me a view of her cushy ass. I have to hold back from grabbing a handful. I'd love to see what it feels like overflowing my hands. Maybe I should fuck her from behind, slam into that plush cushion until she's screaming my name.

I track her every movement as she hops off the tall bed and makes her way to the two massive suitcases leaning against the wall. That's a lot of luggage for a weekend stay away. Maybe she's heading somewhere else after the con.

Her heavy tits hang low as she bends down to unzip the bag. She's rifling through it like a hungry raccoon, and it shouldn't be sexy, but it is. Even her little growl of exasperation is cute as she gives up, kicking the case over and unzipping it the whole way.

Chaos ensues as she pulls out clothes, dropping them on the floor. Finally, she stands up in the middle of the mess, holding a box triumphantly over her head like a warrior princess standing over a vanquished foe.

"We're good."

I seal my mouth into a thin line, attempting to keep in the laugh trembling at my lips. Women don't usually take too fondly to being laughed at while they're naked, but it is pretty freaking hilarious seeing her standing there like that.

She narrows her eyes, tits jiggling as she stalks toward me. "Are you laughing at me?"

"No." Her face pinches in disbelief as I shake my head. "Yes. But only the situation."

Her hands slide down her hips. "You think this is so funny? Maybe it would be funnier if I left you hanging there." She walks toward the window, struggling to drag it open before sticking the box of condoms through the scant few inches of space.

Oh, really. Is that how she thinks this night is going to end? My feet hit the carpet and I'm crowding her from behind. That puts my aching cock between her cheeks. I groan, rubbing against her as I slide a hand up her arm, snagging the box before she can drop it.

"You're begging for a spanking, aren't you?"

"You wouldn't dare." She wiggles against me, and now all I want is to fuck her up against the window. We're too high for anyone to see us. Probably.

"I would."

Her flesh gives under the light warning smack I give her, and she gasps.

"Fuck, Castle. You're going to make me come again."

She's into it. Best news I've had all night. I slide the window shut with my left hand as I smack her again, harder this time. I'm going to explode all over the smooth skin of her back if I don't get inside her, so I snag a foil packet, tearing it open with my teeth and rolling it on.

Pressing her up against the window with my left hand, I give her another smack with my right one before positioning myself at her entrance.

"You ready?"

"Fuck yes." She presses against me, her ass a little rosy from my hand, and that's more than enough for me.

I push inside her an inch. Just the head, wanting to savor the moment. Her tits are pressed against the cold glass, and her head is tilted back, exposing the length of her neck. I lick a slow line from her shoulder to her ear as I slide inside her at the same agonizing pace until I'm halfway in. Her wet heat stretches to accommodate my size.

I run my hands up her sides, wanting to touch every inch of her skin. She shivers as my hands stroke the sides of her breasts. The window fogs up from the heat of her panting breaths.

"You feel incredible," she says.

"Not as good as you."

She's so wet, so ready for me. I plunge the rest of the way inside, and she shrieks. The tingle is traveling up my legs to my lower back and I know I'm not going to last long, so I reach around to find her clit. I use her own moisture against her, sliding in slow circles, easing into a faster rhythm until her moans reach the perfect pitch and I know I've hit the right rhythm.

I slam into her again and again, pulling all the way out, only to thrust back in. She grips me in her hold, trying to keep me there when I pull back, so I slap her ass again and she clenches around me.

"Come for me." Her shoulders jerk as I whisper in her ear, giving her left cheek another slap.

"Dev!" She comes hard, screaming my name as her entire body trembles, and I roar as her pussy squeezes and releases, hurling me off the cliff I was teetering near.

Pure pleasure washes over me in a rush. My cum spills into the condom as my dick pulses and my thrusts slow. Fuck yes. What a way to end the summer.

I stay buried in her warmth, trying to catch my breath until I realize she's shaky under my firm grip.

"You ok?" I ask her.

"Yeah." Her voice is soft and dreamy. "Just sleepy."

Shit, she can't be comfortable pressed up against the glass, all slick with our combined sweat. She squeals as I scoop her up in my arms, carrying her to the bed before I place her carefully down. I reach up to wipe the damp hair off her rosy cheeks, tucking it behind her little shell-like ears.

I'm staring at myself in the mirror, studying each and every one of the tattoos I've gotten over the years. Taking a minute to breathe and try to enjoy the moment. The euphoric haze before the thoughts come racing back to me. I'm not good enough for a girl like her. But it's fine. I'm only borrowing her for the weekend. She's the kind of girl who deserves someone special.

I head back to see her, a little cleaner than before, but my limbs are heavy, stretched out like after a hard game or a tough workout. I'm also starving, so I reach into the backpack I placed carefully beside the bed, fingers fumbling until they land on the baggie of snacks I always keep handy.

"What's up?" she asks.

When I sit up to look at her, she's blinking at me through eyes hooded and content with sleepiness.

I hold out one of my precious granola bars to her. "Snack?"

A laugh bubbles out of her as she twists into a sitting position. "I can't believe I forgot about dinner. I'll order us something. Let me just..." She reaches for the phone, and can't help checking her out, as she leans down.

"It's okay. I'm good." I hate being a burden. She's already bought me food today. I don't want her thinking I'm mooching off her. The rumble of my stomach betrays me and turns her adorable giggle into something more akin to a cackle.

She slaps a hand over her mouth as if she's embarrassed, so I reach out to pull it away. I love the sheer joy of the sound. My laugh might be rare, but it doesn't mean I can't appreciate someone else's.

"Uh huh. Sure you're not hungry." She rolls her eyes as she scans a QR code, bringing up the room service menu on her phone. "I guess I'll have to eat alone, and I'm not afraid to admit I'm freaking starving. I'd eat my brother's dirty hockey socks at this point."

I do a double take. "Your brother plays hockey?"

She groans. "Oh no. Are you a fan? Or wait?" She pauses, narrowing her eyes to sweep a critical eye up and down my body. "Don't tell me I've hooked up with a hockey boy?" Her head falls back to the pillow, a hand falling to her forehead. "I came here for the nerds, the geeks, the weirdos, and artists."

"Don't like hockey players?"

"It's not that I don't like them, but..." My eyes lock on her lower lip tucked between her teeth as she nibbles away, a little crease popping up between her eyes. "I dated one of his teammates once. It did not end well. He was a witness to the aftermath, and he's been pretty good at keeping me away from them ever since."

"Got it."

She tilts her head, studying me, and holds a finger to her lips. There's a mischievous twist to them. "But I've never been a big fan of rules. And this isn't exactly dating. We'll just have to make sure not to tell him." Her laugh is bright and contagious. Clearly, she's gotten over the heartbreak.

I relax back onto the bed, swinging an arm over her soft torso. "Not a word." Nothing to worry about. We already agreed this is only for the con. I'm never going to see this girl again, no matter how delicious she tasted.

"Excellent. Now for the feast." The bright glare of her phone is suddenly in my face as I blink at the room service menu.

They've got an evening menu filled with the usual pub type stuff. Wings, fries, and chicken fingers. And a handful of entrees. My mouth is watering at the thought of a burger. I would do bad things for a big juicy burger right now, but the price is a kick to the gut. How do they justify charging that much for such a basic food item? I shake my head. "I'll just have some fries." My limited food budget runs through my head. I still need lunch and dinner tomorrow. But I'm sure I can find a store nearby to grab some grocery type items to supplement the protein bars and snacks I brought along. There's enough wiggle room to give Cece the money for fries.

The urge is strong to swipe the damp pale blonde strands behind her ear when she tilts her head to the side. "Are you sure? That can't be enough to sustain a guy of your size."

Her eyes dart down to my dick for a moment, and a pink flush creeps up her neck, staining her cheeks as she looks back up at my face guiltily. There is no need to be guilty about that. In fact, my guy twitches to life again in response. He's more than happy with the praise and admiration.

"Nah. I'm good."

"Okay. Well, I'm famished. I'm ordering one of everything."

She picks up the hotel phone, dialing a number, but she doesn't take her eyes off me even as she's talking to the front desk.

I sit up, propping myself on a pillow to snack on the granola bar I pulled out of my bag.

After she hangs up, she accepts the bar I offer her. "Keep your strength up until your feast gets here."

My stomach is still begging when I polish off the bar, but I'm not ready to finish my weekend supply yet. As she leans over me, her breasts press into my chest, causing another kind of sweet ache. It's an excellent distraction until she bends down lower, snagging my backpack off the ground.

"What the fuck!"

She drops it, startled, as I yank the fabric away, tucking the bag under my arm.

"I'm so sorry."

I close my eyes, blowing a breath out to calm the knee jerk panic that stole my breath when she touched my bag.

"No, I'm sorry." She's been nothing but kind and generous and I'm acting like she's some master thief about to steal the shitty belongings and snacks I always keep in my shitty bag.

"I'm still hungry. I was going to see if you had another snack. They said room service is going to be an hour. I didn't mean to touch your stuff."

"It's fine. I overreacted. Sorry."

I'm an idiot, and those wide eyes full of fear and remorse cut right into my heart. I rifle through the bag again, grabbing one of my precious dried fruit bars to hand her.

She shakes her head. "Don't worry about it. I'll grab something from the minibar."

After unfolding herself from the bed, she swings her thick legs over the side, jumping off.

Look at me. Ruining what was promising to be an amazing weekend with my issues.

"The mini bar is way too expensive. Take this."

I snag her arm, pulling until she spins around to face me and offering her the bar.

She glances down at it, hesitating before she takes it from my hand. Her soft skin brushes mine and an electric jolt zips through me. Maybe it's salvageable if I can keep my shit together for the rest of the night.

"I totally get it. I hate it when my brother touches my stuff. We had a constant battle when we were kids to keep our hands to ourselves."

I nod, not really understanding. None of the kids I grew up around were related to me. And I also didn't spend long enough in one place to develop that kind of relationship. The nearest I've gotten is with my team.

Those guys are the closest I've come to a real family. The way they look out for each other is new to me.

"He a pain?"

Her beautiful smile is back on her face as she laughs. "You could say that. But he's also amazing. He's always looking out for me, and I love him. I make him crazy, too. Often intentionally, but don't tell him."

I reach over, peeling her fingers open to place the food in her palm before squeezing them shut. Needing to make it up to her. It's a hundred percent worth it when she smiles at me again, lighting up the room.

We fall quiet. The only sounds punctuating the silence are the crinkle of the wrapper and her munching noises. Loud laughter and the sound of a door slamming invade our peace. She fumbles the ball of garbage she was tossing in the can across from the bed, and it hits the wall two feet from her mark.

"Your brother is the athlete of the family, I see."

"Shut up." Her hand flies out to smack my arm, and I wince.

Luckily, she's glancing out the window, so I think she missed my overreaction to her light touch.

"It's fine. You're an artist. Got anything I can see?"

She spins around exorcist fast, looking at me, then away. Her hands fiddle with the edge of the sheet, and it's a real shame when she pulls the blanket up over all that glorious flesh.

"I don't know. I don't usually show guys my art on the first date."

Even when she's feeling vulnerable, she's funny. "Good thing it's not a date.

Her lips push out, and now I'm remembering what they taste like. I lean in, unable to resist the urge to nibble on that lower one again. Still fucking delicious.

"True," she mumbles when I pull away. "No fair. You're trying to lure me into submission with kisses."

"Is it working?"

"Hmm. Maybe. Want to try harder? A little tongue perhaps?"

That's an invitation I'm happy to accept. I dive in, grabbing the back of her head to pull her in closer. Her hair feels soft and fine, like freshly spun cotton candy tangled around my fingers, and her lips taste just as sweet when I slip inside.

The sheets slip down between us as she arches her chest into me. Those fantastic breasts are so tempting, but I resist the urge to reach down to stroke the curves.

She's all mussed up and glazed over when I pull away. "How was that?"

"What? Where'd you go?" There are two cute little creases between her brows.

"Can I see your art now?"

"No fair. You can't get me all..." she flaps her hands around, "and then... not cool, Castle."

"I never said I played fair."

"You can't leave me hanging here."

I look at her from under eyelids that are still heavy, but I'm determined. I have years of practice controlling my needs. I want to see her art and I'm going to win this one. "What are you talking about?"

"You know."

I shake my head.

"You can't kiss me like that and then stop. What have I done to deserve this cruel and unusual punishment?"

"You want punishment? That can be arranged. We don't have time for the things I want to do to you, anyway. Room service."

"They can wait."

"I tell you what. You show me your art and I'll give you three more orgasms after dinner. If you can handle it."

"Not possible."

I chuckle and shrug.

"Fine. Get my sketchbook. It's in the front pocket of my red bag." Her tits lift and swell as she crosses her arms over her chest and judging by the sparkle in her eyes, she's doing it on purpose, but I won't be swayed.

"You want me to go through your bag?"

"I've got nothing to hide."

And there it is. Now I feel even worse about snapping at her for touching my backpack, but it's clear we've lived very different lives.

My fingers fumble the zip at first, and when I turn around to double check she's okay with this, she startles, tearing her gaze away from my ass.

My right eyebrow arches toward my hairline, and she narrows her eyes, waving me on.

The sketchbook, a few pencils, and a sharpener are the only things in the pocket, so I pull them all out, but I don't open it. She can choose what she wants to show me.

Her mouth twists to the side in thought, fingers dancing on the pad.

I crane my neck for a better look when she finally makes her decision, flipping through the pages until she lands on a blank one.

"I'm not going to show you any of my current works in progress. How about I draw something just for you?"

"Really?" Nobody has ever created something just for me. I'm curious and a little impatient to see what she's going to draw.

It becomes obvious where all the nibble marks on the pencil came from when she tucks it between her teeth, pausing to think.

The flash of inspiration seems to descend on her quickly because she lowers the pencil to the pad and starts sketching out rapid lines. I track her progress and it's incredible how her strokes transform the blank page into something else. Something with depth and texture. The image on the page starts to form into something recognizable, and it's... "A bear?"

Her forehead crinkles in a frown and she shakes her head at me. "Don't interrupt me. No comments until it's done."

Right, she's got her process. I can feel that. I'm the same on the ice.

My eyes still follow the rapid movement of her pencil hungrily, eager to see what she's going to create.

Each layer brings about another level of detail. The bear's eyes start to shine with hunger, and his ears are perked in interest.

She scratches out a few lines, fills in a few more, and brushes at the eraser crumbs, darkening the eyes and the outline one last time. Then she lifts her pencil, tucking her lower lip between her teeth. The whole process takes way less time than I expected.

"Well." She closes her eyes as if she's scared to see my expression, but if she looked, all she'd see was wonder.

I reach out to touch it, pulling away before I make contact. He looks so real, standing on his hind legs. I almost expect to feel the shaggy fur under my fingertips when I touch it. But I resist the ridiculous urge. The ice skates are the best part. A skating bear should be comical, but the way she's drawn it, the life in his eyes. It's perfect.

"It's amazing, but why a bear?"

"That's the first thing that came to mind when I thought of you, Dev."

"A bear? Really?"

"Yeah. You're all massive and a little frowny, but I think you're soft and cuddly underneath."

"I'm not."

"Maybe not, but that's what I see."

"Thank you. Nobody's ever..." Created something like this for me. It doesn't feel right. I don't deserve this.

"What..."

A sharp knock on the door saves me from any further inquiry, and a polite voice lets us know room service has arrived.

CHAPTER SEVEN

DIRTY DREAMS COME TRUE

CECE

W hy is there a single sock in the kitchen? I swipe it off the floor and continue to search every empty nook and corner. Rushing around panic cleaning may not be the best way to live my life, but you think I'd be used to it by now. I don't know where all this stuff came from. All I brought with me to my new house were my two suitcases and an overly large purse. Plus, all the swag I bought at the con last week.

Remembering it puts an automatic smile on my face, and a giddy, bubbly sensation in my chest. Dev. What a weekend. You'd think meeting some of my favorite artists and actors would have been the best part, but no. It was my fling with his athletic body, and the general calm he brought to my chaos. I've picked up my phone a hundred times since we parted ways, some random thought passing through my mind, demanding I send it to him. But that would be impossible. Why did I suggest not exchanging info? There's no way I could have gotten into trouble sending him the occasional text.

I shake my head. Doesn't matter. That was the decision I made. Now I can deal with it. I'm sure it won't be long before he's the star of my dirty dreams and nothing more. That perfect body laid out in my bed the next morning before I had to drag myself away to meet my ride. I wanted to wake him up for one last kiss, but he looked so comfortable lying there naked and peaceful, snoring softly on the white sheets. It was better that way. I might not have left the hotel room if I'd stayed.

I've got more time sensitive problems. Like picking up the assortment of clothes that have appeared on every available surface. Crimson panties are dangling over the brass table lamp that's currently chilling on the cream carpet. Mom would try to make a disappointed face if she knew how I've been living for the past two weeks. Sleeping on an air mattress like a couch surfer. But she's not capable of too many facial expressions any more thanks to the endless units of Botox.

It's been kind of fun. Roaming the place all by myself. The silence and lack of company is making me a little stir crazy. I'm excited for my new roomies to move in this weekend. We've been chatting on video calls to get to know each other better before we have to all move in together, and I think this will be fantastic. They're going to be a fresh change from the friends I moved in with at my former school. Nothing but rich kids and hangers on back there. No wonder I ended up bored and getting into trouble. My new roommates are creatives like me.

But I've got a lot of work ahead to set up this empty house. Thank goodness I enlisted my brother into helping. Volunteered, voluntold. What's the difference when you're family? He's only bringing one of the hockey guys with him, but it's his best friend, Lucy. All I know about him is that they've been tight since first year and he's Beau's defense partner on the team. I don't think he trusts any of the other guys around me. Ridiculous. I'm a grown ass woman capable of making my own decisions. Sure, some of them are shady at best, but he's made his fair share of mistakes too. We're all just fallible human beings struggling to figure ourselves out.

Still, I know he'll flip a lid if he sees the mess, and they're going to be here in ten minutes to meet the moving truck. I snag the undies off the lamp, jamming them into my red bag. After stuffing the last armload of clothes away and plopping my ass on top of it so I can force the zipper to close, I'm out of breath.

I finger comb the limp strands of hair out of the way and search the bathroom for an elastic. No deal. The bulging suitcase is taunting me. No way I'm going to unleash that beast. It'd swallow me whole before it vomited its entire contents back out all over the room. No time. Just gonna have to deal with slightly sweaty locks trying to blind me.

My fingers snag on a hole in my rattiest black leggings. I haven't done any laundry since I got here, so now I'm down to the dregs of my wardrobe. Even the shirt is an old, faded concert tee with holes under the pits. I blow out a breath. It's this or my cutest LBD and that is hardly appropriate attire for my official move in day.

The worst part is Beau always dresses sharply. Even today I'm sure he'll have on a polo shirt or at the very least some high-ticket athleisure. But it's fine. I'm not trying to impress him, or his hockey friend. He won't judge me for it, but it's a constant reminder of why I'll never meet my family's standards of perfection.

I snag an empty pizza box off the kitchen counter, glance around and duck out the back door, chucking the thing on the back porch on top of the big blue bin. *Mental note: buy a small one for the house before my roommates arrive.*

The cheery chime of the doorbell has me skidding across the house. I run a hand through my untidy mess of hair one last time before swinging it open with a huge smile plastered on my face.

"Bo Bo!" I singsong at my brother.

He scoops me up in a hug that warms my soul while crushing my body. Then he drops me back on my socked feet unceremoniously, eyes tracking down straight to my right middle toe sticking through a gaping hole. Is that what you call your second toe?

There's a slight twist of disbelief to his lips when he drags his eyes back up. "Hey, little sis. What happened?

Did you leave your hairbrush at home? Dad cut off your sock allowance? I've missed you."

"Not like we didn't see each other over the summer." I shove him. But I am happy we'll be closer together this year. The past three years while we were at separate colleges was the longest span of time I've been apart from my twin. And even though he drives me bananas sometimes, I missed him.

"This is Lucy. He's going to be the muscle today. Lucy, my little sister Cece."

I laugh, glancing at Beau's tall frame. Not like he can't handle the heavy lifting, but I appreciate the help.

"Not little."

As I'm standing on my tiptoes to peer over his shoulder, my mouth falls open, friendly greeting dying a quick death on my lips. The only part of my frozen body that's moving is my stomach frolicking from my abdomen to my chest and back. I slow blink, trying to clear away the hallucination, but he's still there looking all real, and huge, and... delicious. His stubble has grown out into a short, dark beard and my fingers are itching to run through it.

"Hi, I'm Devlin. You can call me Dev." There was a brief jolt of shock on his face, but he recovers faster than me, holding out a hand past my brother while I'm still grappling to calm my racing heart.

"But." I glance from Beau to Dev, ignoring the large hand hanging in the air between us. This can't be happening.

Beau's brow scrunches in confusion. "Cece? You, okay?"

I give my head a shake, reaching out a tentative hand. We share the fastest handshake known to humankind. I don't think the Flash could have beaten me on this one. There's still a sizzle of awareness at the brief contact. My skin heats, and electricity zips up my arm at the memory of where those hands have been and what they did to me.

"Nice to meet you, Dev. I didn't realize Lucy wasn't your actual name." Not that it's uncommon for the hockey team to have nicknames for each other. He calls his teammates all kinds of crazy things, but a lot of them are based on their real names. I was kind of assuming Lucy was short for Lucius, or Lucas, or maybe it was from his last name. Why can't he be a Lucas? Why does he have to be my Dev? Star of the top three orgasms of my life. He blew away my previous top three all in one weekend. The window... Did that happen, or did I imagine the whole thing?

He clears his throat, shifting on his feet. "Yeah, it's uh, Devlin. Like the devil. Lucifer."

The loud smack of Beau's hand slapping him on the back has me wincing, but he barely rocks on his feet.

"Don't be so modest, Lucy. It's actually because his feet smell like he spends his nights in the bad place."

Dev's lips press together in a thin line, and his already dark eyes are shadowed by his lowered brow. "Fuck off, Bo Bo."

It's a pleasure watching my brother get the shit thrown right back in his face.

"You planning to let us in?" My brother's blond brow arches up toward his perfectly gelled hair. Which reminds me of the hot mess on top of my head I was trying to fix when they showed up early. "If not, I'm sure I can find something better to do with my day."

I glance down at the clothes that didn't seem so bad when it was only supposed to be my brother and some unknown frat boy hockey player. Not his unbearably hot roommate who I happened to see naked a couple of weeks ago. Naked and the embodiment of male perfection.

"Right. I'm so sorry. Welcome to my delightful abode." I step back, swinging the door wide to let them in, and swooping my arm in what I hope is a welcoming sweep. "Over here you'll find the nothing. This room is the void of emptiness. And over there," I gesture toward the kitchen, "the black hole of ingredients. Make yourselves uncomfortable."

Dev lets out a small bark of laughter, while Beau shakes his head, rolling his eyes at me.

"Hilarious. That is why we're here, isn't? Or is this the wrong address? Hang on, I'll tell the driver to head over to my place until I can sort this out."

"Yeah, yeah. I don't know why you keep playing that silly game on skates when you've got such a promising career in comedy. Get to work then. Bring me my stuff. Preferably my couch first. Then I can take a seat like the queen I am and supervise my loyal subjects to make sure they don't break anything."

"You'd like that, wouldn't you? Forget it, little sis, you are helping. Not going to make us sweat while you lounge around like a diva."

I can picture the sweat beaded on Dev's sculpted body. Dripping down his forehead as he slammed into me. Every muscle flexing.

"Hello, Cece. You still with me?"

I snap my focus back on my brother, which is the rudest of awakenings from that brief fantasy. "Yes. I'm here."

"Are you feeling okay? You look a little flushed. You don't have a fever, do you?" My loving brother backs a couple of steps away from me as if I've got the black plague. Actually, he might be less upset about that than he would be if he discovered I slept with one of his best friends. A hockey player, no less.

It shouldn't matter. I'm a grownup. And not some sweet, innocent virgin who had her virtue stolen. But since Deacon... he's kept me away from his hockey friends. Even when I got dragged to practice, he warned them away from me. Which was never really a problem. After I got abandoned for the game and the lifestyle, I wasn't too keen on going back there. My little foray out on the ice turned me off hockey players.

But still, it shouldn't matter. Maybe we should fess up and move on. It's not as if we're planning on keeping it up. It was only one weekend. I study Dev looking for some sign of what he's thinking, but his mouth is pressed together in a neutral line, thick forearms crossed over his chest, and eyes blank. No help there. Looks like pretending it never happened is the vibe.

"I'm fine. Just been running around."

"Got it. Last-minute panic cleaning. I shudder to imag-ine what this place looked like before we got here." His eyes are fixed on my bedroom door. I back up, crossing my arms as I stand guard in front of my room. Even though I know it's fine. I shoved everything into my suit-cases. But I'm sure he'd find something that itched at his brain. And I'd know. They don't tell you about that side of the super special twin connection. Having spent so many years so close together, we can read each other's facial expressions. Hope he can't see the guilt in my eyes.

CHAPTER EIGHT

BROTHERLY LOVE

DEV

A sweet citrus cloud drifts over my shoulder and the smooth fabric of the couch slips in my sweaty fingers. "Shit."

Beau stops in the doorway, looking up at me with concern. "You need a break?"

"No, I'm fine. Just slipped. I got this." We're almost done with the unloading. I can hold it together until the end of the day. Even if it feels like the longest day of my life. Keeping my eyes from lingering on her is taking more effort than lugging all the furniture and boxes.

I resist the urge to turn around, knowing I'll find her staring at me. The liquid pools of her blue eyes are swimming with a mix of confusion and hurt. She's there. I can feel her presence.

There's a warmth and tingle of awareness when she gets closer. It's different from the usual alert mode I'm in. Always aware of the mood in any room, waiting for someone to erupt in anger. Always waiting for the unexpected.

It's easier here. Beau has his own issues, and he may be a little much sometimes, but I trust him in a way I've never trusted anyone else. That's probably why I'm comfortable around her, too. She is his twin sister, after all. All of that shared DNA must make her feel safe, even though I hardly know her.

"Can you put it against that wall?" Her question forces me to turn her way, not wanting to look like a complete asshole, but I drop my eyes to stare at my feet before they lock with hers. They're so magnetic, I'm afraid I'll get dragged in and not be able to tear myself away. Beau would for sure notice something.

"Come on, Sissy. This thing is heavy. Did you stuff it full of free weights before you called the movers?" Beau swipes at a sweaty lock of hair drifting toward his eye.

"Seriously? Big, strong hockey player can't handle moving his sister's things? Suck it up and stop complaining. What's the point of working out every day if you don't actually use those muscles?" She pokes him in the arm.

"Obviously, I use them for hockey. No one told me I'd be obligated to lift heavy shit for my little sister for the rest of my life."

"Two minutes older hardly counts. Nor does this..." She waves her arms down her body, gesturing to the full curves and thick thighs that felt so good wrapped around my hips.

Sweaty hockey bag, that asshole D-man on UPenn's team I'm looking forward to crushing this year. The thoughts are enough of a distraction to soften up the hard-on that's threatening to make its presence known.

"Whatever." Beau reaches over, scrubbing his knuckles over the top of her head in a childish move that has her squealing and slapping at his hands. "You'll always be my little sister. You know. I'm really glad you're going to be around this year. I've missed you." He slides a hand to her shoulder, pulling her into his side a quick hug.

The casual contact and teasing words are foreign to me. I've never shared that kind of relationship with anyone.

I clear my throat. "Maybe I should take those into the bedroom." I gesture to the cardboard boxes stacked next to her door, and she stops slapping at her brother. Her mouth drops open the slightest bit, pink tongue darting out to swipe at her lips as she gets caught in my gaze.

"Yeah, sure. Just watch out for Loki."

Her words disappear into the background as I bury myself in an armload of boxes, needing to give myself a little space from her before I do something catastrophically stupid.

I place the boxes down carefully against the wall before shutting the door and leaning my head against it. The sounds of the siblings bickering in the next room mean they won't be coming in here anytime soon. Good. I need a moment to get my shit back together. I can't bring myself to shut my eyes. Not in a strange place, but I count to five as I drag a deep breath in before blowing it out slowly.

Pull yourself together, Connell.

I got this. The physical barrier of the door provides enough distance to calm me down. All of me. Even the unruly eager part that really wants to see Cece naked again. He's going to have to get used to disappointment.

A quick, dark shadow flickers to my left, snapping my body back into alert mode. "What the fuck?" I jump back, letting loose a high-pitched screech as something skitters across my foot.

There's a flurry of activity. Cece and Beau, rushing through the door, some small creature darting around. Everything's a blur as I struggle to gain control of the quick pants of my breathing.

"Lucy? What's wrong?"

Beau steps over to me, dropping a hand onto my shaking shoulder.

I realize how ridiculous this must look, but I can't help it. "Rat."

Cece bends over by the single table in the room. It was one of the few pieces of furniture in the place before we got here, and I finally spot the two large cages sitting on the surface.

One of them has two shaggy brown and white creatures, nibbling away at a bowl of food. Guinea Pigs. They might be cute if they weren't terrifying, but I can kind of handle them, since they're contained.

When she straightens, stretching her arms toward me, a tiny whiskered face peeks out between her fingers. She plops it into the second cage, and my shoulders ease up the slightest bit at the loud clang that rings through the mostly empty room when she flips the latch.

"Sorry about that," she says. "I did tell you to watch out for Loki."

There's an amused light in Beau's eyes, and he's pressing his lips together to avoid laughing in my face. At least he's trying to contain his amusement. I know how ridiculous it looks. Tough enforcer terrified of tiny fuzzy rodents, but it's ingrained. The fear sunk too deep under my five-year-old skin.

"I need to..." I trail off, stepping away until my back hits the door. I reach down, turning the handle. My eyes stay locked on the innocent looking little creatures hanging out in their cages until I've left the room. The one that accosted me is clearly a ferret.

I don't lift my head up, even when Beau's hand lands on my shoulder. "I think we all need a break. I'm going to grab us some food. Ethel's?" he asks.

"Sure." My voice is still a little shaky, and I'm hot all over, embarrassed at my reaction. Thankfully, my friend lets it go. Stepping away and calling to his sister.

"Heading to Ethel's. Want to come or do you want me to grab you a burger?"

"Burger please," she calls out, still in her bedroom. Hopefully, she stays there while her brother is gone. I'm way too rattled to control myself right now if she gets close.

The door slams shut, a clock ticks in the silence, and then the rumble of Beau's SUV signals his departure.

My body tilts to the side as the couch dips with her weight. The pulse of awareness is back, but she stays silent, not touching me, not speaking, as if she senses I need a minute.

As I concentrate on deep, regular breaths, my heartbeat slows down, returning to a steady rhythm. I can finally lift my head up from hands, but I'm not ready to make eye contact, see the judgment in her eyes that I'm afraid of something so silly.

"You know, when we were kids, Beau thought it was hilarious that I was scared of spiders. He started buying plastic ones and hiding them in my sock drawer, my shoes. It would stop for a while and then he'd spring it on me some random day when I was in a rush to get to school."

She drops a tentative hand on my shoulder, the touch so light it barely registers, but it's reassuring. Helping the fear ebb.

"I'm still terrified of them. Thank goodness we don't live in Australia. If there were deadly ones around, I don't think I'd be able to function. I'd probably start thinking they were fake and get bitten. I'd either die a horrible death of spider venom, or maybe I'd get lucky and a radioactive one would get me. Mutant spidey senses could come in handy." Her weight shifts the cushions and I'm pretty sure she's twisted around to look at me. "You know what, though? I've never been a big fan of Spiderman. Now that I'm thinking about it, I think that's why. Thanks, Beau. Spiderman is actually a pretty cool superhero when you think about it."

By the time she gets through her long ramble, I've almost forgotten the reason I was so scared. Possibly the purpose of her rant.

"Are you laughing at me?" she asks, and I try to still my shaking shoulders.

"No."

"Yes, you are. It's okay. I'm used to it."

She sounds so light and unconcerned when she says it, but I find a flame of anger flickering in my chest. "I'm not laughing at you. With you."

"No, it's okay. I'm aware of how ridiculous I sound. Going off on these crazy tangents. It's just the way my brain works. I get how it sounds, though."

"You're a lot of things, but ridiculous is not one of them." I turn to her. Her cheeks are tinged with pink, either from laughter or embarrassment, and her eyes are sparkling.

Her mouth falls open again, and she searches my face, studying each feature in a way that makes me feel like she can see right inside me. See what's underneath the intimidating hockey player image I've worked hard for.

"Why'd you pretend you didn't know me then?"

My heart pauses at the thought I've hurt her, guilt twisting my stomach. She thinks I'm not interested. That I haven't been wishing for a repeat with every fiber of my being. "It's not you."

I don't love the sharp bitter tinge to her laugh. "It's not you, it's me. Really, Castle? I thought you were more original than that."

"No. That's not. We can't." I'm searching for the words to explain without revealing too much. It's difficult to let go of those little pieces of myself. The hurt, the pain. Everything I've been through that I never talk about. "I didn't have the best childhood. Your brother. He's almost like a brother to me. I can't do that to him. He's all I've got." I'm not good enough for her, but she'd probably try to deny it. I don't need her to defend me, and Beau is a major part of the reason we can't do this thing. Explore all the feelings she sparked in me during that amazing weekend. But even if he wasn't an issue, there's no way she deserves to be loaded with my damage.

"Beau? He's my brother, not my keeper, but you're right. I'm sure he'd give me shit about it, too. And I'm trying to keep myself out of trouble. After what happened..." the words die on her lips, and she glances at me again, curiosity burning in those gorgeous eyes. "You really don't know, do you?"

My brows pull together. "Know what?"

Her fingers tangle in those silky strands, twisting a lock around them as she thinks about whether she's going to share her secret with me. I wish I could tell her to share all her secrets with me, but that's an impossible dream. "I got in some trouble at the end of last year. That's why I'm here at Lakeview. My father pulled me from Cornell. He sent me here, so Beau can keep an eye on me. Like I can't look after myself. Men. Ridiculous. It's fine. Next year I'll be free."

"What did you do?" She can't pique my curiosity like that and leave me hanging. I shouldn't pry, but I can't help myself.

"Ugh." The couch dips again as she flings herself backward, throwing her hands over her face. She separates her fingers for a moment, peeking at me before snapping them shut.

"You don't have to tell me."

"No, it's fine. Not like it isn't all over the Internet. I was kind of drunk, and partying, and I ended up climbing Ezra topless. Someone took my pic and spread it all over, because you know, our family is not exactly under the radar."

"Who the fuck is Ezra?" My back snaps me upright, and I turn to face her. I have zero right to the rage welling inside me at the thought of her riding some guy in public. But it's there, anyway.

She does a double take, shock morphing into amusement. A laugh bubbles out.

"What?"

"The statue of Ezra Cornell on campus. Wait. Did you think I was getting it on with someone in public? Give me some credit."

"Shit." I duck my head.

The memory of her gorgeous tits flashes in my head, and I suck in another deep breath, reaching up to cover the still tender spot on my side. An angry red cloud descends over my vision at the thought of them on display for the entire world, but then I check myself. What about her? The impact it had on her. Having her privacy violated. I can't stand it when someone touches my bag, but that. That's unimaginable. Never knowing how many strange eyes have seen you in a vulnerable position like that.

"I'm sorry."

"What?"

"I'm sorry that happened to you." It's all making sense now. How edgy she got when I teased her about taking her picture. I can't imagine how hard it's been for her. Growing up with so many eyes on her.

Her laugh is nervous this time. "It's fine. My bad. I should know better than to do careless shit like that. I've been in the public eye my entire life."

"It's not your fault. Have they caught the person who did it? It was their fault, not yours."

"Oh." The surprise in her eyes has an uncomfortable knot forming in my chest. "Most people roll their eyes and tell me I shouldn't have been so stupid. Thank you for not..."

Fuck. Humans can be so crappy to each other. I nod, pretty tapped out on words by this point. It's easy to talk to her, but hearing her voice makes it harder to resist reaching over to pull her into my side. Drop a kiss on top of her head to feel the silky strands against my lips. Ask her for one more night before I let her go. Because I'm not going anywhere near my best friend's twin after today. I won't be able to keep my hands to myself if I have to spend any more time around her. Especially when she's looking so vulnerable. If I could even hug her. But no. Terrible idea.

She stares at me for a little while longer. The silence isn't uncomfortable, but I think she's expecting some kind of response I'm just not capable of right now. Too dangerous.

Her knee is bouncing double time, and she's nibbling on her bottom lip. "You're right."

"About?"

"We should not let that happen again. As fantastic as it was, we both agreed it was just for the weekend. That doesn't have to change just because we're going to the same school now. You don't want to mess with your friendship. I'm already on shaky ground, and Beau's already going to be keeping a closer eye on me than usual. Staying away from each other is the smart choice." She nods her head, then leans in until I'm engulfed in her. Her scent surrounds me, her soft breath brushes my cheek, and her lips are so close I can almost taste them.

I drag in a lungful of her sweet aroma, locking it away in the part of my brain where I keep my positive memories. The scattered few from my childhood. The more frequent ones since I got to college. The ones I dredge up to chase away the darkness in my past.

"Maybe one last kiss..."

She leans closer until the space between our lips is paper thin, and it's sweet agony, but I don't make a move. Not wanting to destroy the moment.

The scraping of a key turning in the lock is like a gunshot, sending me flying back in my seat before I make contact.

"Shit." Cece jumps up, running her hands down her sides, fussing with the already disheveled mess of a bun on her head.

I'm still slumped back on the cushion, heart racing again as she bounces over to the door. Her ass jiggles in those tight leggings, and I know I can't see her again and definitely not alone. I would never be able to resist the temptation, no matter how much is at stake.

"Beau!" she calls out, voice overly bright and loud. The glaring opposite of her last whispered words. The promise in them is going to linger in my mind for the rest of the week or year. Taunting me with the missed opportunity. "Let me help you."

That kicks me into gear, and I push myself off the couch. The food smells amazing, and even though I'm not that hungry anymore, I'm going to demolish that burger. Ethel makes the best burgers, and thinking about her homemade fries has my mouth watering. My hand brushes Cece's as I'm snagging the bag Beau holds out, and I pull it back like I've been burned, retreating to the floor beside the couch. If I take the couch, she might sit next to me, and breathing would be difficult with her soft body so close to mine. Even with her brother sitting beside us.

"Why are you sitting on the floor? Plenty of room up here." My friend gives me a weird look, but I shrug at him.

"Whatever, dude. You do you. Did you get anything else done while I was gone or were you too afraid to go into Cece's bedroom?" Beau asks before taking a tidy bite of his burger.

"What?" Does he know?

"The animals. My sister's rodent collection too much for you."

I'd completely forgotten about the ferret. That's how much she transfixes me.

"Hey! Don't say that about my sweeties. They're not rodents. They're my family."

"They're not your family. I'm your family."

"I guess I'm stuck with you, but Rogue and Gambit never give me noogies."

"That's because they don't have knuckles," Beau says, between mouthfuls of fries.

There's a painful lump in my throat as I swallow down a too large bite. "Rogue and Gambit?" I tilt my head to the side, questioning Cece.

"Yes. Those are my guinea pigs. Because they have the same everlasting love for each other. Minus the sexy times, because Gambit is neutered. I adopted them at the beginning of last year. Loki puts up with them, but they don't mind his indifference because they've got each other."

"Loki is the ferret?" A little shiver runs up my back remembering his tiny paws skittering over my socked feet, but I try to hide it, because she obviously loves the creature.

"Yup." There's genuine affection shining in her eyes. I've never had a pet. A couple of my foster families had dogs or cats, but I never stayed with them long enough to get attached. Maybe I should get a cat now? But then, probably not a great idea. I sometimes travel for games now but next year, once I'm in the pros, I'll be traveling constantly. Not exactly a great lifestyle for a pet owner. Not unless you have someone at home to look after it. And that will not be happening for me.

After cleaning up dinner, we head back to her room to finish our last job before wrapping up for the day. Assemble her bed. Not at all a torturous proposition knowing I'll never get to spend the night in it with her.

I'm hovering in the doorway when she waves me in. "Ca... I mean Dev come in. It's safe. I swear all critters are safely tucked away in their cages this time."

Beau barely notices her slip, but it almost rocks me back on my heels. He would have had questions if she blurted out a nickname for the hockey player she supposedly just met. And he's well aware of the Punisher costume I wore to the con. Not that there's any chance he'd connect those two dots. Now I'm being paranoid.

"Give me a sec. Gotta wash my hands." I dart into the ensuite bathroom, scrubbing the grime off my hands, then gasping at the shock as I splash cold water on my face.

Something silky slides under my hands as I'm reaching behind for the towel.

Beau shoves the door open wider. "Come on, dude, I... what the..."

Water droplets sting my eyes when I blink them open. Emotions flash across his face. Eyes narrowed with suspicion, followed by amusement. And suddenly he's full out laughing.

"Sissy!" he yells.

Now she's peering in the doorway and I'm still clueless. Until I glance down to find a bright red bra hanging from my fingers.

Her cheeks flame up, turning the color of the garment she's snatching out of my hand. She stomps off without a word, leaving me standing awkwardly next to her brother, who is doubled over in laughter.

"Don't be getting any ideas. That's my sister," he says, slapping me on the back and hustling me back into the bedroom.

Chapter Nine

My Kind Of Weird

Cece

The chime of the doorbell has me leaping to my feet, knocking the half empty bowl of popcorn sitting beside me to the floor. Crap. I was stuck in waiting mode and got trapped in a loop of endless doomscrolling. What time is it? My roommates are all due to arrive at any moment, and I was planning on getting changed into something, anything. Of course, that would have required doing laundry, which I fully intended to do this morning, but couldn't find the motivation for such a mundane chore. Nor did I bother to figure out which box contains the rest of my wardrobe.

And now, here I am, once again, brushing popcorn crumbs off my fuzzy pajama pants. It's like I'm living in that old Groundhog Day movie Beau forced me to watch when we were kids. He loved the endless repetition. My tangled hair is hanging loose around my shoulders after a restless night of sleep. There's at least one hair elastic in this place. I was using it yesterday when the guys were over.

The guys. Thinking of Dev reminds me of the reason I got no sleep last night. I spent two hours reviewing every detail of our weekend, followed by every glance and expression on his face yesterday. And when I did fall asleep, I had some of the most vivid, spiciest dreams of my life, starring his perfect hockey body. My nipples are tingling at the mere memory. But it's only a shadow of the real thing.

The doorbell sounds again, a little longer this time, but not past the point of politeness. "Crap."

I run over to the door, suck in a deep breath, and throw a smile on my face. I'm hoping it's not too unhinged, but they've already signed the rental agreement, so they're stuck with me either way.

A blonde with curly shoulder length hair is standing on the other side of the door. She's got a Barbie pink rolling suitcase by her side and a beaming lipsticked smile on her face.

"Georgia. Welcome." My volume of my voice has me wincing. *Too much, Cecelia. Don't scare them away on the first day.*

She doesn't seem to mind, throwing her arms around me in an effusive hug.

"Cece, so nice to meet you." Her southern accent is as welcoming as her bright smile.

"You too. It's great to meet you in person. Finally. A video call isn't the same as a flesh and blood meeting, is it?" She's perfectly put together. From the smooth perfection of her pink polished nails to the styled curls held back from her forehead by a wide blue headband.

She's rolling her suitcase through the hall toward the living room. The living room. My stomach hits the floor. The popcorn. I dart ahead, glancing around, trying to remember where I stashed the broom. There's no sign of it, so now I'm hunched over, scrabbling around on the floor like a scavenger, scooping popcorn back into the bowl, when my perfectly polished new roommate steps in.

"Oh," she says.

"I'm so sorry. I was having a snack when you got here, and the doorbell startled me." No need to let her know the bowl of popcorn was actually my combination breakfast and lunch. Clearly, she can already see what a hot mess I am. No need to drive the point home any harder.

"Not a problem. Let me help you." And then she's dropping down to crouch beside me, shoulder brushing mine as I'm picking up buttery kernels off the floor.

"Not the first impression I was hoping to make."

"I don't mind. It's kind of refreshing, actually. My mom would have a positive conniption if I dropped a single toast crumb on the floor. College life has been very liberating."

I dig the last couple of pieces out from under the couch, dropping them in the red plastic bowl and dart off to the kitchen. Georgia has settled right in, sprawled on

the overstuffed beige couch, socked feet up on the shiny
new coffee table when I get back.

"Feel that. Your mom is a bit much?" I ask her.

"I love mama to death, but she needs everything to be
perfect all the time, but prim and proper is not really me.
I like to dress up and look nice as much at the next lady,
but I also like to let loose. If you know what I mean." She
winks at me with one of her impossibly long, thick lashes.

"Awesome. Me too."

I drop next to her on the couch. "So, you're working
on your MFA, right?" After going through endless appli-
cations and a series of video calls that drained me for a
week, I selected a group of roommates I could live with
who also passed my father's scrutiny.

"Sure am. Writing is my passion."

"And you write horror and paranormal stuff?" My eyes
travel down the pink highlights on her outfit, the perfect
blonde hair and shimmery eye makeup.

Her laugh is like a tinkling bell. "I sure do. I love a
spooky story."

The doorbell rings again, interrupting my curiosity,
and she joins me to greet our next arrival.

It's actually two arrivals. Anna and Blake are both waiting on the other side with smiles on their faces. Did I
neglect to mention Blake to my dad? Maybe. I'm a hundred percent certain he would not be all in on the idea of
me living with a guy, but he and Anna came as a package
deal. They're best friends and have been living together
since they started at Lakeview. Their last rental house got
sold and they couldn't renew their lease for senior year,

so here we are. Anna slid through his background check, and I told Dad I needed to use the fourth bedroom as a library. I'm sure Blake will keep some books in there, and my father won't take the time to drive all the way from Fox Chapel for a visit.

"Anna, Blake. Nice to meet you."

"You too." Anna's smile is a little more tentative than Georgia's was, and she's dressed much more casually in a graphic tee that says Game On paired with worn jeans. Blake's got on a similar outfit and his blue eyes are shining with warmth behind his dark glasses. He steps ahead of Anna to hold out his hand for a shake.

Blake is craning his neck, taking the place in, while Anna untangles herself from Georgia's embrace.

"I'd love to check out our rooms and grab the rest of our stuff." The deep tone of his voice catches me by surprise.

"Umm, I'll show you the rooms and you can take your pick however you want. Swords at twenty paces would probably be my choice, but it's up to you."

That steals a giggle from Anna.

"I'm more of a pistols girl myself," Georgia says.

Blake holds up his hands. "I'm not getting involved in this. I'm sure either of you ladies could take me down. If it's anything more serious than rock, paper, scissors, you can count me out."

"Chicken." Anna smirks at her friend, and there's a teasing glimmer in her eyes when she looks at him.

She's more tentative and quieter than Georgia, but I'm pretty good at getting people to open up. Look how many words I dragged out of Dev. I have got to stop letting every single thing remind me of him. It's not happening.

"I'm going to make a suggestion before this comes to blows. How about if I show you the rooms and you three can decide if you have preferences. You never know. It might all work out with no one spilling any blood."

Everyone traipses upstairs to check out the rooms, and after some discussion and a minor dispute between Anna and Blake, they all settle on their choices.

"I'll let you guys unpack and settle in. I'm ordering dinner for everyone tonight. Want to make it an easy pizza night? Any vegans? Gluten-free?"

"Nope, Anna and I are pizza sluts. We'll eat anything except for jalapenos or green peppers," Blake says.

"The more meat, the better. I like a little sausage." I do a double take at Georgia, not knowing her well enough to read her tone, but the smirk twisting her lips gives her away.

"Got it." I scribble on an imaginary pad. "Extra sausage for Georgia."

"I think I'm sleeping here tonight." I flop back against the couch with a groan, patting my aching belly. "Unless someone can roll me up the stairs."

"You're not going to sleep yet. We have to get to know each other." Georgia bounces in her seat, turning to face me. "Tell me about the best sex you've ever had."

She is one surprise after another. "Way to dip your toe in the pool. We can't start with something the tiniest bit less personal. Like, I don't know. My favorite color or something? It's red, by the way."

She waves me off with her pink-tipped nails. "No way. We're going to be living together. I'm all for diving right in. Then there are no surprises. If you need me to, I'll go first. His name was Damon." Her dramatic pause has me tapping my foot impatiently. "Black hair and dark brown eyes, but that's hardly important. It was last summer. We went on a family vacation to Florida to visit my gran. He was a lifeguard. Yum. You can not imagine the muscles on him." She closes her eyes, a dreamy smile spreading across her face. "He took me up the lifeguarding tower after it closed for the night, and I'm pretty sure several people reported hearing a banshee that night. I may never scream that loud again. Sadly."

That was informative. "You're lucky he didn't murder you and throw your body out to sea," I say.

"Don't tell me you haven't had a one-night stand?"

"Of course I have. In fact, my last one was only two weeks ago..." I trail off, unsure if I should share this. It's one thing to share a story about an anonymous guy you're never going to see again, but talking about someone that is now so close seems a little dangerous. As if I'm going to invoke his spirit or something and he'll show up at my doorstep. Or he'll overhear me.

"Ooh. Do tell. This sounds juicy." Georgia is egging me on, and both Blake and Anna are leaning forward.

The couch cushion bounces under the weight of my head, and I scrub my hands down my face. The words are ready to burst out of me, but I'm still hesitant. If I put the experience out into the universe, will he know I'm talking about him? Will I be able to look him in the eyes when we run into each other? Beau typed his number into my contacts. Just in case my dear brother isn't around to bail me out of whatever situation I end up in. As if I haven't been living quite capably on my own for the past three years.

"I'll share if you share."

My eyes pop open at the softer voice, and I catch Blake glancing curiously at his friend. As if he wants to find out her secret confession. That's enough to convince me. He's not a ghost. I'm not going to summon him by speaking his name out loud.

"Fine. I was at the Great Lakes Con."

"You were?" Blake asks. "Anna and I were there too. If we'd known, we totally could have hooked up with you."

"That would have been epic." Except... then I might not have ever met him. Although with the recent turn of events, maybe that would have been for the best.

"Shush, Blake." Anna lands a friendly smack on his arm before turning back to me. "Go on."

"Right. I was supposed to go with my friend, Tess, but she ended up having to bail out last minute. So, I was waiting in the registration line, and there's this guy in front of me. Massive." In all the right ways.

"Tall? Muscular? Like a bouncer, or more beer gut? What are we talking about?" Georgia asks.

"Like athlete. Tall, muscled. He's a hockey player."

"Ooh. Nice catch. Nerdy and a hockey player. Put a ring on it."

"Um, no. It was a strictly one weekend kind of thing. We were both heading back to school. But honestly. The things he did to my body. The places... against the window, the shower. I didn't think it was possible to come that many times in a twenty-four-hour span."

Blake's eyes are wide, and heat zips up my neck to my cheeks. Maybe that was too much information for our first day as roommates. I need to learn when to stop.

"Amazing. You win. I mean, we still need to hear Anna and Blake's stories, but this sounds like a winner to me. Did you get his deets so you can hook up with him again, or is he just going to be future fodder for your sexy dreams?" Georgia asks.

"No. Definitely never happening again. That's a hard no." My brains are as rattled as my thoughts from the vigorous shake of my head. I got so caught up in the story I almost forgot who Devlin is. And that information is far too intimate for this fledgling friendship.

"Too bad. You could have introduced me to one of his hockey player friends. I'm not a skater, but I'd share the ice with one of them any day."

"My brother plays."

Her whole being lightens up at my offhand remark. Her big blue eyes sparkle, her blonde curls look even shinier. If that's possible. "Really? I'm going to need you to introduce me."

"Ew. Not my brother."

Her curls bounce as she shakes her head. "Well, no. That might be weird. But there's an entire team to get to know. I've tried out a couple of the football players, and I even dated a soccer player for a coupe of months, but sexy hockey player is at the top of my TBF list. Preferably with all teeth currently intact."

"TBF?" Anna asks, looking about as confused as I am.

"To be fucked. Obvi."

Hearing all the dirty thoughts spilling from Georgia is a little jarring when you compare it to her perfectly demure designer outfit but, I love it. She's my kind of people.

"My brother doesn't like me near his hockey friends. Ever since..." I trail off.

"Ever since what?" Anna asks.

I tilt my head up to inspect the ceiling. It's flawless, not a single crack or tiny bug to fixate on.

Georgia snorts. "Honey, if I listened to everything my overprotective brothers told me to do, I'd be wearing a nun's habit right now. And honestly, I've never been into LBDs, much less BBDs. I'm fond of a little color in my wardrobe."

I may have just met the girl, but I cannot picture her in chaste nun's clothing, that's for sure.

"I guess I can snag us tickets for the first game of the season. It's October seventh, if you can wait that long." Beau can't object to me attending one of his games. He doesn't need to know the real person I'm there to watch.

"Excellent. It'll give me time to do some research."

"Hockey research? I can fill you in on the rules if you'd like. I may not be into the game, but I've been dragged along to enough of them over the years that I could hold my own against some of the most avid fans in a trivia game."

She laughs again. "Not that kind of research. Unless you're familiar with the Lakeview players. I'm going to dig into their social media. Check out their pics, see if they any of them are off limits. I am not a cheater."

"Gotcha. Anna, Blake, want me to get you tickets too?" I turn to them. Might be fun. A bit of a bonding experience with my new housemates.

Anna laughs. "No, thanks. The only sports match we've ever gone to is Quidditch."

"Respect." I nod. "Okay, Georgia. It's a date. I'll snag some tickets."

CHAPTER TEN

EMOTIONAL SUPPORT DEFENDER

DEV

T he last few weeks have crawled by as if time decided to mess with me. And JJ seems to have latched on to me as if I'm his emotional support defender. That guy can not take a hint.

Tonight's season opener couldn't come soon enough, but here we are at last, and I can not wait to get out on the ice. Hopefully, I can pour some of the guilt and frustration that's been riding me out on the ice. Practice is great and all, but there's nothing like a game to work through things. It's been my coping mechanism ever since I was lucky enough to find the sport. Who knows where I'd be right now if it wasn't for Coach Neeland introducing me to hockey? Nowhere good.

I'm relieved Beau headed to the arena early to deal with captain business. There's some shit going on with the team right now. It's keeping him busy enough to consume his attention. The relief is a double-edged sword. It makes the knot of guilt residing in my chest press against my heart in an even tighter vise. I've been spending a lot of time on campus, so I don't have to look my best friend in the eye, which only compounds the feeling. The things I did to his sister. He's given me his trust and his house. He's the most important person in my life, and I betrayed him. It doesn't matter that I was in the dark about her identity at the time. Ignorance is no excuse for breaking the bro code.

I clock Beau sitting on the bench having a chat with Cole. He was a mere blip on the radar of the team last year. Newly transferred to Lakeview with a murky past, but he kept to himself. This year some girl drama seems to be coming back to bite him in the ass. Not ideal for the team, but it's keeping Beau's attention occupied at the moment. Between him and that cocky freshman Hail, I'm a little less worried about my best friend catching on to me.

I ignore JJ and Grant even when our illustrious goalie ends up at my feet, half dressed. He hurled himself on his friend for an unannounced piggyback ride gone wrong.

"Iceman! Nothing's going to throw you off your game, is it, Lucy?" Grant asks despite the laughter shaking his shoulders.

I don't bother to answer, instead replying with a slight lift of my brow. It only ratchets his laughter up to the next level, almost sending him to his knees.

JJ jumps to his feet, bounding over to me like the excited puppy he is. "Lucy. I was worried about you. You're always one of the first ones to arrive. What happened?"

The bus was late, that's what happened. "None of your business, JJ."

"It is. I need you out there. My brick wall. Jameson is out on the ice tonight. He's sent more than one goalie flying."

He was worried. Jameson is a dick, and I'd be happy to be the one to teach him a lesson if he tries to pull any shit on my goalie. "Don't worry. I got your back."

He smiles, walking back over to his stall with a swagger. "See, I told you he's my friend." He's trying to be quiet, hissing the words to Grant and Mack, but he's not great at volume control and the room is small. I shake my head, turning to grab my equipment so no one notices the twitching of my lips.

Even though I got in later than most of the team, I'm the first one out the door and into the tunnel. The thump of skates on rubber echoes behind me as I make my way to the ice. My favorite place. I need it more than usual today. The weightless feeling of gliding on the icy surface, freshly smoothed out by the Zamboni. I'm not interested in being the center of attention, but once the buzzer sounds, the crowd melts away as I'm consumed by the game.

I'm waiting for Beau to catch up and lead us onto the ice, scanning the packed arena just in case Cece showed up. Even though I know she's not interested in hockey, there's a miniscule part of me that is hoping she's out there. An icy shock hits me in the guts when I spot someone else familiar out there. He's sitting in the stands to the left of the tunnel. Not in the friends and family section, but too close to it for my liking.

His smile falters when he catches my glare. I shake my head and get jostled from behind, not realizing our captain slipped by me and we're on the move. I stomp the rest of the way, hopping onto the ice with a thump and racing past Beau.

"Hey, you okay?" Beau's hand lands on my shoulder as he catches up to me.

"Fine."

I'm sure he'll spot the lie if I turn to look at him, so I keep my eyes fixed on the path. He's the only person who can read me. Who can see past my carefully cultivated veneer of calm.

"You sure? You haven't been around as much, Lucy. Leaving me with those children." I follow his glance to catch sight of JJ and Grant still jostling each other. Cole is storming along behind them, brow pinched in a frown as he stares at Hail's back.

"Exactly. I don't have the time in my senior year to deal with those hooligans." I'm practically growling not.

"Thanks, bestie. Appreciate the support."

"Hey, you said yes to the captain's gig. You laced your skates, now you've gotta hit the ice on them."

He slaps my back with a laugh, and there's a strained look on his face. "I guess you're right, Lucy."

That was shitty of me. I should be supporting him. I'm not his alternate, but I am his friend, and instead of helping him out, all I can think about is his sister.

"Shit, I'm sorry. Let me know if you need anything." I tap gloves with him, settling back a stride behind for our lap of the arena.

The conversation was enough of a distraction I almost forgot this isn't just a practice. The sweeping spotlights and rumble of the crowd as we skate the perimeter is a brutal reminder, and my nerves ratchet back up to the level that always sets in during a game. Especially an important one like this. The first and last games of every season are always significant to me.

I'm conflicted. Back in the place I love. Competing, proving myself. That I'm better than my past. Better than my upbringing. Better than the names the other kids called me when I'd show up at school wearing second-hand clothes. Out here, on the ice, with my team, we're all in it together. But there's still doubt. That I'm not good enough, and never will. That I don't deserve this. My only solution when those doubts creep in is to work harder, go the extra mile. Prove myself with my actions.

I slip across the slick surface as our names boom out, echoing through the cavernous space.

The crowd is riled up, cheers and stomps booming across the clean sheet of ice. Freshly groomed ice is the best. So much potential in front of us. Senior year for me and Beau. Our chance to claim the glory of a trophy, proving our worth without the heavy hitting stars who moved on to the next level after winning the champs last year.

Jameson, UPenn's massive defender, starts the game off quick and dirty, hooking Grant in a subtle move the ref misses. Big mistake. I'm always determined to win, but if you're going to pull dirty shit on my teammates, I'm gonna take you down. Guy may be big, but he's a hothead. And nothing makes a hothead lose it faster than playing hard, but fair. And not caving to their taunts.

Beau glances at the ref, calling out for justice, but he doesn't push his luck. I can't say I blame him. This ref has tossed players for smaller sins than fighting a missed call. He's got beady little mouse eyes. Maybe that's why he misses so many calls.

My eyes dart back and forth, tracking the puck and all the other players as they zip over the slick surface in a familiar dance.

Alarm bells scream in my head when their top scorer Luchek snags the puck. I drive my legs into high gear, pushing off the ice at what some might say is an impossible speed for someone of my size. But I've spent years defying the odds, and I'm not about to stop now.

Working three jobs this summer didn't stop me from getting in as much ice time and cardio as I could manage. I pushed myself to the limit of my endurance every day. That's one good thing about having the house to myself all summer. No distractions. Every spare minute of time I've had has been devoted to improving my speed and my game, other than that one weekend. I catch sight of Beau, stifling the thought immediately.

Luchek's eyes widen when he realizes I'm almost on top of him. He's got no chance as my momentum sends him crashing into the boards in a clean hit that thunders into the stands, sending the fans near the front flying to their feet.

There's no time to pause, even see the look on his face. I skate off, but my lips twist in a satisfied smirk when I pass the dirty defender. That's how it's done.

Excitement is swelling. This is looking promising. Cole snatched the puck and is racing down the ice clear of his tail. This could be it. First blood. But then he falters, frozen into place, staring at the crowd. Split seconds matter in hockey, and the pause gives the other team time to swoop back in for the steal.

Fuck. What the fuck was that all about?

I turn to Beau, but he's already on it, dressing down Cole with an angry shout as the play continues.

Jameson sets his sights on our rookie with an attitude problem, while I'm trying to figure out what the fuck is going on with Schaeffer. I sigh, nope. Not on my watch. He might be a big guy, but I'm bigger and, even more important, smarter. I blast up behind him and interfere with his plans, whatever they might be. He backs off our winger, glaring at me. His face is red, and I'm sure his knuckles are white under his gloves he's clutching his stick so hard.

I shake my head at him, skating away as Hail pulls away from the snarl.

Whatever extra speed I've gained is nothing to Schaeffer and Hail. Before now I would have said Schaeffer's got the edge this year, but honestly, the way Hail moves on the ice is almost liquid. Shame he's such a shitty team player, because that cocky asshole is going to be a star one day. If he can scale that massive ego.

They spend the entire game trying to one up each other, which only makes my job harder in the long run. I have to keep a constant eye on both of them when they're on the ice together. Cole's a bit distracted by his own drama, and Hail seems hellbent on proving his dick is bigger, so they keep getting themselves in dangerous situations. Situations I have to handle as the enforcer on the team. Nothing I'm not used to. I may not always get the glory as a D-man, but half these goals wouldn't happen if I wasn't looking out for these guys.

My constant vigilance pays off. I'm distracting the defender that was tracking Hail, leaving him open to snag the puck. The lamp and our home crowd lose their shit at the same time before the puck has bounced off the back of the net.

Fuck yes. Beau barrels into me with a quick hug and we count down the seconds to the end of the game, playing a game of competitive keep away. He rips his helmet off, running a slightly shaky hand through the damp strands of dark blond hair.

"You okay, man?" I ask him quietly. The shakiness could be the adrenaline, but the glittering sheen in my best friend's eyes sets off an internal alarm.

He laughs off my concern. "I'm fine."

I narrow my eyes at him, but he skates away to congratulate the rest of the team before I can dig deeper.

The team's riding on a high after kicking ass in our first game of the season. As a result, the shenanigans in the dressing room are extra even for these guys, so I'm trying to slip out the door without anyone noticing me. At this point, I'd rather take the bus home than deal with JJ and Grant anymore. Not to mention Hail's attitude. Cocky fucker.

Unfortunately, sneaking around is not such an easy task when you're my size, and Beau, our ever-vigilant captain, catches sight of me as I'm pushing the door open. He breaks off his conversation with Cole to call me out. "Lucy, you got somewhere to be? If you hang out a little longer, I can give you a ride. I'm going to finish up here and have a quick convo with Coach, but I won't be long."

I duck my head down, rubbing a hand over my close-cropped hair to avoid looking him in the eyes. I've gotten surprisingly adept at that since the start of our senior year. "Nah, I'm good. I've got a couple of things to do before I head home." Great. Now I'm going to have to stall and hang around campus for a while when all I really want to do is collapse on my bed with my graphic novel.

"Okay, man. I'll text you before I leave, in case you're still on campus and ready to head out."

"Thanks." I dip my head, trying to ignore the sour curdling in my stomach.

I'm in such a hurry to escape I'm pushing out the back door without thinking. I was planning on leaving out the side entrance in case my dear father is still lurking out back.

Looks like my carelessness didn't bite me in the ass this time. I glance around the parking lot. A handful of students loiter near the small grouping of statues in the little grassy area off to the right of the building, but that's it.

I breathe a sigh of relief and pick up my pace, legs eating up the pavement as I make a beeline for the North block of buildings where the library is located. I can hang there for a while, catch up on some of my assigned work before I head home.

But I'm only halfway across the lot when someone walks around the side of a black pickup. The low-level dread that's been lurking in me since he first showed up on my doorstep flares into a helpless mixture of fear and rage. I hate that he can still make me feel this way.

"Devlin," he calls out. His all too familiar eyebrows are lifted in a pleading expression. Everything about him is familiar, like a reflection in a warped mirror. He's an older, more faded version of me, with all the evidence of his rough life etched into his features. It's an unsettling reminder of what I could become if my luck runs out. If someone realizes I don't really belong here. At college, and especially not in the pro hockey league. I don't deserve that. Everything about my upbringing taught me that.

"I told you to leave." My spine stiffens, and I cross my arms over my chest, taking an involuntary step back even as I'm glaring at him.

"Please, I just want to talk. I stayed for the game. You played so well. Without you, your team never would have gotten those goals."

"I don't need your praise." The time for that would have been a decade and a half ago.

"Just one drink. We can grab a coffee and talk. And then if you never want to see me again, I'll leave you alone." His brow is pinched together, lips tight. If I didn't know better, I'd think he was sad at the thought of never seeing me again. But I do know better. Didn't he tell me he wished I'd never been born enough times? He can't fool me with this act.

But I waver. If I say yes, there's a tiny chance he'll follow through on his promise and I'll never see him again. *Isn't that what I want?*

As I'm going back and forth, shifting from one foot to another, a shiny red car coasts up beside me, and a familiar face stretches through the driver's side window. I swallow hard as I take in her features. Her white-blonde hair is pulled back in a high ponytail, curved cheeks stretched in a smile to show her shockingly white teeth. Her eyes are narrowed, flicking back and forth between me and him as if she can sense the tension.

"Hey, Dev. Need a lift?"

Chapter Eleven

Something Sweet

Cece

I'm tugging at the hem of the jersey I wore to the game. I wasn't planning on it, but Georgia snagged them for us from the campus store. Hers says Hail on the back. She said he was the hottest player that's not in a relationship based on her in-depth research. Hail is an outstanding player. He's fast on his skates and aggressive toward the goal. No surprise he scored one for the Lightning tonight, but he's not my type at all. Not to mention it's a bit of a cradle robbing situation for Georgia.

I ducked out after the game, though. Georgia heard the team was going to Wright's. Apparently, that's where the hockey players and fans hang out after games. She asked me to come, but I begged off, not really feeling like hanging out somewhere to watch a bunch of fanboys and puck bunnies waiting in court for my brother. Been there. Done that. Not for me.

On the plus side, she told me I could take her car home, and she'll grab an Uber later, so she can have a few drinks. I sent Beau a quick text to keep an eye on the southern belle. He can be an arrogant asshole some of the time, but I know he would never let one of my friends, or any woman, get into trouble if he could prevent it.

A sense of freedom washes over me sitting behind the wheel. Finally, a chance to shake the pent-up restlessness of not having my own vehicle. I know I've been totally spoiled having my own car since I was sixteen, but that's the way it's been. And losing my ride chipped away at the independence I've had since I started college.

I'm coasting by the back of the arena when something snags my attention. There's something familiar about those broad shoulders. I slow down, turning into the parking lot that's designated for staff and players. But-terflies are stirring in my chest. Their swirling dance gets more insistent the closer I get to the figure. It's him. My comic con tryst.

A different kind of anxiety takes over when I pull up beside him. He's talking to someone. His shoulders are tense, arms crossed over his broad chest as he shakes his head at the man. The older man looks familiar for some reason, and as my eyes dart back and forth between them, something clicks. He's like an older version of Dev. They've gotta be related, but nothing about Dev's posture gives me any indication this is a joyful family reunion. I've seen that look on Beau's face before when he wants to escape some stuffy dinner with my dad and his uptight cronies.

"Hey Dev. Need a lift?" It's not like I can leave him here like this. I'm sure Beau wouldn't want his best friend trapped in an uncomfortable situation.

Shock registers on his face when he catches sight of me. His hesitation is not so flattering. Would he rather be here, trapped in this tense conversation, than accept a ride from me?

But his shoulders soften, features relaxing as he nods. "I'd love that."

The other man reaches out for him as he's stepping around the back of the car. But his legs are so long he takes all of two seconds to make it to the passenger side door.

His eyes are fixed straight ahead as if to avoid looking back at the guy after he folds himself into the seat, swearing as he conks his head on the door frame. But the veins in his neck are standing out, jaw clenched.

It takes him a minute to fold his large frame into the tiny sports car. A guy of his size needs a fuck-you truck or big-ass SUV like my brother's.

"Sorry." I shrug as he struggles with the seatbelt.

I drive carefully off in case the man does something stupid like step in front of my car, but he doesn't. Just steps away, shoulders dropping in defeat as we make our way back to the ride.

"Thanks," he says.

I'm gnawing on my lip, debating whether I should ask him about the confrontation.

"You okay?"

He drops his head back against the headrest, eyes shut. "I'll be fine."

Clearly, he's not into sharing any more details, so I ignore my curiosity. "Great game."

His eyelashes flutter open, mouth popping open with surprise, as if he forgot all about his team's win.

"It wasn't bad." His brown eyes fix on me. "I thought you weren't a hockey fan?"

"I'm not. Not really. My friend Georgia wanted to come. Apparently, she's got some sort of athlete bingo card on the go or something. She needs to check off hockey player, so she was excited to learn my brother is on the team. I told her I'd get us tickets for a game."

"Gotcha. You're still not a hockey fan. Guess if all those years at games with your brother didn't convince you, you're a lost cause."

"Actually, after tonight. I think I might be persuaded to come over to the dark side." Probably a bad idea to tell him I've never been so invested in a hockey game as I was tonight, but it's the truth. Even when I was dating Deacon.

"Really?"

I can feel him turning toward me, his eyes locked on me, but I don't turn my head. Yes, I have to keep my eyes on the road, but really I don't want to see the heated gaze that's washing my neck in warmth.

"What was different about it?"

My lips are pressed together so tightly I think they might stay that way. It's the only thing keeping the secret from spilling out. Him. He was the reason my attention was locked on the ice. I was tracking his movement, gasping when he took or gave a hit, cheering when he cleared the ice for one of his teammates or snatched the puck. I've never considered sports to be a turn on. Until now.

Finally, I can't stand the tension anymore, so I flick my eyes over to him for a brief glance. A small grin curves up his lips. Not quite the full-blown smile I caught a couple of elusive glances of while we were at the con, but it's there. Is he laughing at me? Unsure. The only thing I know for sure is that even the hint of a smile has a fluttery heat uncoiling low in my belly.

"Want to grab a coffee or something? Ooh! Maybe some dessert." I could do terrible things to a chocolate cake right now. A poor substitute for the things I want to do to Dev, but maybe it would help take my mind off that.

He's silent for so long I'm about to repeat the question.

"Probably shouldn't."

Heat crawls up my neck at the rejection. "Oh. Sorry. I shouldn't have..."

Warmth climbs up my leg when his hand lands on my thigh. The thick denim is no barrier.

"I said we shouldn't. I didn't say no."

"Oh." I risk a glance at him when we hit a red light. He's staring at me, and I can see how wrong I was. His pupils are so blown out his eyes are almost black, and his full lips have fallen open.

A horn jerks my attention back to the road and we're jolted forward when I step on the gas a little too hard.

"Where should we go? We're not too far from Ethel's. Or there's that dessert place on Main. What's it called? Pie in the Sky. We could do a coffee shop. A little more casual."

There's a low rumble next to me.

"Anywhere you want."

"Right." *Cece stop it.* Babbling. One of my less stellar qualities.

My fingers are tapping out a frenetic rhythm on the wheel as I execute a perfect parallel into a spot on the street. I glance around, hand reaching up to run through my hair, but pausing on the smooth surface when I remember it's pulled back into a neat ponytail. His hand stills the motion, and I jerk back to him.

I pull away from him. The flutters have morphed into a liquid heat and I'm going to jump his bones in my roommate's car on a public street if he keeps touching me. Terrible plan. This man is going to be my downfall if I'm not careful.

"Dessert place is right there. Let's hit it up."

I leap out of the car, pressing my body against the door when another vehicle whizzes by.

"Careful," he says, a hint of something like anger coloring his tone.

But it's not anger that has him yanking me away from the road and back against his hard chest. I'm melting into it as his right arm presses me back. My heart is thumping in my chest as if I the doors were about to open for an art show. I'd like to think it's the adrenaline from my near miss, but I'm pretty sure his proximity is also sending my pulse into overdrive.

"Don't do that again, please." His words caress my ear.

"I won't." I shake my head and squirm, trying to escape his arms. Not because I don't welcome his touch. Rather, I welcome it too much. I want his arms around me so badly I'm afraid I won't be able to hold back. If I just tilted my head the slightest bit. Leaned in toward him, his lips...

The shock of cool air yanks me out of the moment. He's pulled away and taken a step back. His fingers close over my arm in a softer hold than I would have thought the tough hockey player would be capable of. Especially after I saw the aggressive way he was taking down his opponents in the game earlier. He doesn't let go until he's dragged me away and lifted me up onto the safety of the sidewalk. I'm not sure I've ever had someone that concerned with my safety before. At least not someone who wasn't getting paid to look after me.

"Good."

He's back to rubbing his hand over the short strands of dark hair, avoiding eye contact. "Maybe we should go."

My stomach sinks. Not yet. I'm not ready to say goodbye. We might not get another chance. "I could use something sweet. Could we maybe stay? If it's not too much of a hassle for you."

He tilts his head up to stare at the sprinkling of stars in the sky, his Adam's apple bobbing as he swallows hard.

He mumbles something under his breath, and I take a step closer, trying to catch his words. "What?"

"Not a hassle. You're not a hassle."

I'm swallowing hard and blinking away the burning behind my eyes. I shake it off. "Good. Let's go. It's on me. A thank you for saving my life."

He shakes his head. "I didn't save you. And you don't have to thank me."

"Who knows what could have happened if you hadn't grabbed me? That car could have skidded and slid into me. Escaped elephant could have come pounding down the street and flattened me. Iron Man might have swooped down to fight crime and knocked me into the multiverse. The possibilities are endless. Accept the thank you already."

This time, the full-blown smile creeps up his face. It's a slow bloom. Takes its time curving up his cheeks as if it's rusty from lack of use, but it's worth the wait if you're paying attention. No missing teeth. One of the advantages to college hockey. They're required to wear the helmets with cages, so not as many missing teeth as the pros. But I think he'd be hot even with a few gaps in his rare smile. It's so rewarding when I tease it out of him.

"Welcome."

"Since we've got that settled, come on." I grab his hand, pulling him toward the little cafe.

Two diminutive trees frame the front door, twinkling lights glowing from their branches, and it gets worse as I duck under his arm to enter the place. Everything in here has been carefully curated to create the perfect ambiance for a date. Dim lighting. Check. Bud vases with multicolored carnations on each table. Check. Soft jazz in the background to set the mood, and a flickering display of candles on the hostess stand. Check and check. Great idea, but I'd look like the crazy person I am if I backed out now, so I step boldly up to the hostess.

Her smile is all for Dev, eyes trailing across his shoulders and down lower. He hunches forward as if he's trying to make himself look smaller under her hungry gaze.

"For two?" she asks his abs.

"Yes, please." I step into his side, sliding an arm around his waist, and turn to gaze up at his face in what I hope is an adoring way. Although, in all likelihood, I look more like a serial killer sizing up her next victim. "It's our first anniversary. We'd love that private little table in the back corner if that's okay." I bat my eyelashes at him. "Right, sweetums?"

All the discomfort on his face is gone, replaced by bemusement. His lips are twitching. "Yes, cupcake."

When I turn back to the hostess, she's hiding her disappointment behind a bright smile. "Aw, that's so sweet. Of course. Follow me."

We trail behind her, weaving through the crowded tables to reach my requested one. There are only a handful of occupied tables, anyway.

I'm staring down at the laminated black menu she handed me when Dev leans in. "Sweetums? What was that all about?"

"I don't know, cupcake." I put a little extra emphasis on the ridiculous nickname. "I was trying to get her to stop ogling you."

"Oh."

He sounds surprised. Why does he sound surprised? Surely, he knows half the campus must be lusting after him. He is a star of the hockey team, and hot as the devil he was nicknamed for. "You didn't notice?"

"Yeah, I'm used to that. I don't love it. The attention. The thought of people prying into my life is the one part of playing hockey professionally I'm not looking forward to. But it's part of the gig."

My stomach drops. He doesn't like the attention. The publicity. He's uncomfortable in the spotlight. The kind of spotlight that would be amplified by having me in his life.

"Right. I don't like it either. Sometimes I wish I'd been born into a different family."

"Me too."

I reach across the table, dropping a hand over his and giving it a squeeze, and he flips his over, closing his fingers around mine to return it.

"So, if you noticed her checking you out, why were you surprised?" I circle back.

"I'm just not used to anyone stepping in for me."

The honest confession hurts my soul, but I try to lighten the mood, not wanting to drag him back into whatever weird place we were sinking into. "Do you need me to kick my brother's ass? Isn't he your best friend? Best friends are supposed to stand up for each other."

Epic fail. The laugh I was angling for never makes an appearance. Instead, his brown eyes widen, and he leans back in his seat, going so far as to inch it back as if he needs to put that extra bit of distance between us.

"Right. Your brother. Yes, he looks out for me."

He leaves me hanging there, waiting for him to expand on his thought, but the invisible shield around him has snapped back into place again. Shut himself off from me and I know exactly what it was. The giant brick wall named Beau that stands between us went incognito for a moment, but now it's back in full force. Fantastic. Great thinking, as always. I sigh, turning my face down to study the menu full of things that sounded amazing before. Now I'm not so sure I'll be able to choke any of them down.

Chapter Twelve

Like A Cheap Jersey

Dev

What was I thinking? Letting her convince me to come out with her? Who am I kidding? That required zero convincing. I folded like a cheap jersey when she asked me to. One look in those gorgeous blue eyes, and I'd agree to anything to spend a moment with her.

But now I've fucked it all up. Led her on. Come out here with her, and now I have to put a stop to it. It doesn't matter how protective I feel for her, how much I want to pull her into my arms, or how incredible her soft curves felt pressed against me. I can't. We can't. I can't betray Beau like that.

She's clearly upset now. Eyes turned down, lids half closed, with her thick lashes almost resting on her full cheeks. I almost reach out to tilt her chin back up, wanting to wipe away the hurt I caused her, but I check myself.

"What are we having?"

She looks up. "We?"

"You pick whatever you want, and I'll share a bite or two." I can't express the words I want to say to her, so I'm hoping this will be something of a peace offering.

"Don't you want to pick something yourself?" she asks.

"Nah. I can't eat much dessert. Not in the plan." No matter how delicious it all sounds, it's not in the protein rich athlete's diet I try my best to stick to during the season.

"Plan?" She tilts her head. "The athlete thing. Gotcha. You weren't sticking to that when we were at the con."

I shut my eyes, trying to contain the groan. A flash of her naked body underneath mine has my cock waking up. The deep breaths I drag into my lungs offer no help to cool the fire, either. She's still there, etched into the back of my mind. Her plump thighs wrapped around my waist, lush ass jiggling as I pounded into her from behind. Those pretty lips wrapped around my cock. Not helping. I shift in my seat, but it fails to ease the uncomfortable ache.

"Are you okay?"

She's back to studying my face. Maybe we should take it to go? I don't think I can handle the sweet agony of watching her scoop bites of dessert between those lips. No, I've got more self control than that.

"I'm fine."

"Just get something yourself. I don't want to share. You don't have to eat it all." Her tone is all sass now.

The server walks up before I can reply. He's got a bored expression on his face. "Can I take your order?"

"I'll have a hot chocolate and the caramel apple cheesecake, please. Sweetums?" She looks at me, fluttering her lashes, even though her words are threaded with venom.

"I'll have a black tea... and the chocolate mousse, please."

He scribbles our order, eyes trained on the couple having a heated discussion two tables over. We don't even get a glance as he walks away.

"Well?"

Conversation not forgotten, apparently. "I'm sorry. It's hard to be near you."

She winces. "Harsh. That's a new one. I've been turned down by plenty of guys, but that was pretty brutal."

I'm not explaining myself right. I'm shit with words. Feelings. But I have to try. I can't hurt her or let her feel like I'm not into her. "Not because I don't want you."

"What?" She's shaking her head again, glancing at the door.

"Because I want you more than I should."

Her eyes flick back to me. "Is that a thing?" She's nibbling on her lip now and I want to snatch it away, tuck it between my teeth, give it a gentle nip.

"It is when you're you, and I'm me."

More confusion. Why am I so bad at this?

"Your brother is my best friend. My closest friend. The closest thing I have to family. I can't lose him. No matter how much I want you."

I lean over the table, getting a noseful of her sweet lemon scent. "And do not underestimate how much I want you. All I want right now is to drag you by your hair to the bathroom and slam into you from behind while I watch your tits bounce in the mirror."

She inhales a gasp, pink flooding her cheeks, eyes sparkling under the soft lighting of the glass chandelier.

"Then maybe you should." It's a challenge. One I should refuse, but I don't think I'm strong enough.

"Fuck, Cecelia. Don't tempt me."

I'm ready to protest when her small hand lands on my thigh, sliding up to find my cock. It's hard as steel, protesting its confinement, and I shut my eyes as need races through me when her hand makes contact.

Her fingers trace a path along my length, teasing and taunting me as she leans in closer. Her top dips to a deep v in the front, revealing a tempting expanse of plump flesh. "I can keep a secret."

Her lips curve up in a sly smile at my groan, and my hands are clenched so tight the tendons in my wrists are protesting.

"We shouldn't." It's a weak protest, and she knows it, continuing the long strokes that are setting my nerve endings abuzz.

"But we could. He never needs to know. We'll enjoy each other like the grown adults we are and not worry so much about what other people think." Her hand tightens in a squeeze.

"But..."

"Why not? Life is short, Dev. Might as well live it to its fullest. I spent the first half of my life trying to live up to other people's expectations. And what I discovered was that it was an impossible task."

Her words hit home. Life is fucking short. I still want to say no, protest a little more, but I'm weak. I can't. I need to get my hands on her again. My mouth. We can do this. I think. Beau doesn't need to find out.

"Oh, God. I can't think when you're touching me like that."

She releases my twitching cock. "Don't want to sway your decision." Her smirk doesn't back up her words.

"Too fucking late." I snatch the water glass off the table, icy water stinging my throat as I gulp down half the glass in one go.

I lean back in the wooden chair carefully. It feels too delicate for my bulk. I'm scrubbing at my scalp, taking a moment to compose myself. "If we do this, how would it work?"

"Well, you see. Boys have something called a penis, and girls..."

"Careful, Cece. You're already asking for a spanking. Don't make your punishment worse."

Shock replaces the wide-eyed innocent look she was giving me before, her mouth popping open. I lean in closer, unable to resist the temptation of running the pad of my thumb over her lower lip. It's as soft as it's been in my dreams.

"Promise?" she says.

"Uh huh."

Her little pink tongue swipes across her lip as if she can't wait for a taste of me after I pull my thumb away. "I don't know. We could wing it."

I shake my head at her careless shrug. "No. That will never work. We need a plan."

"I'm not much of a planner. More of a doer. Kind of like Yoda. Do or do not, you know."

"I'm pretty sure that weird little green creature still made plans. Okay. How do we make it work? Obviously, I can't bring you back to the house." I don't love that idea. She's the kind of girl who deserves to be flaunted, not hidden away like a dirty little secret.

"My roommates are chill. Art nerds. Not the type of people in Beau's inner circle. And of course, there's that other place you were just talking about." She smiles, twisting around to glance at the back of the restaurant toward the restrooms.

We can't do that. Can we? What if we got caught? I have to reach down to adjust myself in my pants. Something about the idea of taking her here and now is really fucking hot, and I've never been an exhibitionist.

"That's a terrible idea. Didn't you get sent here for that sort of thing?"

"Yes. I guess. We have the rest of the meal to think about it, anyway."

It's a good thing the waiter is still paying zero attention to us when he comes back with our food, because anyone less oblivious would have noticed the thick cocoon of tension our table is swathed in.

Steaming liquid sloshes out of the silver teapot when he places it in front of me. I idly dip the tea bag in and out, eyes locked on Cece as she takes a slow lick of the cocoa sprinkled whipped cream on top of her hot chocolate. I wish I'd ordered one too, but I had to exercise some self control. I'm not doing so well in resisting her, so the least I can do is stick to my meal plan.

She buries her face in her drink, moaning as she takes a swallow. A slash of the cream marks her upper lip when she comes up for air. On anyone else, it would be amusing. On her, it's fucking delicious.

Now she's taunting me. I reach over to wipe it away, slipping my thumb between her lips when I've got it. Her mouth is warm and wet, as she sucks the cream off.

"My cock is going to love slipping between those dirty lips of yours."

The waiter does a double take as he sets our desserts down in front of us, and Cece giggles. At least we know he's not a ghost. Something finally cut through his ennui.

Don't love the attention, though. That was for her ears only. I hunch over my mousse, studying the patterns in the shaved chocolate.

"Cock? I'm just here for the dessert, right?" Cece has no problem pulling the attention back to herself. As if she can sense my unease.

The waiter makes a humph noise, stiffens his spine and walks off muttering about college kids, causing her to erupt into giggles.

"Poor guy." I shake my head at her.

She laughs, scooping up a mouthful of her apple concoction. My mouth waters, watching her slide the morsel between her lips, but it's not the caramel oozing off her fork that's got me interested.

She's half finished hers as I'm taking small bites, savoring every mouthful of the sweet but light mousse. I jerk it back toward my chest when her fork swoops in to steal a bite.

"I'm so sorry," she says, pulling away.

Guilt steals my air as the joy slides off her face, leaving it crumpled and unsure. I did that to her.

I shut my eyes. "It's not you. It's me. A food thing." The explanation is lame, but I can't tell her why I'm so protective of my food. Why I savor every bite, and begrudge anyone who tries to take any? No matter how innocent. I know she'd give me her entire portion without batting an eye, and here I am, a massively damaged asshole unable to share. But there's no way she can understand the way I grew up. She and Beau have never suffered a single day of hunger in their lives. She'd never understand.

"Oh. Well still. I'm sorry. Do you want a taste of mine? You don't even need to trade. I probably shouldn't finish this entire thing, anyway."

"Thanks, but I'm good. Why shouldn't you finish it?"

Her head tilts at me, and she's staring at me like I'm not the sharpest blade on the ice. "Um." I follow her hands as she waves them in front of her body. "Don't need all those calories."

It dawns on me. She's referring to that gorgeous body. As if there's something negative about those curves. "I hope you're not saying what I think you're saying?"

"That I could stand to lose some weight?"

"Don't say that. Your body is perfection. Like everything else about you. If I hear you saying anything negative about it again, I'm going to have to have to show you just how wrong you are. Those thighs, those hips. That fucking ass. They've been haunting my dreams all month."

The deep pink flush of her cheeks doesn't give away whether she's embarrassed or turned on by my words, but the way she's squirming in her seat gives me some idea. I bet if I slid my hand down her pants right now, I'd find her wet.

"Maybe so, but it's kind of hard to shake a lifetime of people telling you that you need to lose weight. I try to be all strong and confident, but you know, sometimes those insecurities creep in."

"I get it." She arches a brow at me. "Not that, but your past creeping in to tear you down."

Her lips are pressed together, and she's frowning. That's not where we want this night going. Maybe I need to show her how excited I am to make her come.

I mirror her action from before, slipping a hand up her thigh. She's wearing jeans under the Lakeview jersey, but there's an obvious damp patch even through the thick fabric. She lets out the softest moan when I make contact, but it's not enough. It's a bit of a struggle to snap open the button, but I pull it off one handed.

Her eyes drop to my left hand that's still scooping tiny bites of mousse into my mouth.

"You've got skills on and off the ice."

"Too many words." I need to get her to the point where the only word she can whisper through those lips is my name.

As soon as I've got her zipper gaping open, I slide a slow trail over her mound until I reach the top of her cotton panties.

"This okay?" I ask.

She nods. "God, please."

"I'm no god, and I'm certainly no angel, haven't you heard? They don't call me Lucy for nothing."

My hand dips beneath her underwear. Her neatly trimmed hair is smooth under my fingers, and she's already soaked.

"Holy fuck."

"Shh." Her hips jump as my finger circles her entrance, then slips in and out in a shallow tease.

Good thing we snagged the shadowy corner. I'm pretty confident we're safe from ogling eyes here. I continue my tease, circling my thumb around her clit as my finger plunges into her slippery tunnel a little deeper with each thrust. I scoop a solid bite of mousse onto my spoon, sliding it between her lips, and as she's swallowing it down, my thumb presses down on her clit.

She gasps, arching toward me. See, I can share my food. Under very special circumstances.

I add a second finger, dipping into her heat, stretching her out. Getting her ready for my cock. She slides a foot up my leg, inching toward it as if she wants to return the favor, but I brush it away. This is already too much. It would be fucking embarrassing to blow my load in my pants.

She makes a small, frustrated noise when I pull away from her, leaving her empty and wanting. She was too close, hanging on by a rapidly fraying thread, and I want to make this last. I take another bite. The smooth chocolate treat is almost as sweet as her.

"You really are the devil," she hisses at me.

I smile, walking my fingers back up her trembling thigh.

This time I go in hard and fast, thrusting two digits inside her clenching pussy. She gasps, eyes blazing. I keep up a steady rhythm, thumb bringing her closer and closer as I curve my fingers up to press on the sweet spot on her inner wall. Benefits to long fingers.

She's almost there again, letting out a gasp as the waiter walks back. I turn my head toward him, but don't make eye contact, stilling the movement between her thighs.

"Everything okay here?" he asks, lips pursed.

"Fine. Check. Please." Her words come out in quick gasps as if she's struggling for breath, but the apathetic lines of his face never change.

"You've got to stop," she whispers at me. "I'm going to come right here in the middle of the restaurant."

"Kind of the point."

"Seriously. What if someone sees?"

I glance around the handful of other tables draped in flickering shadows. There's one four top full of giggling girls, and a few other couples who are completely absorbed in each other. "I think we're safe."

"But..." she's biting her lip again, and the strands of hair that have escaped from her ponytail are damp.

"Fine. I can wait."

I stare her directly in the eyes as I lift my hand up and pop my fingers into my mouth.

"Dev!"

"What? You taste better than any dessert in here... Cupcake." I tell her.

Her cheeks are flushed as she pushes up from her seat, a little shaky. She fumbles with her purse, tossing a pile of cash on the table.

"Don't make me wait." She stares me down, then turns around, hips swaying as she threads her way to the back of the restaurant.

CHAPTER THIRTEEN

WRONG NUMBER

CECE

I'm gripping my wristlet in my hand, staring at myself in the bathroom mirror. I hope Dev takes me up on the offer. At the same time, I'm hoping he's smart enough to put the brakes on this runaway train. Haven't I gotten myself into enough trouble already this year? One year, Cecelia. You only need to keep it together and be on your best behavior for one more year. Then you're free.

Good behavior is overrated, though. Each toilet has its own little room. No one's going to see us in here. No one is taking any pictures. It's fine. And there was no way I could wait until we got home. I don't think I've ever been this keyed up. The anticipation sending little shivers up my spine as I brace my hands on the counter, staring myself down in the mirror. I've never had sex in front of a mirror.

My eyes have a glossy feverish quality to them. Lipstick a bit smeared from nibbling on it.

I reach up to release my hair from its tight ponytail. The door gives a gentle creak as I'm finger combing my long blonde locks, trying to wrestle the elastic back on. The lock clicks and the heat from Dev's body surrounds me on all sides as he reaches up to still my busy hand.

"Leave it down," he says, voice raspy.

I give up, dropping my right hand back down to brace myself on the counter.

A shiver runs down my neck as he tenderly brushes the long strands aside, exposing my neck. He bends down to plant a trail of light kisses from the dip of my shoulder to that spot under my ear that always gets me going. My pussy is clenching on nothing. His long finger brushes under my chin, tilting my head to the side as he leans in closer.

His lips are inches from mine, hovering, waiting. For what, I don't know, but I can't take it anymore, crashing into him. He tastes like chocolate and raspberries, and me, and that is a way hotter combination than I would have thought. Our tongues clash in a war for control. He was always going to win, though. He takes control, delving deep, nibbling and sucking. One hand cups my chin, squeezing it until it's verging on this side of pain. I squeak as my insides clench.

He pulls back. "Let me know if it's too much. I'll stop. You sure about this?"

"I've never been more sure of anything in my life." I tell him. If he doesn't get inside me right this second, I think I might melt into a puddle.

"Let me just get this shit off you." He rips the jersey over my head, tossing it into a corner. "Don't ever wear that thing again."

"What?" I glance at the mirror to see him glaring at the jersey. His team's jersey. "Don't you want me supporting your team?"

"I don't want to see another man's name on your back." His dark brows are pulled together as he glares at the harmless piece of fabric.

"Umm. That's my name. You know that, right?"

"Yes, but it's his number."

"Yeah, my br..." He places his finger over my lips before the word slips out, and it hits me. It's not just one of those possessive guy things. He doesn't want the reminder of that inconvenient barrier between us.

But I can't keep my mouth shut after he lifts the finger. "I can't exactly wear yours if I go to another game."

His face seems to soften and fall a little, all the anger draining away. "I guess not."

Did I spoil the mood? What is wrong with me? I should have let it go. Not stirred the pot. He's leaning back a little now, eyes shut, breathing hard as if he's trying to get control of himself again. That won't do.

I reach behind myself to slip open my bra. The satiny fabric dangles down my back, and I do a little shimmy to work the straps down my arms. A little yank drags the underwire out from under my heavy breasts and it falls to the floor in a heap. I bend over a little until my ass bumps into his groin to find him still hard.

As soon as I make contact, his eyes fly open, pupils dilating as he catches sight of me in the mirror. His mouth parts and all the heat rushes back, turning his dark eyes into velvety pools of night.

Score one to Cece. We are back in the game.

The pained groan comes from deep in his chest, and he lifts his arms, hands hovering in the air for a moment before he reaches around to land on my hips. He squeezes tight then slides them up sides, sending shivers running through my body as he traces a pattern over my sensitive skin. I shut my eyes to avoid looking at the extra flesh. I try to embrace my extra curves, but it's not always easy when you've grown up in the world I grew up in. Constantly told that you don't fit in. That you're not thin enough. Somehow less, because you're too much.

"Don't shut your eyes on me, pretty girl. I want to see those gorgeous blues on mine."

"But..."

"No, buts. Open them up and watch or I'm not touching these luscious tits." His hands stop before he reaches my breasts, but I can feel the heat from them. He's so close to making contact. "You don't want that, do you?"

"No," I whimper, dragging my lids open.

His lips reward me with the hint of a smile, and he stares at me as he slides a little further up until he's cupping the underside. "That's a good girl."

I moan, arching into his touch, and when he finally makes it to my taut nipples, I grip the counter to make sure my knees don't give out on me. I've never been this needy for a guy. But then he's not just any guy. I still have dreams about his hands all over me, his mouth exploring my body. The way he slammed into me from behind, pressed against the window. Best sex of my life hands down. And I never thought I'd get to experience it again, but now here we are. This is our moment, and I don't want to miss a second.

I reach back one arm to loop around his neck, as he bends his head to nibble and lick that spot behind my ear again. I'm on fire for him. The way he knows just how and where to touch me after our brief encounter is incredible.

He's pinching and plucking at my nipple, and it sends a sizzling trail down low in my belly. His other hand slides down my abdomen, kneading and squeezing the flesh on its way.

"God, I love this body."

My face was already flushed from the need, so I don't think he notices the blush that forms at his words. The way he worships my curves is unreal.

I'm so desperate for his touch down lower that I reach down to unsnap my jeans, but he's smacking my hand away before I can accomplish the task.

"Hand back on the counter. I'll take those off when I'm ready. I want the privilege of uncovering that exquisite flesh of yours.

My groan this time is frustrated, but he doesn't leave me hanging for too long. One long sweep up and down my sides with a pause to squeeze my tits has a low moan coming from him.

He slips down to cup my mound through the pants one last time until I'm pressing up on my toes, arching my back into his hand.

My skin is on fire, every whisper of his breath on my neck, the slight breeze from the vent, every touch amplifies the burn.

Finally, he's unsnapping my jeans, sliding the zipper down in a slow crawl.

"Please, just get them off."

"Oh, I'll be getting something off very soon. You. But only if you're patient."

The sounds of the restaurant are dim in the background, but I'm vaguely aware that we are in a public place. "We can't stay here too long. We'll get caught." That's an excuse to force him into sending me over the edge I've been dancing beside for too long.

He sighs, closing his teeth in a gentle nip at the base of my neck. "I guess. You win this time, Beauty." He yanks my jeans and underwear down so fast I'm jerked back into him, and my feet lift off the ground.

His left hand closes around my waist, keeping me steady as he tussles with the denim to drag it over my foot. The pants fall to the floor.

"Spread those legs for me. I want to see that beautiful pussy of yours before I sink my cock into it." His voice is rough around the edges, and there's a rustle of fabric as he fumbles with his zipper.

The hard flesh of his dick presses into my ass once he's free, and he reaches around to find my slick center. He toys with me, swearing when he finds out how damp and ready I am for him.

"You need my dick so bad," he says as he's sliding the tip of his finger into my opening. "But you're going to have to be patient for one more second.

I hear foil tearing, and another groan as he slides the condom on. Once he's ready, he grips my hips again.

"Close your eyes. Just until I get inside. I want you to feel every inch of me sliding inside you, tearing you apart until you come to pieces around my cock."

A shiver rips through me, and I grip the counter until my knuckles whiten, closing my eyes, waiting.

"Good girl." He's leaning right up to my ear.

Every sensation is heightened by the loss of my sight when I shut my eyes. I can feel him tensed behind me and can almost picture the ridges of his abs tight and ready. His hands grip my hips, the tip of his cock poised at my entrance.

His thrust is intense and deep, taking me by surprise even though I was waiting for it. He's so thick he stretches me to my limits, and the pressure would be too much if I wasn't so ready for him. The teasing at the table, the slow build here, has me dripping and ready to take all of him in one go.

My eyes fly open, and I see myself, and him, melded into one person. I'm flushed and slightly damp with sweat, but he's staring at me like I'm something special, eyes shining, taking in every inch of my body.

He fills me perfectly, pausing to kiss the back of my shoulder. "You good? Ready for me?"

I nod. "Fuck, yes."

There's a slight sting on my ass that sends another wave rolling through me. I'm so close already. One move and I'll plummet off the cliff.

His thrusts start off slowly, a steady drag deep inside me, opening me up for him. I'm already trembling and fluttering around him.

"Hold steady for a minute. I don't want to lose it yet."

The pressure returns to my clit, matching his quicker thrusts. It builds and builds. Steady heat and need tearing at me.

I'm leaning into my hands, afraid my legs will collapse under me as he brings me closer and closer.

I don't think I can take any more of the torture when he leans in, his entire body pressed into mine.

"Come for me." His fingers dance a rapid step over my clit, and I give in, shattering around him.

As my legs are failing me, he grabs my hips, pulling my legs off the floor as his rhythm picks up. He pounds into me as I'm clenching around him. The orgasm rolls into another one,

"Fuck." His soft whisper is more powerful than if he screamed my name as he follows me over the cliff. He buries himself deep shuddering as he's pulsing inside the condom deep inside me,

I don't know how he's possibly steady on his feet while I'm ready to melt right into the floor.

He holds me tight to him, head thrown back as he pulses, buried deep inside.

Maybe he's not as unaffected as he appears. He lets me slip from his grip until my feet hit the floor again but doesn't pull out or otherwise move from the position.

It could have been two minutes or two hours before he's gripping his length and sliding out. My walls clench around him as if they're not so eager to let him leave. Can't say as I blame them. People talk about getting their world rocked, but I didn't think this was actually a thing until I met him.

It's like the earth has shifted under my feet. Nothing else matters but us. It's him and me, and the rest of the world fades away when we're together like this. How am I ever going to stay away from him?

CHAPTER FOURTEEN

EVERY MISSED SHOT

DEV

T hings look a little different in the daylight. I came home with her. I couldn't say no. That seems to be the case with her. I can't say no, and I can't stay away. No matter how bad of an idea being with her is. I'm drawn to her.

When she tilted her head up to look at me this morning, her eyes were shining, blonde hair tangled in a heap around her head. And her tank top was all twisted up around her chest. She looked like my version of perfection.

And now I have to leave it behind. Go home. Every step I take toward the front door has that guilt swelling up in my chest.

"See you later, handsome." Her redheaded roommate has been teasing us all morning, but it's good natured. I hate that I can't take her home with me. Show her off to the guys.

"Wait." Cece's small hand lands on my shoulder as I'm about to push the front door open.

I turn back to her, the longing ache in my chest deepening. Her hair is now piled on top of her head in a purple scrunchy. It's a perfect match for my jersey, and that need to see her wearing it kicks back up. She's darted off and is rifling through a pile of papers on the hall table.

She gathers a bunch up and skips back to stuff them into my hand.

"What's this?"

She pulls her lip between her teeth, and it looks like she's second guessing her decision, about to snatch the papers back from me.

I pull them away before she can act on the thought, glancing at the first page.

It's her art for sure. There's a sketch of a woman on the first page standing with her legs spread in full superhero garb. It's a black and white sketch, but the details are exquisite. Clearly, she drew this. Next to the woman is a series of barely legible scribbles as if ideas were flowing through her brain faster than her fingers could write them down.

"It's my character, and some of the ideas I have for my series. I shouldn't have." She shakes her head, reaching toward the papers. "I don't know what I was thinking. You don't have to look at them."

I clear my throat. There's a burning sensation in my chest. She's entrusting me with her precious work. I don't deserve that kind of trust, but I need to see this. See the ideas that are lurking in her brain? I've got no artistic skills myself, but comic books have always been my escape. Even before I had hockey, I could escape to the comic book store to get away from whatever awful situation I found myself in.

"No."

"What?"

"Don't. I'd like to look at them." I'm hoping she doesn't notice how thick my voice has gotten.

"Oh, okay. Cool. So, maybe we can get together soon, and you can tell me what you think?"

I nod. "Sounds like a plan." She doesn't need the excuse to tempt me into a return visit, but I like the idea that I've got something important to her. She's definitely going to want it back, so that means she wants me back.

I lean in, cupping her cheek in my hand. My hand is so big it spans the length of her head. Her lips are soft under mine, and this kiss is different. Not like when we parted in the hotel. That was a goodbye. This is a promise that we'll see each other again.

Everything is a little colder when I pull away, heading out the front door.

"Bye, puck boy." It's Georgia again, getting in her two cents.

"Bye, ghost girl."

The redhead tilts her head back with a raspy laugh much better suited to a chain smoking grandmother than a southern belle. "I like you, puck boy. You should keep him, Cece."

Cece mentioned her roommate is into the paranormal, and this morning she had some podcast playing at breakfast. Two women talking about ghostly encounters. It was pretty fun, not that I believe in ghosts. There are enough monsters in the real world without worrying about what might be lurking in some other plane of existence.

Normally I don't mind the bus. You get the occasional weirdo causing a fuss, and it doesn't always smell the best, but I've smelled worse than a little bus funk. There are benefits to my six feet five inches of muscle. Nobody bothers me. Unless they recognize me from the team and want to chat hockey.

Today I'm fidgeting with my bag and shifting in my seat. Usually, I have my comfort book in my hand to hide behind. But I finished my last read and haven't hit the library yet, so I'm at loose ends, staring at the slow progress of tidy houses as the bus passes by.

I'm on my feet, hanging onto the railing with a loose hold three stops early. My body sways to the rhythm as we hit a pothole as easy as if I was balancing on my skates when we finally ease up to the stop near our house. Usually, I'm the only one who takes advantage of this. Beau's got his fancy ride, JJ and Grant each have a decent car, and even Cole has one now. Jacks offered me his old car, Mabel, before he moved off, but I said no. No point in keeping something that's going to cost me more money than I have. I can handle the bus or hitch a ride with any of the other guys. So, Cole ended up with the beater. I never told him I got the first offer from Jacks. What would be the point of that?

The sidewalk jars my knees as I leap down, skipping the stairs. I'm in such a hurry. However, now that I'm here staring down the road to our house, I'm wondering why I was in such a hurry to disembark. There will be questions. I haven't been out with a girl all semester.

Even dragging my feet, my legs cover so much ground that I'm staring down the cheerful front doorway too soon. Dragging in a deep breath, I slip my key into the lock. Before I've had time to turn it, the door swings open, and I stumble inside, hand still attached to the key in the lock.

"Lucy!!! Where have you been all night? I thought you were going to be late for practice." It's JJ, of course. Our overenthusiastic goalie can't help himself. Normally I'd shoot Beau a look, and he'd dart in for the save, but I'm not so eager to look him in the eyes after the things I did to his sister last night. *Fuck, what were you thinking?*

As if I was telegraphing my thoughts, he steps in behind JJ, grabbing him by the shoulder and tossing him to the side. "Leave him alone."

"Thanks." I mutter, still not glancing up from my feet.

"Seriously, though. Finally broke your dry spell? I thought maybe you were going with abstinence to improve your game."

That gets my attention. I glance up to see my best friend with his arms crossed over his chest. He's got a cocky grin on his polished face. I'm trying not to compare to his sister's. I can't help myself. His hair is a much darker shade of blond than her pale locks, but they've got the same piercing blue eyes. He's obviously much taller, but they share a nose straight in that blue-blooded kind of way. He has a pronounced bump in the middle that didn't come naturally, though. Broken noses are a hazard of the game, and lots of us share that feature.

"You think my game is off?" I can't help the worry in my tone. Deep down, I know he's joking around, but I can't help the constant edge of worry that rides me. Always afraid I'm not good enough. That I'm going to get rejected before I even get a chance to prove myself.

He tilts his head to the side, studying me as if he can't quite figure out if I'm serious. "Obviously not. I don't think your game has ever been this strong. You've been showing the rest of the team up every single time we hit the ice. You may not think I've noticed, since I've been dealing with those other two jokers so much, but I have."

I blow a breath out, but my shoulders stay tense. "Good." I nod, brushing by him to head up to my room. He claps me on the back as I walk by, but otherwise leaves me alone.

"What? You're not going to make him spill? I want to know who he went home with?" JJ comes bouncing back over, ignoring the vague threat in Beau's eyes. "Was she hot? I bet she was a redhead. The quiet ones always like them spicy. Maybe a brunette, no blonde. I think Lucy is definitely into blondes. It's that devil and angel thing."

My head snaps up to glare at JJ, but he just laughs, even as I'm balling my fist up and slamming it into my palm.

"Ding, ding, ding! We have a winner. A hundred percent he's got a blonde under his skin. What can I say? It's one of my special skills. It's like I'm some kind of sexual psychic. I can always tell what shade of hussy someone got inside. If you know what I mean?" He gives an exaggerated wink, while he pumps his hips at me, and my limbs get all hot and shaky as I step toward him.

Beau's hand lands on my shoulder to restrain me from seriously damaging our star goalie. I know he's trying to signal to me he'll deal with it, but I've never been so fucking furious at our dumbass teammate. Sure, he never shuts his mouth, and has zero filter, but I usually don't let it get to me this hard. But the thought of him turning Cece into a dirty joke enrages me.

Beau pushes past me to confront him. "First. What is wrong with you? If I didn't know better, I'd say you've been playing goal without a helmet and taken too many pucks to the skull. Second. Who says hussy? And third. If I ever hear you disrespect a woman like that in my house again, you'll be out on your ass faster than you can say Zamboni."

JJ's mouth falls open in a comical oh. It's not unusual for Beau to lay down the law as the team captain and owner of the house we live in, but I've never heard him threaten to kick anyone out.

"Sorry, Captain."

"And apologize to Lucy as well."

Our humbled goalie turns back to me. "Sorry, Lucy."

"Don't let it happen again."

"Thanks." The word is a mumble on the air as I dart past Beau, heading for the stairs and the safety of my room.

Thank fuck. I burst through my door, stretch to the top of the bookshelf, and pull down my ancient copy of The Boys of Winter. It's the one thing I've kept from my childhood, and I read it any time I need a reminder. Of how and why I survived this life. It's this sport and the one foster parent who cared enough to find me an outlet that wouldn't land me in jail. The title is barely legible anymore, cover scratched, and pages torn, but it's still my most valuable possession.

Before I crack the bent spine to lose myself in the pages, I pull the sheaf of papers Cece handed me out of my bag, idly flipping through her artwork, and it sucks me right in.

My favorite book is still sitting on the corner of my desk when there's a knock on the door.

"Come in." I'm so drawn into the world she's created that the automatic response slips out. I spin around in the luxurious office chair that came with the house as the door swings open.

Relief is my initial reaction. I wasn't thinking when I granted passage to my inner sanctum. If I had been, I might have been more concerned that it was JJ about to wreak havoc on my peace.

"Hey." I fold my arms, leaning back in my chair, but avoiding eye contact.

"Hey, man. What's going on? I feel like you've been avoiding me."

I guess my attempt to fly under the radar and act like everything is fine has been failing. Am I even surprised? Beau and I have been tight since our freshman year. He probably knows me better than anyone else in my life. Maybe it was wishful thinking that he would be too distracted by his captain role and the rest of the team to notice me pulling away.

"Just been busy."

He leans back on his heels, and I can feel his eyes locked on me. Finally, when I can't stand the scrutiny anymore, I look up.

"There you are. Seriously, what's up? Is it a girl? Something else. You've been catching rides with the other guys, not coming out as much. You know you can tell me anything."

I mash my lips together to keep back the bitter laugh. Pretty sure he suspects nothing, because if he knew about Cece and me, he wouldn't be standing there casually digging. I'd be the one out on my ass instead of our goalie.

Something. I've got to give him something. I squeeze my eyes shut, take a deep breath, and spill. "My father showed up. In the summer, when you guys were all gone. And again at the game yesterday."

Beau gasps. He knows how I grew up, bouncing around houses. He knows my home situation was bad, and my biological father is the reason I don't drink, but he doesn't know all the details. If he assumed both my parents were dead, I never contradicted him.

"Your father? I didn't know. Are you okay?"

"Yeah." He keeps staring at me. "Sort of. I will be. I told him to get lost. I don't want to see him again. I'm sure he's looking to snag a ride on the pro hockey gravy train."

"I'm sorry, dude. If you need any backup. Let me know. I'll pull the entire team to scare him off if you need."

I shake my head. "No. Please don't tell the rest of the guys. They don't know... It's in the past. I don't think he'll do anything too crazy. He actually seemed okay. Said he was sober, has a fiancée. Probably won't cause shit."

He takes a few steps toward me, dropping a hand on my shoulder. "I won't tell anyone or get anyone else involved. And feel free to call me a crazy asshole, but do you think maybe if you talk to him, he'll leave you alone?"

My head tilts back, eyes seeking the ceiling. "Maybe. But I don't want to see him. He's not worth my time."

"I gotcha. But if you need anything, let me know."

The seat squeaks under my shifting weight. As if I didn't have this intense guilt dragging me down already. Why does he have to be so understanding? It only makes it worse. What I'm doing behind his back. Maybe I should stop. Tell her I can't see her again, but every time I close my eyes, her face appears in my mind. I can't shake her. And I don't want to. No matter how much of an asshole it makes me.

"Will do."

I chance a glance at him. His brows are pulled together in a slight frown, dark blond hair a little less groomed than usual, as if he's been running a hand through it on repeat. Maybe he needs me, and I haven't been there for him? Hiding away.

"What about you? You okay? Those fuckers aren't too much for you to handle, are they?"

He's frozen for a moment, almost as if he didn't hear me, then he reactivates with a toss away laugh. "Nah. I've got it under control."

"Let me know if you need me to rough them up a little. Especially that cocky fucker, Hail." The rookie has really been testing Beau's captain skills, but he paired him up with Cole, and they seem to have formed an uneasy truce.

"Will do."

He steps in a little closer, leaning over me with a deepening frown. "What's that?"

I follow his gaze to the pile of papers I left carelessly lying on the desk. His sister's artwork. Something I'm sure he's very familiar with. Fuck. How could I be so stupid?

I'm whipping around, scooping up the papers, and stuffing them into my desk drawer, hoping he didn't catch a good look. My heart is pounding so hard I can hear it.

"Nothing. Just part of an assignment."

When I look back at him, he's staring at the wall behind me as if it's going to spill my secrets.

"Didn't think you were taking an art elective."

"I'm not. It's for my psych elective."

"Oh, gotcha." The lines on his face smooth out and it's painful how easily he believed the lie.

Because he trusts me. I'm supposed to be his best friend, and instead I'm fouling him behind the ref's back.

Chapter Fifteen

HAUNTED CLOSETS

Cece

I've never been so aware of the students hustling down the halls between classes as I have been over these last two weeks. It was lurking in the back of my mind that there's was a chance I might run into Devlin around here, or maybe he'd even be in one of my classes. We are both business majors, after all. That was me being overly optimistic. He's majoring in accounting, while I'm on the marketing side of things. Given the limited options laid out for me before I started college, marketing was the most creative. I can even slip in some graphic design courses that will still advance my career. Not that I'm planning on spending my life in the marketing department of some soulless corporation, especially not my father's. But I may need a stable income to pay the bills while I pursue my dream of publishing my own comics and graphic novels.

In our senior year, things have gotten way more specific, so we haven't crossed paths since our last encounter two weeks ago.

My ringtone cuts through the reverie, wrinkling my nose when I glance down at the number. I am so not in the mood for one of my father's lectures. But if I don't deal with it now, he'll be all over me, so I accept the call with a sigh, bringing it up to my ear.

"Hi."

"Cecelia. How are your classes going?"

I'm doing great. Thanks for asking. Is what I want to say. "Good." Is what I actually say, wondering where this is headed. I've been doing fine. I'm actually acing my digital marketing class, and I've got no economics on the docket this semester.

"I heard you turned in a B paper for your strategic marketing class." He gets right to the point of his call. No fucking around with small talk. Even with your daughter. Probably especially with your daughter. I'm pretty sure he could make small talk about golf or some new restaurant with his cronies all night at a cocktail party.

"Where did you hear that?"

"I've worked with some of the faculty before."

Isn't there such a thing as student professor confidentiality? I'm quite certain they're not supposed to be sharing your grades, even on the golf course. And also, who cares? I'm getting the degree he wants me to.

"I'm doing my best, Dad."

"If you need any help to pull that up, talk to your brother. He's still at the top of his class. I'm sure he'd be happy to help you."

"He's pretty busy with hockey already, but I'll talk to him if I need to." I absolutely won't.

"Excellent. I've got a meeting in ten, so I'll be talking to you soon. You will be home for Thanksgiving, right?"

It's not a request, and there's only one correct answer. "Of course."

"Excellent, see you then."

My sign off lands on a dead line, and I lean back against the wall, but seek comfort in my messages.

The string of texts I've shared with Dev has grown into the hundreds over the last couple of weeks since our encounter after the game. Last night, he sent me a text to wish me a good night, and he asked me what I was wearing. So, I sent him a pic of my head on the body of some model in sexy lingerie.

He sent me back a WTH meme and told me he'd rather see a pic of me wearing a paper bag if it was the real me. I responded with a real selfie, flannel pants in a glorious bright yellow with lemons all over them, and a Marvel tee with a small tear below my right boob. My hair was tangled, and I'd already taken my makeup off, so I went all in, making a derpy face with my eyes crossed and tongue sticking out. That's trust. Not a picture I would ever want getting out into the world.

I'm still smiling at the gif he sent back of a cartoon dog with its tongue rolling out when I glance up, and a shock ripples through me.

There he is, walking toward me. The man himself. He looks as hot as usual in a pair of black track pants. The matching hoodie is pulled down over his forehead, casting deep shadows over the sculpted lines of his face. A shiver runs through me at the sight and my lips curve up in a smile.

"Dev," I call out, walking toward him.

His brown eyes lock with mine for a moment, and I'm sucked in. Until he breaks the contact, whipping his head back as someone walks up behind him, clapping a hand on his back. Beau. Shit. Right. Of course they share some classes. Stupid of me to think I could just walk up to him in public like that. I mean, it is reasonable. We met, and Beau told me I could call him if I needed something and he wasn't around. But as far as my brother knows, we've only met that one time.

Dev's expression doesn't change much. There's a subtle tightening of his features that most people wouldn't even notice, but that's all.

Beau is still turned toward his friend. He hasn't seen me, but it would be weird if I rushed off without saying hi, so I push myself forward toward the guys.

"Hey, Beau... and Derek, was it?" I force my lips into a big smile, interrupting their conversation.

"Cece!" My brother turns toward me, eyes skating from my face down my body. He takes in my baggy purple sweats and long-sleeved black t-shirt with a dancing skeleton on it. It is spooky season after all. "I would kill to see Mom's face if she saw you wearing that in public."

I shrug, lifting a finger to my lips. "But I know you'll never tell."

"Of course not, but it would be so much fun."

"I can get you one and we can wear them home together. Or just take a snap and send it to her. Probably safer."

He shakes his head. "I wouldn't put that thing on even for a pic, but you go wild. Just let me know when you're going to do it so I can clear my schedule."

I can't help turning back to Dev, and our eyes lock for another moment. It's hard to tear myself away, but I do, focusing on my brother's blue eyes that are so similar to my own.

"We were heading over to the UC for some lunch if you want to join us?" Beau tilts his head at me, but his gaze is straying over my shoulder, and his fingers are twitching in a steady rhythm.

"Nah, I'm going to meet Anna at Northman. We've got something to work on."

My brother nods. "Cool. Catch you later."

"Yup. See you."

I resume my walk toward the east exit, passing by the guys. My skin ripples as large fingers trail down my arm, and I swivel my head around as Dev squeezes my hand in his. The calloused fingers are scratchy but reassuring. I smile at his back, almost bumping into another student as his fingertips slip from mine, leaving only a pleasant warmth behind.

"Sorry."

I apologize, hustling on by with a dreamy smile on my face, floating out the door and across campus.

Heat embraces me as soon as I walk through the doors into the hall. It's in the quiet zone between lunch and dinner, so not too crowded. I scan the handful of tables, searching for Anna, but it's a raspy laugh that catches my attention. The dining area lights are glinting off a head full of bright blonde hair. My other roomie is sitting across from Anna.

"Good afternoon," I say, plopping into the seat beside Georgia, and giving Anna a bright smile.

"Well, well, well, what have you been up to, darling? You're always a ray of sunshine, but there's something of an extra glow about you today." Georgia pauses with a fry halfway to her mouth.

I reach up to rub at my heated neck, hoping there's no blush to give me away. "Nothing. I came from class. It was a sales class. Not my favorite."

"I don't envy you that," Anna says, going along with my deflection.

But Georgia is not deterred. She purses her lips into a perfect bow. "Cute guy in your class?"

"No." I shake my head.

But she continues to stare at me, and it almost feels like she can see into my mind.

It doesn't take long for me to crumble under the scrutiny. I glance to the left, and the right before I whisper. "I ran into Dev." Obviously, I couldn't keep my tryst secret after he emerged from my room after our last encounter.

She lights up like a birthday cake. "Ooh. Did you get up to some in class shenanigans? Be careful of sneaking into any storage closets in the Jameson building. There's an entrance to the secret tunnels under the school that is super haunted."

"Of course not. I don't sneak into closets between classes for a little make-out sesh. Not my vibe."

Her perfectly arched eyebrow curves almost up to her hairline. "Of course it's not." She turns back to Annie. "She's more of a restroom kind of gal."

Annie does her best to muffle her laugh, but she can't quite do it and it comes out in a snort.

I shake my head. "Wish I never told you that one."

"Well, guess what? You did. And you should know that a southern lady never forgets a bit of hot gossip."

And that's one more reason not to tell Georgia any more secrets I don't want thrown back in my face for the rest of the year, or probably my life. We haven't known each other that long, but I think these ladies are in it for life.

"Actually, Beau was with him, so even if I was about to sneak into a haunted closest, twas not to be."

"You should just tell your brother. He's going to find out eventually, and it's going to be so much worse if it comes from somewhere else."

I'm looking at Annie for help, but she glances at her hands, avoiding my gaze. Clearly, she agrees with Georgia. "I can't. I promised Dev I wouldn't tell him. This whole thing hinges on secrecy." The thing I really should do is break it off. Whatever it is, we haven't exactly discussed the details yet. But every time he sends me a funny text, or I think of him, I get all hot and bothered. I confessed more things to him about my life when we met at the con than I have to any of my other friends over the years. I want to peel back the layers he's still keeping tightly wrapped around himself, and I want to explore every inch of his body. I think I might actually be addicted to him.

Annie looks back up at me, and she looks conflicted. "The only thing I'm worried about is the fact that he's keeping you a secret. That never ends well. I'm worried about you, and I don't want you getting hurt."

It's a bit of a cold shock hearing that. Does she think he's got someone else on the side? I mean, he could. He's a very private guy and I really don't know that much about him, but he never seems to leave the school, so I doubt he has anyone long distance.

"It's not like that. We're only keeping it a secret from my brother. Besides. I don't want my dad finding out, either. As amazing as Dev is, I'm sure he wouldn't approve." A shitty but true fact.

"Okay, but be careful please, Cece." Her hand is warm and comforting when she places it on mine.

"I will. It's all good. I got this. Now, should we get to work on this novel?" We're t minus 45 days from the deadline.

Georgia pops her last fry in her mouth, her tongue darting out to lick the last bit of salt from her lips. "That's my cue to leave. I've got an art history lecture to get to, anyway. You gals have fun."She waves the tips of her manicured fingers at us, standing up and sashaying off.

"Later, G," I say.

"Ta ta."

"That was a surprise." I'd only been expecting one roommate, but I got two for the price of one.

"I ran into her in Keefe after class, and she said she was going to waste away to nothing if she didn't get some food, so I invited her for a snack. But I told her we were planning to work, so she couldn't linger." That's right, they both take most of their classes on the west side of campus where most of the art centric buildings are.

"It's all good."

"We should get to work. I was thinking about what you said about Zane, and the relationship between him and Eliza. I'm thinking we could slip their tryst into this story arc, but I think it ends in a betrayal. We can leave it on a cliffhanger and then decide where we want to go with it in the next arc."

I never intended for my superhero to have a love interest in my graphic novel, but after Annie and I started talking and agreed to a collab, it sort of clicked. It felt right for her. It's not her entire identity, but she is a woman with needs, and I love seeing her take charge. The romance is a side plot, but it's been working and adding depth to all the characters. Especially her rival and potential lover. He's one of the bad guys, but that's the thing about life. Everyone has a little hero and a little villain inside. It's the actions you choose that define what kind of human you are. Or in her case, half alien.

"Amazing. Did you read over the Offset guidelines for submission?"

"Yup. And I think it's going to be tight to get a finished product ready to go by the deadline, but with the two of us working together on it, we can do it."

It's hard to believe I'm getting my first graphic novel finished and polished to submit to a publisher. Offset Inx may be a small press, but they're looking to add some new local creators to their team. I had a chat with them at the con. When they first posted a call for submissions, I didn't think I'd be able to make the deadline. But working with Annie, I'm confident we can do this.

"Fantastic. I sketched out a couple more panels. Let me know what you think." I'm chewing on my lip, hoping she likes them. Dev told me my work was amazing, and asked to see more, but I think he's biased because he's seen my boobs.

She actually squeals as she's flipping through my notebook. My new friend that usually has all the chill squealed at my work. I release the breath I was holding and lean back in to see what's got her excited.

"This is perfect. I know we were talking about adding an edgier look to the design, and I think you've got it here. This scene is perfection."

Pride swells in me. Other than the odd enthusiastic high school teacher, praise for my artistic skills is not something I'm used to. I'm kind of loving this teamwork, and I can't wait to see where our collaboration leads.

CHAPTER SIXTEEN

RESCUE MISSION

DEV

Another day, another win for the Lightning. I was flying high on the ice after the game, but now that the adrenaline has won off, the ache has set into my left side. I had to hand out some pretty tough set downs to our opponents and my arm is feeling the brunt of the punishing hits.

Coach gave us the morning off training to recover before our next game, so the guys are celebrating a little harder than usual during the season. I lift my cola to take a sip, but my mouth stretches in a huge yawn.

Beau has had a few, but he's not too sloppy. Still keeping things under control as the captain.

"How are you doing?" He leans closer, so I can hear him over the noise of the crowded bar.

"Pretty wiped. Might head out."

He nods. "I'd come with, but someone has to keep an eye on these jokers. Take my car. I'll call for a ride later."

I breathe a sigh of relief. All I really want right now is a quiet room to recover in with some ice for my shoulder and a book.

"Sure you don't want to come with? They're all adults. They can look after themselves."

As if to prove me wrong, there's a loud clatter as Grant knocks over a glass of beer, and JJ laughs hysterically as he's trying to sop it up with the shirt he whipped off.

Beau grimaces. "Nah, I'll look after this disaster scene. Make sure it doesn't escalate. Coach would take my C if I let that happen."

I nod, trying not to visibly wince as I stretch my arms over my head.

Beau's ringtone pierces the air as I'm pushing up from my seat, but he doesn't silence it like I thought he would.

"Cece? What's the matter? Slow down." His shoulders are tense and he's speaking clearly again. Sobered up by whatever the emergency is.

My heart leaps out of my chest, leaving me breathless. What's wrong? Is she sick?

"Okay, okay. It's going to be okay."

"It's okay. It'll be fine. I promise. But I can't come right now."

I'm so focused on his conversation, the sounds of the bar fade away.

"I've been drinking. I know. But maybe. Give me a sec."

He pulls the phone away from his ear, and my leg is bouncing as I lean toward him, but he places it back.

"Hang on. I'm not ditching you. I'm just going to ask someone else. I'll be right back."

Beau slides the mouthpiece away, leaning toward me. "Dev, can you drive Cece to the vet? Her guinea pigs are sick and she's freaking out. You're the only sober one here. If it's too much, I can send an Uber for her. I know you're not so fond of rodents."

"Yes. Of course." My entire body eases up a little at the news that Cece is not hurt or sick. The things that flashed through my mind weren't pretty. She could have been attacked, lying hurt in the middle of nowhere, burst appendix, intruder to her house. At least she's safe. I'm sure she's freaking out, and I feel for her, but selfishly I'm glad it's not her that's sick.

"If it's too much..."

"It's not. On my way." I'm pushing past JJ to slide out of the booth before he can finish the thought. JJ stumbles and falls to the ground when I shove him, but I ignore his complaint, reaching over the table to snatch Beau's keys.

"Thanks so much, man. I owe you one. Let me know how it goes. I'm not sure she's going to be up for calling me. She loves those little creatures."

He doesn't owe me anything. I'm doing this for her.

"Hey wait. You need her address?"

"Got it." I have been there after all. No need for him to be suspicious about why I remember where she lives.

I push Beau's fancy ride a little faster than is wise to get to her house. The streetlights are lit up, and the houses all look the same. It might have been hard to identify which one was hers if she wasn't standing on the porch glancing anxiously up the street. I wish I could have been there sooner for her.

She recognizes Beau's car as soon as I swerve into the driveway and rushes back into the house to emerge a moment later with a plastic cat carrier.

I leave the car running but jump out to open the passenger door for her.

"Dev," she says, sounding surprised.

"You, okay? What's wrong with them?"

She settles into the seat, pulling the carrier on her lap, but doesn't bother with her seatbelt.

I don't start backing out.

"Hurry, we've got to go."

"Need to do up your seatbelt." I reach over her and the big container in her lap to grab the belt, pulling it carefully across her, weaving it around the carrier to snap into place. I know she's upset, but I would not be able to handle it if anything happened and she got hurt.

The streetlights highlight her tear-streaked face when she turns to me with a pleading look.

"What's the address?"

"Oh, I'm sorry. I wasn't thinking. The only emergency vet that takes small animals is an hour's drive. I hope that's okay?"

"Of course."

She grabs my phone, punching in the address, and I peel out of the driveway, neck stretched back to do a shoulder check.

"So, what happened?"

The adrenaline from the game had just released me from its clutches when Beau got the call, and it ramped right back up to a hundred.

"They're not breathing properly. It's my fault. They both seemed a little listless earlier, but I've been so busy working with Anna that I didn't really pay attention. I should have taken them to the vet right away. Guinea pigs are really susceptible to respiratory infections. They could die, and it would be all my fault."

"No, it wouldn't. I know you take good care of them."

She shakes her head, clearly not buying my line. "Anyway, it started getting worse. Rogue was gasping for air. They breathe through their noses; they're not supposed to breathe through their mouths like that. Gambit wasn't even moving. I didn't know what to do. Georgia was on a date, and Anna and Blake are at a concert tonight. I didn't have anyone else to call."

"You could have called me first. I would have found a way to come for you."

She sniffles as we stop at a red light, and I turn to see her swiping a shaky hand across her cheek. "Even though this is secret? What if Beau found out?"

I shrug, stepping on the gas as the light turns green. "He told me to be available to you if you needed anything. This wouldn't be a surprise for him.

"Oh. Right." Is she disappointed? Is it bothering her we're keeping this thing between us a secret? What am I even doing? She deserves to be shown off, not hidden away in a corner.

"I'm sorry." I'm tapping an anxious rhythm on the steering wheel, and I fall silent for a few minutes, but I can't stand the soft sniffles. I'd do anything to distract her from her fear.

"How's the novel coming?"

"What?"

"How's it coming? I'd love to see more of the story."

"Um. We finished another few chapters. Annie and I work surprisingly well together."

She's tentative and distracted, but the conversation keeps her mind off her worry for the rest of the drive and that's a win in my book.

But as soon as we slide into a parking spot at the well-lit vet's office, she's climbing out of the car, struggling with the large container.

I'm glad to see there's only one other anxious looking woman in the waiting room when we get there. She reluctantly lets me grab the carrier from her, holding it carefully while she talks to the receptionist, and fills out the paperwork.

I place the plastic box on the counter to peer in at the little creatures. An automatic shiver runs down my back when I see the little rodents, but as soon as it passes, I feel sorry for them. They're both lying there, mouths open, and I can hear their breathing. That can't be a good thing. Cece loves these little things, and if I'm going to be in her life, I think I'm going to have to learn to love them too.

"Hey," I say, poking a finger into one of the holes in the side to touch the soft fur. I'm not sure which one is which, but it doesn't even blink at me. I really hope the vet can help them. The thought of Cece suffering is causing an ache in my own chest.

She slides her small, chilly hand into mine after we settle into some chairs to wait for the vet to call us in.

"Hey, we're here now. It's going to be okay."

"I hope so." Her breath catches on the words, and silent tears are streaming down her face again.

I'm not great with sick people, with crying girls. The only emotions allowed in my house growing up were fear and anger. But I've got to do something, so I reach over, sliding an arm around her shoulder and dipping down to plant a kiss on her head. I think it's the right thing to do. She leans into my touch, shoulders giving the occasional shudder.

The vet finally makes her way out to see us, walking right up.

"Cecelia, let's get these guys into the exam room to see what's up."

When I don't rise from my seat, she grabs my hand, pulling me with her. "Come with me. Please?"

I would never say no to her, so I unfold myself from the uncomfortable waiting room charge and follow the two ladies into the exam room.

As soon as we walk down the sterile hallway, I get anxious, feeling a little lightheaded. I've had to deal with my fair share of injuries playing hockey, but I've never gotten used to being in hospital settings. I don't even remember visiting my mom in the hospital before she passed away. I was too young, or I blocked it from my memory, but it must be imprinted in my memory. That fear of watching someone you love fade away. Not even old enough to understand what was going on.

My breath is coming faster, and I realize I've missed out on the entire conversation between Cece and the vet.

Her pets look so helpless, lying there too still and tiny on the stainless-steel table. Why am I even afraid of them? They're so small, helpless. Granted, they've got some weird teeth, but they're not out to get me. I need to get over that shit.

"Okay, I'm going to run some fluids into them and get them checked out. All signs point to pneumonia, but I'll do some tests to confirm and start them on a round of antibiotics. It would probably be best to keep them overnight. Then if all goes well, you can take them home in the morning and start administering the rest of the course of antibiotics yourself."

"Okay." Cece nods. "Are they going to..." She stumbles over the words.

"You did good bringing them in right away. There's a high probability they'll pull through with the correct treatment, but this is the most crucial time."

I get it, but I hate how doctors have to hedge their words and not make promises. And I really hate seeing Cece on the verge of tears with worry.

"You should probably head home for the night and get some rest. I can call you if there are any changes."

Cece shakes her head vigorously. "No. I don't want to go. Can I stay here and wait?"

"You can."

"Good."

At least the vet is kind. She's a young woman with an understanding look in her brown eyes. Her black hair is pulled up in a bun, and she talks in a soothing tone. She reaches a hand out to pat Cece on the shoulder.

I grab Cece's hand, squeezing it as we make our way back to the waiting room.

"You can go. I'll call Beau to pick me up when they're ready to go in the morning."

"I'm not going anywhere," I say, but I reach into my pocket to grab my phone. "Just going to give your brother an update.

She nods, dropping her head onto my shoulder.

It rings a few times before Beau's sleepy voice comes on the line. "Hello."

"It's Dev, just wanted to give you an update."

"How's Cece?" he asks, sounding a little more alert.

"She's okay. The guinea pigs probably have pneumonia. The vet's going to keep them overnight, so we're going to stay here if that's okay. I'll bring your car home in the morning."

"Yeah, no problem. If you'd rather, I can Uber out there and you can drive my car home. You can pick us up in the morning or we can grab another ride home."

I know he's being nice and trying to do the brotherly thing, but it sets my teeth on edge. I'm the one who needs to be here for her. Comforting her. Even if it isn't exactly my place. "Nah, I'm good."

"If you're sure." I can hear him yawning through the line.

"I'm sure."

"Okay, can I talk to Sissy for a sec?"

The childhood nickname slips out of his mouth so easily.

I hand the phone to her, and she grabs it with her right hand, leaving her left entwined with mine. I give it a squeeze to reminder her I'm here for her.

"Yeah. I think so," she says, swallowing hard.

"Uh, huh."

"No, I'm good. Thanks for offering."

"I'll let you know."

I don't know what her brother would do if he saw the way I was staring at his sister, but I don't think it would be good. I should end this before it gets more complicated, but I've got to be here for her now. No matter what. She needs me. Or someone, and I happen to be here.

"Okay, I'll call you tomorrow. Love you."

Her smile is tentative, and her pretty blue eyes are still glistening, but she looks a little better now.

"Bye."

She hangs up, handing my cell back to me, and drops her head back on my shoulder. I slide an arm up hers, pulling her head in for another kiss. Her hair is soft and silky under my lips, and she fits there perfectly. Like she was meant to be there. But that's wishful thinking. I'm not good enough for her, and I never will be. I may have the privilege of borrowing her love for a time, but I'm not worthy of it on a permanent basis.

Chapter Seventeen

Work In Progress

Cece

A wash of cold air hits me, startling me awake. There's a sharp pain shooting through my neck, and I blink away the gauzy film blurring my vision. I'm resting on a pillow that smells calming. A leathery, sage scent. It's warm and moving gently up and down.

"Hey, sleeping beauty."

The familiar voice is a little softer and gentler than his usual rasp, as if he's trying not to startle me. Where am I? My fingers get all tingly and my eyes fly open when I remember. My piggies!

"How are they?"

"No word yet. I would have woken you up."

"Right. How long was I asleep for?" I can't even believe I fell asleep while my poor babies are lying in there, helpless and sick. It feels like a betrayal.

"Not too long. Half an hour or so," he says, fingers lightly stroking my head.

I struggle to sit up, but he's holding me tight to his chest.

"I should check on them."

"I'm sure the vet will come out soon with an update. She's probably busy working with them. You don't want to bother her, do you?"

"No, I guess you're right." He loosens his hold to let me sit up but keeps his arm firmly resting on my shoulder.

There are a couple of new people in the waiting room now, and the door is swinging shut after the newest arrival.

"Thanks again for staying with me."

"It's not a problem, Cece. I'm not a huge fan of hospitals, but I'm here for you."

"That makes me feel even worse. Bad experience?"

I tilt my head up to look at him, and his eyes shutter in that way they usually do when he's about to shut down a question about his past, but he surprises me.

"My mother."

His features are tight, and I hate to see the pain in his eyes.

"I'm sorry. Was she sick?"

"Yes, she died when I was little. I was too young to remember, so you don't need to feel too bad about it. But that's when things started getting bad with my father."

I'm not sure if it's the lack of sleep, or the closeness we've shared tonight during a tough situation, but he's opening up to me for the first time and I don't want him to stop.

Carefully, though. Don't want to scare him. "Is that when he started..." I trail off, not wanting to word this wrong.

"Drinking. Yes. I think. It's hard to say because I was so young, but I'm pretty sure that's when things went downhill."

"I understand why you don't want to see him."

He nods.

"Do you think it might help, though? Not for him. I'm sure he doesn't deserve anything from you, but maybe for you. Some closure. A final goodbye, or fuck you, or whatever you need."

I keep my voice low so no-one around us can hear, but I can see him shutting down.

"I'm hungry. Where's my...?" He looks around, half standing and then looking toward the door.

"What?"

"My backpack. I don't have my backpack. I must have left it at Wright's. I always have my backpack. Maybe it's in the car." He rushes off, leaving me in his wake.

The cool breeze hits me again as he walks outside, but then he's back in a minute, shaking his head with his arms wrapped around himself in a hug.

"I'm going to call Beau. Maybe I left it at Wrights. I hope. What if..."

I've never seen him this agitated before. He's pacing the waiting room, long legs taking him across the room in a few strides. I see him shaking his head as he talks to my brother.

Finally, he hangs up, running his hand over his short hair.

"He got it. He brought it home. It's okay."

"I'm sorry. This is my fault. You never would have lost it if Beau hadn't made you come out here. Is your wallet in there? I know how much it sucks to lose your ID. It happened to me when we were traveling in Europe one summer. It was such a pain in the ass to get sorted out."

His shadow passes over me and the heat from his body brushes my side as he settles next to me. He remains still and quiet as I'm babbling on, staring at my hands. It's not a surprise, really. He is the strong, silent type. But my words slow as I realize it feels different. There's a tightly wound tension in the silence. I cut myself off, turning toward him to see his elbows propped on his knees, head resting on his hands. There's a slight tremor to them.

"Devlin?" I reach up, placing a tentative hand on his back. There's a slight shudder running through it. "Is it something else? Something about the bag?" I don't understand, but this feels like more than the stress of losing his wallet. And this isn't the first time he's reacted to having his bag touched.

He lifts his head but doesn't turn toward me.

"Sorry." His voice is gruff, hands shaky.

"What is it? Can I help?"

He tilts his head back, exposing his throat, and my eyes are fixated on his Adam's apple as he swallows hard.

"No. You can't. It's fucking stupid. It's just a backpack. Nothing important."

"Then... what is it? Please tell me. Maybe I can do something."

"You can't do anything. I'm fucked up. No one can do anything for me."

"I'd like to try. Maybe you can tell me about it?" I'm pleading now. Seeing him like this slashes my heart to shreds.

"I'm going to sit in the car. You don't need this right now. You've got your own worries and I'm dragging you down. Like I knew I would." He jumps up from the seat, hurrying back toward the door.

I'm stunned for a minute, my butt glued to the seat. But no. He doesn't get to do that. Take off without talking to me. That's not the way this thing works.

A vicious wind kicked in while we were inside, almost knocking me on my ass, but I push through. His hands are braced on the hood of my brother's car and his shoulders are shuddering. It's cold, but I don't think that's the problem.

"Dev, let's sit in the car. We can talk or be silent. Whatever you need. It's too cold out here and you've only got that thin shirt on."

His complete lack of movement is starting to worry me. "Come on, Dev. Just get in the car with me. I'm cold."

A touch of guilt nags at me. I'm using my own comfort to push him, but it works. He finally stirs, arms flexing as he pushes off the hood. "Right." He comes around my side of the car, opening the door for me, and then settling into the driver's seat. His hands are gripping the wheel so had his knuckles have gone white.

"What is it, Dev?" I place an arm on his shoulder, giving him a soft squeeze and letting the heat from his body seep into my chilly fingers.

It takes everything in me to control all the thoughts and questions racing through my brain from bursting out. That's not what he needs right now. He's like a wild animal. I need to give him a moment to trust me. Then hopefully I'll get something, anything, out of this stoic man.

A shiver ripples my skin as the cold sets in again. It's better in here, away from the powerful bite of the wind, but it's not warm.

"It's stupid. The backpack thing." His voice creaks out a little rusty.

I rub circles on his arm but hold my tongue. Waiting for him.

The harsh breath he blows up fogs the windshield. "My mother died when I was tiny. Don't remember anything about her. Except the smell of the hospital room where we visited her in those last days."

"I'm so sorry."

"It's fine. Like I said. I don't even remember her. How can you miss someone you never knew?"

"I think you can. You can be sad about the things you missed out on. The chance to get to know her."

"I guess. My dad always drank. I'm pretty sure. He was a blue collar go to work, come home and crack a few beers everyday kind of guy, but after she died, he got out of control. He spiraled. He stopped looking after himself. He stopped looking after me. He lost the house, and we started moving around to a new apartment every few months."

His words slam into me in a rush of pain. I'd gathered he didn't grow up well off or have an amazing childhood. But this is worse than I thought. He was just a kid who had lost his mother, and then his father abandoned him too. I can't even imagine. My parents are not great at being parents, but at least I had a stable home. I had Beau, and people who cared about me. I can't imagine the pain he endured.

"Sometimes there was no food in the fridge. Sometimes there was no heat in the winter. Sometimes he left me alone for days at a time. Off on some bender, or God knows what. The apartments got worse and worse. The last one had rats, and I'd wake up to a creature skittering across my arm in the middle of the night."

"Oh, Dev." No wonder he's scared of my pets. I thought it was... I don't even know what I thought, but that is something I never could have guessed.

"Anyway. A teacher finally noticed, and they took me away. I didn't want to go. No matter how bad it was, he was still my dad. He was all the family I had. I was already angry, and it got worse after that. I lashed out at every family that took me in. So, I bounced around a lot. Some of them were nice. They tried to help me. They tried to be nice. Others... not so much."

The moonlight shining through the window bathes him in a pale glow as he tilts his head back, leaning in his seat.

"I probably would have ended up in jail if it wasn't for the Neelands taking me in when I was ten. Wayne was a former college hockey player. He ran a local league and coached a couple of teams, including a group my age. I'd never even been on the ice when he brought me to the rink with him. He was nice, but he didn't put up with any of my shit. And as soon as I hit the ice, I knew."

"You knew you wanted to play hockey?" Wow, that's incredible.

A bar of a laugh comes out. "God no. I hit the ice so hard I had bruises for a week that day. But a couple of the other kids laughed at me flailing about there and Wayne got super pissed at them. He gave them a lecture, and..." he pauses. "I think that was the first time anyone had stood up for me. It changed something in me. I felt like I needed to prove myself. To make him proud. I started showing up every day. I practiced until I had blisters up the backs of my heels. I'd skate until my legs were numb. And it didn't take long for me to get the hang of it. A year in and I was playing better than the rest of the eleven-year-olds."

"I'm glad you found someone." I don't think this is the end of it, though. His eyes have a distant look in them as he deliberates over his next words.

"By the time I was fourteen, I was playing with kids older than me, but then my foster mom Jenny's mother got sick, and they moved back to Florida to look after her. They had a lot going on, and they couldn't take me with them."

"That's terrible. I am so sorry." To finally find stability and a home where people care about you, only to have it torn away again must have been heartbreaking for him.

"Just how it is. But Wayne made sure I could play hockey. That was the only thing that saved me. He arranged a free pass to the club, equipment, and a team until I graduated from high school. And that's what I did. I spent all my time at the rink. Sometimes even slept there while I bounced around between families."

I've got an overwhelming urge to wrap my arms around him and never let go. But I can tell he's not quite finished, and if I move too fast, he might not be able to get the rest out.

"There was so much uncertainty moving from one family to the next. Sometimes the foster families had their own kids, or there were other fosters around. Sometimes I had to share a room. And some of the other kids were in even worse shape than I was. They'd learned to steal to survive, and they couldn't stop the urge. The only things I still had from my own childhood home were that backpack, a few photos, and a stuffed bear. I kept it with me at all times, and whenever I could grab extra food, I did. Whether it was from the nutrition bin in a school classroom or at the arena if a parent brought extra snacks. Any time I got my hands on any money, I bought myself food to keep on hand. I don't know if I'll ever shake that empty hollow feeling of hunger. So, I still do it. Keep snacks with me, extra socks and underwear, a toothbrush and toothpaste."

My stomach is churning now at his story. No wonder he freaked out when I touched his bag at the hotel. I chalked it up to some compulsive tendencies like my brother has, but it wasn't that. It was genuine fear.

"I'm sorry."

"No. It's not you. It's all me and my fucked-up childhood. That's why I'm no good for you, Cece. I'm broken. Can't even go anywhere without a stupid backpack."

I wince at the sound of his hand banging on the steering wheel. "That's not true. I've never suffered a day of hunger or physical need in my life, so I can't even fathom how terrible it was for you. But my parents were hardly emotionally available. I know what it means to cling to people and things for comfort. Probably the reason I collect animals. You're not broken. You're just in progress. Like all of us."

His shoulders slump and he leans toward me, seeking comfort. "I'm so sorry. I've fucked this all up. Your pets are sick, and you're worried about them, and I had to go make it all about me."

I pull him in even closer. It's a little strange comforting the massive guy, but we're all human. We're all vulnerable, and the way he opened up to me meant something. He trusts me with secrets he keeps tight to his chest. Secrets his best friend probably doesn't even know.

"It's fine. You were here for me. And now I'm here for you. That's the way it works."

He relaxes into me for a moment before pulling away, clearing his throat. "We should go back in. Check on your pigs."

Sensing he needs the distance from the conversation, I nod, leaning in to plant a kiss on his cheek and then I open the door, bracing myself against the wind.

He walks around the car, grabbing my hand in his, squeezing it tight as we make our way back in to check on my pets.

Chapter Eighteen

Secrets And Tats

Dev

I 'm still operating on not enough sleep as we're dressing for our game. After that long night with Cece at the vet's office, she was able to bring them home, but they've demanded a lot of attention all week. Antibiotics, a vaporizer. The lengths she's willing to go to look after the weird little creatures hits me hard. So, I've been over there a lot, helping her. The one good thing about the situation is my fear of rodents is ebbing away. Something about seeing them helpless, relying on her to look after them, eased it. Gave me a clean start. I still might not be too keen on spotting that mouse darting around, but I think I could handle it better.

Even thinking about her brings a small smile to my face. Never a good idea when you're in the middle of a room full of guys who are used to your glower.

"Is Lucy smiling? Lucy, are you okay?" JJ asks. "I think he might be possessed or something. Anyone know an exorcist. I think the devil really did let something in. We need to help him."

"Shut your mouth, JJ." I'm almost snarling, but as usual, my threat does nothing to deter him.

Beau steps between us as I'm rising out of my seat, fists balled up. "When did you get that new ink?" I twist around, hand flying up to my newest tattoo. It's on the left side of my chest, wrapping around under my arm, so it's tucked away near my heart but not too visible. Only about four inches tall, it blends into the mass of tats already imprinted on my skin. It escaped his notice for a couple of months, but of course Beau noticed it.

"End of the summer." I yank my shirt down over it as he's moving in to get a closer look.

While I appreciate Beau's intervention, now I'm even more on edge since he's noticed the tat I've been keeping on the down low. Somehow even his sister hasn't noticed it yet. Might be because I'm usually the one in charge when we've got significantly fewer clothes on, but still I thought she'd see it. And if she does, I'm not sure what I'll say.

"You trying to hide something? Let me see. The style looks different from your usual. Did you go to a new artist?"

"No."

I'm rolling up my socks and throwing every fuck off vibe I can muster his way.

"It's like that, is it? Okay. Have it your way. No questions."

The problem here is that he knows all my tattoos have some kind of meaning. And if he happens to recognize the art style, we're all going down.

"Boys. Stop fucking around. I need your asses out on the ice!"

Coach walks in, he's got his give-them-hell face on. Usually reserved for playoff games. Must be something going on.

I grab my helmet, jumping up from the bench. Never thought I'd be glad to see angry Coach, but it's a temporary reprieve from my best friend's scrutiny.

"We've got some VIP donors and alumni in the stands tonight, so best behavior. No fighting, no dirty play. You can save that for our away game next week."

Hail snickers, giving Grant a shoulder check as he walks by. Coach doesn't catch it, so I step in, arms crossed over my chest, glowering down at the little shit of a rookie.

He backs off Grant, but pretends he's not scared of me, puffing his chest out.

The game starts off fine. We're playing Boston. The only problem is they're an aggressive team. And since my job is to keep them in check, it's going to be twice as hard to keep things clean for Coach and the donors. I wish we didn't have to care about these things, but someone has to pay for the fancy arena and all the new equipment that flows through the system.

There are problems from the start. They come in fast and hot, clipping Cole behind the refs back barely a couple minutes into the first period. Beau's got his hands full keeping their other D-man off Hail, so I swoop in to mete out some punishment. I push the offender away from where he's harassing Cole, shoving him into the boards.

Backing off, I scan the ice, racing up to the action and then hanging back a bit. Cole swept up as soon as he was clear, but they got in his way again, tangling him up while someone snatches the puck from between his legs.

Skate blades cut the ice in a flurry of snow as we all push ourselves to the limit to get to the goal. They've got too much of a lead, though. Their wingers are tossing the puck back and forth, searching for a shot.

Beau gets up in their center's grill, trying to steal the puck, but he tosses it to the right. Beau doesn't react. He's leaning in, shouting at the opposing team member. Shit. He never loses it, but it looks like he's about to drop his gloves. I have no idea what that guy said to antagonize our cool, collected captain, but it must have been worse than the usual chirping. I'm heading over to help when a collective groan from the crowd sinks my stomach as the horn blares, and our net lights up. JJ. Fuck. He let one in. And none of us did anything to stop it. We haven't played this bad all year. Something is off.

The other team is sharing a victory hug. Coach is screaming at us to get our heads out of our asses.

"Fuck, Beau. What the hell was that about?" Usually, he's the one dressing us down when we fuck up, but as his best friend, I have to take over the job when he loses it.

"He was talking trash about my sister." Beau blows out a breath, shaking his head. "I know better than to let that get to me but fuck man. My sister is off limits."

I can't even focus on the warning in his tone. Some asshole was talking trash about Cece. "What did he say?"

"I can't even repeat it."

"What did he say?" I repeat. Needing to know. It can't be worse than all the things running through my head.

"He said he heard she gives good head, so he might try her out later. Fat bitches are always the best at sucking dick, and from what he's seen, she's got nice tits."

"From what he's seen? The fuck?" My entire body is on fire, trembling. My head is swimming with a level of rage I haven't felt in a long time. "Why is he still mobile?"

"I can't let that shit get to me," Beau says. "I know better. It's all bullshit talk. My sister would never let that piece of shit near her, but it still gets me going. I think he's seen those pictures of her from the summer."

"You're right, he wouldn't." Because I would disassemble him tooth by tooth if he laid even a pinky finger on her.

The buzzer sounds the end of the first period, and we head off the ice.

The disgusting words are still running through my head when we get back out there, and I am laser focused on number 33. The one who clearly doesn't value his face.

"I'll look after it, Beau." I tell him as we settle in for a lecture.

"What did I tell you, boys? You've been playing decent all season and today you choose to play like I let a pack of dusters on the ice. Beau, you should have gotten that puck. Hail, get your head out of your ass and pass the puck. You shouldn't have even had possession when they stole it from you. Get back out there and smarten the fuck up or you're all losing your spots."

Beau stands up, running a hand through his sweaty hair. "You're right. I let myself get distracted, and it cost us a goal, but there's still time to turn this thing around. They're playing like a bunch of thugs because they're not as good as us. We got this."

The agreement is not as enthusiastic as usual. Apparently, the rough start to the game has taken its toll on us.

"We got this!" He raises his voice this time.

"You better," Coach says.

It's fine. They were bullshit words. I don't need to make that asshole pay. That's what he wants. To rile us up so bad we get ourselves into trouble. I'm trying to convince myself, but my hands are still a little shaky.

The second period starts out a little smoother. Cole and Hail have slipped back into a smooth rhythm. Their teamwork has been smoother since Beau got them doing some extra practice together. Not as smooth as Seb, and Woodsy, and Jacks last year, but they were the dream team, and that kind of chemistry takes time to build. I miss those guys.

Beau and I are working the back end, cutting back and forth, trying to keep the way clear for our offensive line when it happens. Number 33 gets handsy again with Cole when he's trying to receive a pass to make a run for the net. Beau and I advance on him like a couple of tigers slinking up on their prey. We get in close, pressuring him.

I'm about to drive him back into the boards when he chirps at Beau. "Look, your sister showed up. Guess she couldn't resist the offer of my dick tonight. Don't worry. I won't give her my jersey. She's okay but not hot enough to wear mine. Plus, everyone has seen her tits now. I know I've got a pic saved on my phone."

The rage I shoved down earlier comes roaring back and my skates clear the ice as I make a run at him. My entire body is trembling, limbs numb, all reasonable thought long gone from my brain. All I can think about is how hard I'm going to take that fucker down.

"Lucy, stop!" Beau's warning comes way too late. And I don't think I'd have listened to it even if it was in time.

There's a thump, and pain spikes down my arm as my body hurtles through the air, slamming into him with a crunch.

We hit the ice, and he gets an extra slam when I land on top of him. At least he broke my fall, but now there's chaos all around us.

I'm flying back as someone yanks me off him before I can get a punch in. I want to pound his face in until it's unrecognizable.

I'm still struggling against the hold on my arms even as I'm dragged away.

The ref calls it a major and I'm sent to the penalty box, but it takes three of our guys to drag me off the ice. I'm not even sure who takes me. My vision is so blurred by my anger.

"What the fuck, man? Thanks for defending my sister's honor and all, but now we're fucked."

I blow out a breath. "Sorry." Even as I say it, I know it's not true. I would pound that asshole into the ice again if he said anything about Cece. He was probably lying. She's probably not even here.

But I look up toward the friends and family section, and my heart skips a few beats when I spot her. She is wearing a jersey. I'm sure it's not mine, and that chafes, but the horrified look on her face cuts deep. I don't want her to look at me like that.

The audience is going crazy. Some of them are riled up and pounding the floor, some of them are booing now that the away team has the advantage of a five-minute power play.

It's painful to watch the next five minutes from the box. Boston scores two more goals before I'm out, and then Coach immediately pulls me.

"The fuck was that all about, Connell?" He gets in my face. "All I asked was for you guys to play a clean game, and you had to go out there and play the worst you have all year."

"That asshole was playing dirty the entire game, and then he was talking shit about Beau's sister. Family is off limits, Coach."

"You know better than that. He was talking trash to get you riled up and gain an advantage. They know we're better than them. Not that anyone could tell from that travesty. And you fell right into his trap. She's not even your sister. I appreciate loyalty but not at the expense of the team."

Now that the adrenaline has worn off, I'm shaky, cold, and tired. I lift a hand to swipe my hair away before I nod. "I'm sorry."

I am, but only because I cost us the game. Not for what I did to him. It's not like I actually started a fight. That would have been an immediate DQ.

"Get out of here. I'm not even going to make you suffer. I'm sure your team will take care of that for me, and the fans as well."

Right. I don't even bother to shower. Ripping my equipment off to change clothes, and slamming my locker shut on the way out. No way I'm waiting for Beau. That's an uncomfortable conversation I'm not ready for. I'll head home, grab a hot shower and hide out in my room until this blows over.

Except, when I storm out the back door, there's someone waiting for me.

CHAPTER NINETEEN

FALLOUT SHELTER

CECE

"Dev?" I keep my tone soft, afraid to spook him. He doesn't look angry anymore. Just defeated and sad. "What happened?"

He shakes his head. "You really don't want to know."

My back snaps up into defensive mode. I don't appreciate being told what I want and don't want. "Yes, I do. I've never seen you like that on the ice. It was terrifying." My hands are clenched at my sides to hide the slight tremble, and my heart still hasn't quite settled from the fear. I don't want him to think I'm scared of him, though. He looks upset enough as it is.

"I can't." He shakes his head.

"Tell me. It might help. Beau looked more riled up than usual too, so it must have been bad."

"Oh, fuck. It was." He shifts on his feet, staring at his toes. "He was talking trash about you."

I reach up to rub at my chest, trying to ease the breathless pain. Not exactly what I was expecting. I'm way too sensitive to the judging eyes of random strangers, but being the target of one of my brother's competitors on the ice is new. Or maybe it's not. Maybe Beau has been dealing with this for a long time and he never wanted to hurt me. Ever protective. But then, it wasn't Beau who lost it. He was mad, obviously, but he didn't get himself sent to the penalty box. That was all Dev. A different kind of tingle skitters across my skin. It shouldn't be hot, but it kind of is.

"What did he say?"

He looks up, brown eyes pained. "You don't need to hear that. It was disgusting. He's a piece of trash. Glad I took him out to the curb."

"That can't be good for you. I don't want you getting in trouble for me."

"Hey." He closes his hand around my chin, tilting my face up to his. "You're my girl now. No one talks about my girl like that. Ever. You're worth the risk." His eyes are shifting around, though. He looks nervous, and I hate that me being in his life could jeopardize his future.

I don't say it out loud. That I don't think I'm worth fighting for. Not worth risking things for. But it's like he can see inside the tangled mess in my brain. The dark thoughts, and self doubt that I usually keep to myself. Because nobody needs to hear that. Or wants to hear it. A lady never complains, as my mother is fond of saying.

His face scrunches up in pain. "And he's seen the pictures. They might be circulating again. I'm so sorry, Cece."

My skin crawls. I'm never escaping those. That one stupid moment. Stupid mistakes like that shouldn't be able to follow you for the rest of your life. But in this day and age, they do. And we're back to that place where I'm bad for Dev. The man craves his privacy. Something he never had growing up. He shouldn't have to carry my burden as well as his own. "I've got to go. Georgia is waiting for me in the car."

I'm reluctant to leave him like this. He looks so upset, but the team usually goes out to celebrate a win or commiserate after a loss. He won't want to come to silly old games night with me. And it's probably better if he keeps his distance.

But his face falls, eyes drifting away, but not before I catch the lost look in them. I can't bear to hurt him by pushing him away when he's already down.

I guess it doesn't hurt to ask. "You should come. We're having a games night. Unless you've got other plans with your team."

He dips his head to mine, capturing the lip I was nibbling on, and it steals my breath. His kiss is slow burn, fingers reaching up to tangle in my hair, pulling me closer until his tongue slips inside to trace mine, and the world fades away. When we're together like this, nothing else seems to matter.

The metallic squeal of the back door shocks us apart. What am I doing? We're out in public. Right behind the arena full of Dev's teammates, including the one person who can't find out about this.

Don't be Beau. Don't be Beau.

"Hey, Lucy, need a ride?"

I'm too scared to turn around. It's one of his teammates, but since I've been avoiding them, I'm not too familiar with their voices.

Dev straightens. He reaches casually behind me, hands resting on my lower back for a moment before he slides one up my back, pulling my jacket's hood up and over my ponytail, until it's shadowing my face.

"I'm cool. I've got plans tonight. See you later."

I'm resting a hand on his chest, and his heart is pounding as fast as mine. Georgia. I need her asap. I slip out my phone, sending a quick SOS.

Boots stomping on the pavement get closer and closer, and Dev pulls me in, tucking my head against his chest to conceal my face. His shirt is soft under my cheek, but I'm hyper aware of every movement behind us and can't enjoy the proximity.

There's a low whistle, and the disembodied voice is even closer this time. "Sure, drop the bomb out there and leave the rest of us to deal with the aftermath. Honestly, good on you. Beau is going to be a nightmare tonight. He hates losing. He'll be beating himself up over it, and that's no fun for anyone."

Georgia's bright red car in my peripheral vision is a beacon of safety as she squeals up in beside us.

"Nice ride. Are you sure I can't come along?"

"Fuck off, JJ." Dev's words rumble against my cheek.

"Fine." There's an exaggerated sigh. "Catch you later. Or maybe not. If you're smart, you won't come home until tomorrow." The footsteps finally start to recede.

"It's safe." It's a low whisper in my ear.

Dev moves beside me, keeping me blocked from prying eyes as I step toward the safety of the car. I duck my head down, reaching out to fumble for the door. It swings open, and I slip into the back seat, leaning to the side until I'm almost horizontal.

One door slams and then another, while I remain hidden. The engine rumbles to life with a smooth purr that matches the laugh of its owner coming from the front seat.

"Hey, Dev. Cece, what are you doing back there? You look like you had an encounter with one of the ghosts that haunts the arena."

"Close call with one of Beau's teammates. For a minute, I thought it was him. I think I may have actually had a near death encounter. Pretty sure my heart stopped for a minute or two there."

The car is shifting under me as we make progress out of the lot and onto the street.

"You're safe now," Georgia says.

But I wait another couple of minutes, exercising extra caution.

"You coming to games night with us, puck boy?"

Dev actually lets out a rare chuckle. Georgia has that effect on people.

"I guess."

"Good. We could use some fresh blood. I was thinking of breaking out the Ouija board."

That has me sitting up fast. "No, you're not. Aren't you the one who told me you're not supposed to fuck around with those things? A demon in the house is the last thing we need."

"There she is."

She was messing with me, got it.

"Why are you bringing one home, then?"

Her head is cranked around to look at me rather than the road she should be focusing on.

"What are you talking about?"

"Don't they call this one Lucy? For Lucifer? He sure looked like he was possessed tonight. What was that all about? I'm still a hockey newbie, but judging by how fast he got sent to the penalty box, I'm assuming that move wasn't legal."

I laugh. Why am I not surprised she's done a deep dive into the team, including the origins of their nicknames?

"Asshole deserved it."

"Fair point. No further questions. Let's get home. We're making Penne Vodka for dinner. You two can be in charge of the salad."

The rumble of Dev's stomach travels all the way to the back seat, and he reaches in his backpack for a snack. "Trail mix?" he offers. "If you don't mind me eating in your car?" He turns to Georgia.

"No problem, sugar, but I'll pass. Saving up for our delicious meal."

I shake my head so he's the only one munching away on the short ride back to our place.

"Hey, you brought the jock!" Anna pulls her head off Blake's lap as soon as we step into the house.

I come to an immediate halt when Dev freezes in place. I tug on his arm, trying to encourage him through the door.

"Don't scare him away, Anna." The other few times he's been over, we were kind of occupied in my room and only emerged for brief periods to avoid starvation. While death by sex might seem glamorous, I'm not ready to check out yet. So, he hasn't had much contact with my roommates yet. Now that I'm thinking about it, he may have been avoiding them.

"What? We're not used to athletic types around here. Most of our friends have only played hockey with a video controller in their hand. If that."

"Well, he plays video games, too. Obviously, he's more well rounded than the rest of us."

"I'd say he's well rounded." I give Georgia the stink eye when I turn to catch her appreciating his rear end with a covetous look in her eyes.

I lean back to hiss in her ear. "Mine. Eyes to yourself."

She laughs, marching by us. "What are we playing? Clue, Cards Against Humanity, Risk?" I tilt my head up at Dev. "What do you feel like? We have pretty much everything you can think of. Our board game closet is epic."

He's shifting from one foot to the other, arms crossed over his chest. I'm worried if he doesn't relax, he's going to leave, and I'd really like to keep him for the night. Or maybe the week. If only we had zero responsibilities. Snowed in for a week doesn't sound so bad if I'm with him. But that is unlikely to happen in October.

"Whatever you want."

"No, you're our guest. I think you should pick. Come on."

Blake is eyeing him curiously. "We pulled out a handful to choose from. Because I know you girls. If we don't at least narrow it down, we'll spend the rest of the night debating the merits of Scrabble versus poker and end up playing nothing. Check it out. You each get one veto."

We make our way into the living room.

"I am absolutely not playing CAH while sober. Then you'll know what a terrible person I really am. At least under the influence, I can blame the alcohol," Georgia says.

"Fair. But I'm pretty sure we all know what a terrible person you really are, G."

"Maybe, but Dev here still thinks I'm the angelic southern belle I pretend to be."

That earns a short bark of a laugh from my guy, and I squeeze his hand.

"Risk is a hell no for me. Blake gets way too competitive, and I don't want to be stuck at the same game all night. Dev?"

He grunts.

"What's your veto?"

"Oh, I don't..."

"Yes," Anna says. "We all get one veto. You're one of us now, so pick your no go. Then we can choose one and get dinner started. I'm famished. I've been saving up room for this meal all day."

Our weekly Friday night roommate dinners have turned into something of a tradition. It's nice. We all cook together and play games. The kind of family I always wish I had. Beau and I did things together as kids, but more often than not, he was at hockey practice or games, and our parents were hardly ever around. I can't even fathom the thought of them playing a game of Monopoly with us. And if they weren't out for dinner, our cook was making something too fancy for our childish tastes. What kid wants to eat quail with all the bones and blackened Brussels sprouts? Not me. That's for sure.

Anna's plea gets him to admit his preference. "I don't really like Charades. Not much of an actor."

Georgia grabs the Charades cards and tosses them toward the closet. "Beautiful. Anna and Blake know each other too well, anyway. It's like they can read each other's minds. Not exactly a fair competition. What's it going to be then, puck boy?" She lifts a brow at him, brushing a stray curl behind her shoulder.

He turns to me. "Your pick tonight. Choose wisely. Those feral creatures might not give you another chance. First time privilege."

"I kind of like Catan."

"Yes," Blake says. "Good choice. Anna, want to get it set up with the extension while the pros get dinner started?"

She nods, scooping up the rest of the games to stow in the closet, and the rest of us head to the kitchen for dinner prep.

Dev leans in closer, lips brushing my ear. "How are Rogue and Gambit doing?"

My insides get all warm and fuzzy at his concern for my pets. The pets he was terrified of the first time he saw them.

"They're doing so much better. Do you want to go say hi?"

He hesitates. "Sure."

"Amazing. Come on."

I was a little suspicious that he was only doing this to get me alone, but instead of pulling me in for a kiss like I thought he would, he scoots over to the cages, bending down to peer in.

"Hey, guys. You doing good?" Rogue looks up, twitching her nose, and Gambit ambles over to sniff his finger.

The squeal that comes out of him is more suited to a sorority girl than a big tough hockey enforcer. He pulls away, then reaches out again to boop the twitchy nose.

"They like you." Loki is weaving around in circles, giving me an affronted look. Such a diva. He really takes after his namesake, expecting immediate attention as soon as I walk through the door. He inches up to me when I go over. "Sorry boy. I'd normally let you out, but we've got company."

"It's okay." Dev's voice is so quiet, I think maybe I mis-understood him.

"What?"

"You can take him out and let him run around the house. Your roommates don't mind, do they?"

There's a pinching sensation in my chest. "No, but I thought you..."

"I don't mind. They're important to you, and you are important to me. Take him out."

The pinching turns into a full-on squeeze. He's got my heart in a vice, and my insides are melting. "Are you sure?"

"I'm sure. I l... like seeing you happy." He stumbles over the words, ducking his head.

CHAPTER TWENTY

BEGINNER'S LUCK

DEV

I'm not sure what I was going to say, but she's looking up at me with those big blue eyes shining, and I'm starting to realize I would do anything for her. Even get used to the tiny creature that almost gave me a heart attack the first time I came over here.

"Really. It's okay. He can deal."

"He shouldn't have to."

That's the smile I love. The one that takes over her face, spreading right to the corners of her eyes. She hops up onto her toes, flinging her arms around my neck, lips crashing with mine. It starts out sweet. Lips closed, hands pulling me down, but like a rising tide, heat washes through me, and I can't help searching for more.

My hands go to her hips, kneading and yanking her in closer. My dick comes to life, jumping to attention. I need more. Closer. So, I slide down those lush hips over the round ass. She squeaks when I close my hands around it, pulling her up into my arms. Her legs fly around my hips, keeping me close. Our lips never part. Never come up for air. What started as a spark of thank you is turning into a raging fire. Everything she does sparks that flame, though. I can't be around her without wanting to feel every inch of her naked skin against mine.

"You feel fucking amazing. Remind me why I ever leave the house?" I ask her, backing up until that incredible ass is hanging over her bed.

"Hurry up, guys. We need help in here." I groan, reluctant to break the kiss.

"Ignore them," she mumbles against my lips.

"Seriously, put your clothes back on and come out here. It's Roomie Fun Night!" Blake is getting involved now. We're screwed. Or maybe not so much.

"We should go out there." I'm saying the words, but not releasing my grip on her ass.

"Do we have to?" She's pouting now and I really want to take a bite out of that lower lip.

"I think so. They're your roommates."

"Right. Fine. Georgia won't let it go. If we're not out there in five, I'm sure she'll be unscrewing the hinges on the door. She's surprisingly handy like that."

"Really?" Surprising, but then ghost girl seems full of surprises.

Her eyes are still locked on mine, hands wrapped around my neck. "Are you going to let me down?"

"I guess."

"I mean, you could carry me out there like this, but then they'd definitely have something to mess with us about, and I don't think we need to give them any more reasons to tease."

"Fine. But this is not over." It's a promise I intend to keep. Like all my promises. Except the one. The most important one. The one where I told Beau I would never touch his sister. "Tonight, I'm going to lay you out on that bed and I'm going to drag my tongue over that sweet clit of yours. I'm going to enjoy my dessert until you're so wet you barely feel it when I slide my hard cock into your pussy. And then, I'm going to fuck you so hard you'll still feel me when you wake up in the morning. Or maybe you'll still feel me in you, because I'll be fucking you again."

Then I release her, letting her slide down my body so she can feel every inch of me ready to keep my word.

She gasps. "The fuck, Dev. Don't say shit like that to me, and then put me down. Now I have to go out there all red and flustered and help my roommates make dinner. Not fair."

"All's fair. I'm just giving you something to look forward to."

She shivers as her feet hit the floor, then she shoves me. Her touch barely rocks me on my feet, and I smirk at her.

As she's walking out the door, I look back, catching sight of the weird little creatures she shares a room with.

"Forgetting something."

She turns back to me, lips reddened and swollen from my kiss, eyes extra starry. "What?"

I nod toward the cages, and she comes rushing back. "Loki. So sorry baby. The bad man made me forget about you. How rude."

The latch on the cage snaps open with a loud clang and she reaches in to scoop up the slithery little thing. He snakes his way up her arm to perch on her shoulder. I could swear his little pointy whiskered face is glaring at me, but that's impossible.

I'm jealous of the ferret as she strokes her hand down his furry length. "Want to pet him," she says, advancing on me.

"Nope." I back up a step, throwing my hands in the air. I'm not ready for that. I can handle being in the same room as him. Progress. But I don't think I could handle touching him, no matter how soft and small he is.

"Suit yourself."

She puts Loki down on the floor by her bed and walks toward me.

"Hurry up." Her hands are shooing me out the door. "He's gotta stay in here until we finish making dinner. He's way too much of a pain in the ass while we're cooking. I've been tripped more times than I can count. He'll have to stay in my room until after. Then he can roam free."

There's an indignant squeak as she shuts the door before he can escape.

"Now. How are you in a kitchen?" she asks.

"Decent." I've had to learn to look after myself, and since I got to college, I've spent some time watching cooking shows and reading recipe books. I've learned some things about making food. Something about the process is soothing. It makes me think about my childhood and reminds me it doesn't have to be like that. Always a little hungry. Sometimes a lot. Never knowing if it's going to be a good eating week or a bad one. Leaving a decent family who kept me well fed to move in with one who doesn't always remember to give me lunch money.

"Good. Because I'm terrible. I've always wanted to learn how to cook, but I'm a hot mess. That's why we got salad duty. I'm not to be trusted with the oven. So, you'll balance it out. Maybe they'll even let us boil the water."

"A hundred percent no, sweetie." Georgia is looking at me with suspicion. "Last time I let you do that, we had to spend a week scrubbing the stove top."

"But Dev..."

"Is a wild card," Blake finishes my sentence. "No offense man, but we can't trust Cece, and we don't know you yet."

"None taken." I shake my head. "Whatever you need."

"Okay, grab the romaine, cucumbers, and green peppers out of the fridge. Start chopping." It's Blake again. He's clearly in charge of the activities in the kitchen at their place.

He tosses me a bright yellow apron with sunflowers and a little ruffle around the edges. I know he's fucking with me. Thinks the big tough hockey player won't stoop to wearing an apron like this, but I'm happy to prove him wrong.

Cece bursts out laughing as she reaches back to tie the plain black one around her waist. I can't resist stepping in to help, taking a moment to smooth her hair off her neck and bending down to place a gentle kiss on the back of her neck. Goosebumps form under my touch.

"Get to work lovebirds," Annie says. Apparently, she finished her set up job and now she's sliding the cutlery drawer open.

She rattles it around, gathering up supplies and heads over to the expensive looking dark wood table beside the big window. The last gasp of the sun for the day is casting a rosy glow through the windows, and it's a perfect picture of domesticity.

Georgia joins Blake by the oven and the easy familiarity with which they move around the kitchen is surprising. Anna and Blake were the only ones who lived together before, and yet they've already formed this little easy family.

For me, the only time I've ever experienced that kind of dynamic is on a hockey team. The way sport binds you together and the shared goal of winning unites you in a special sort of way. But even though I've been on several hockey teams before, it's never been quite as intense as with the Lightning. I miss Seb, and Woodsy, even Jacks, who delighted in driving me crazy. I hope there's something similar in my team when I go pro, because I'm not a pro at making friends in general.

"Can you grab the Parmesan out of the fridge, Dev?" Cece asks.

I'm rooting around in the fridge looking for a container and coming up empty.

I can feel her presence behind me before she speaks. "What's taking so long?" Her head appears under my arm, and she joins in the search.

"Are you sure you have Parmesan? I don't see the container."

She reaches past me to pull open one of the drawers. "It's right here."

Heat crawls up the back of my neck when I see the yellow triangle of cheese. I've never seen it in that form before, and it's kind of embarrassing to admit I don't recognize the fresh ingredients.

"Sorry," I mumble.

"It's all good. Now put those muscles to work and grate it. Sorry we don't have the already grated stuff, but fresh is so much better."

"Hey, Dev, tell me about your teammates. I'm doing research into hockey players."

Research. That's weird. "For a project?"

"You could say that," Georgia replies, spinning away from the sauce she's stirring on the stove to give me a long-lashed wink.

"Really, Georgia. Trying to dig up dirt on his team. He's more loyal than that."

"Not dirt." She waves a hand. "Information. Hasn't anyone ever told you that information is the world's most valuable commodity?"

"Well, they're people, not commodities, and I highly doubt Dev has the information to help you lure one of them into your bed."

"Ah well.

"Why don't you tell us about that ghost tour you did on campus last week? I think the only way I can handle it is if I've got Dev here."

Georgia launches into a story about a couple of ghosts that lurk in a closed-off tunnel in one of the residence halls. She's a fantastic storyteller. Changing her voice and inflection as needed. Setting the scene with great detail. I don't even believe in ghosts and my eyes are watering. Cece might think she needs me to comfort her tonight, but I think it's the other way around. I'm not going to sleep ever again if I'm alone.

Dinner is incredible. I think it's the best pasta I've ever put in my mouth. The rich flavor bursts in my mouth. We made a homemade Caesar dressing with an outrageous amount of garlic, and Blake even whipped up some crispy, buttery garlic bread.

I'm groaning, hand resting on my over-inflated stomach, but still eyeing the big bowl of pasta in the center of the table.

"Go ahead, take another helping," Cece says.

"I shouldn't." But I reach out anyway to fill up my bowl. I can't resist.

Making the dinner was fun, cleaning up less so. We pile whatever we can in the dishwasher and leave the rest for morning.

"Beau couldn't handle that." Cece waves at the pots and bigger dishes we left on the counter.

"Nah, definitely not. Even just living with him has sparked an itch in me that's hard to resist. I really want to clean it up so it doesn't upset him, even though he's not here.

We plop down on the dark grey couch. I helped move in here and roll to see who starts first.

"Me. Yes." Cece bounces, clapping.

"I think I need a refresh." I tell them, picking up the rule book.

I won the first game. It's always that way. Beginner's luck or something. But no one gets upset. The team has tried playing board games at our house, but it always gets way too competitive, so the only ones we can handle are party games like Cards Against Humanity.

We're on our fifth or sixth game, and I'm yawning hard. A quick glance at my watch tells me it's past midnight. I don't want to be the first to suggest bedtime, but I don't think I can keep my eyes open any longer.

Cece drops her hand over mine. "Let's call it a wrap. I'm going to pass out in the popcorn bowl if I don't hit my bed soon. I need my beauty sleep." I shoot her a thankful look, and we say our good nights, heading for her room.

My stomach tries to leap out of my throat when a tiny blur zooms at us when we open her bedroom door.

Cece bends down to scoop up the fuzzy little trouble-maker.

"Loki, calm down. Ready to pet him yet?" She holds him out to me, and I reach out to see if I can do it. But my stomach clenches with dread. Nope, no way. Not happening. Yet. I'll get over it. I have to.

I shake my head, and she gives him a few more pats before dumping him in his cage. I'm ripping my socks off when she bends down to give me a kiss. "Let me wash my hands. I'm sure you don't want ferret germs all over you."

I rip my shirt off, stretching my arms over my head. She left the door open so I can hear her singing along with the sound of running water, but I can't make out the words. I could get used to this. And that is a serious problem.

The gentle hum that whispers through my body whenever she's around picks up to a roar when she walks back in wearing a scrap of red satin and lace that hides nothing. Her heavy breasts hang loose, straining the fabric, and the fabric barely brushes the top of her thick thighs. I love that body so much.

Her lips curve up in a mischievous smile, the swaying of her hips is hypnotizing me. Making me forget all the reasons this is a bad idea. For me, yes. But mostly for her.

"Hey, there. Come here often?"

She leans in, dropping her hands to the bed beside me. My eyes are drawn to the creamy flesh displayed for me, and I reach up, needing to feel them in my hands.

I groan, and her eyes close, head tilting up to reveal the long line of her neck as I knead her breasts, brushing my thumbs over her hardened nipples.

My phone rings, shattering the moment.

I pull my hands away from her, glancing at it guiltily. It's Beau's ring tone.

"Ignore it. Please." She grabs at my hands, trying to bring them back to her body.

I want to. There is nothing I want more than to rip that skimpy fabric off and explore her. Spend the rest of the night worshiping her, but I've got to get it. I don't think she'd understand if I explained it to her. How important it is to answer the call. Because the one time you don't, you might get home to find it was your last chance.

"I can't. I'm sorry." I hope she can read the apology in my eyes.

"Hello?"

"Hey, man. Where are you? I thought you were sulking in your room, but I got worried when you never came down. It was a rough game, but I wanted to at least touch base. Make sure you're okay?"

The guilt that's been riding me since I started sneaking around with Cece grips me hard, tensing my shoulders, clenching my jaw.

"Sorry. I went home with a girl."

"A girl?" Beau sounds surprised. "Is this thing getting serious? You've been disappearing a lot lately. Anyone I know?"

"No." The lie causes me physical pain.

"No, it's not serious, or no, I don't know her?"

"Neither. Both. It's nothing. Just a fling." Now I'm digging myself deeper. Cece is probably hanging every word.

"Okay. As long as you're okay. Everyone's pretty pissy tonight anyway, so it's probably good you're not here. It'll blow over tomorrow. We'll kill it next game."

"For sure."

"I'll let you go. Just wanted to check on you. Make sure you're good. And one last thank you."

His voice is getting a little rough around the edges, like he's holding it together with a fraying rope.

"Thank you for what?"

"For defending my sister. And for looking after her last week. You've been there for her when I couldn't, and I can't tell you how much it means to me that I have someone I can count on to help look out for her."

Fuck. I can't do this. I can't be here with her. Each word digs my well of lies deeper. How am I ever going to get out of this?

"Don't thank me."

"Of course I will. My sister is the only true family I have. And now you're like a brother to me. So, thanks. Enough of this. Get back to your lady. I'm sorry for interrupting your night."

He's sorry. He has nothing to be sorry for.

My numb fingers can't hold my phone anymore, and it slips to the carpeted floor with a soft thud.

"Is something wrong?" Cece sounds worried about me now too, and I don't deserve any of it. I'm an asshole.

"I'm fine. You know I'm pretty tired, and I've got early practice tomorrow. I should probably go to bed."

I drop my head into my hands, avoiding looking at her. Seeing her again when she looks like that won't help. I can't resist her ever, but especially not like this.

"Oh. Okay. I thought. Fine. Yeah, we'll go to bed. I'm tired too."

I can hear the soft thuds of her feet on the carpet as she walks to the bathroom, but I don't look up. Instead, I slip under the thick duvet on her bed, dropping an exhausted head on her pillow.

When she returns, she slides in beside me, but I feign sleep. Because if I open my eyes. If I see her all soft and sexy. If she slips in beside me and snuggles up, I know I'll be lost.

CHAPTER TWENTY-ONE

THE THREE C'S

CECE

We're only a few days away from my favorite holiday of the year. Not everyone considers Halloween to be a holiday, but you'll bring me over to the dark side. Cosplay is life for me, so I think it follows that the one day a year that even the masses wear costumes is a cause for celebration. Usually, it's just the cosplay crowd.

The details of what I'm going to wear are running through my head as I idly chew on the end of my pen.

"Miss Whitaker."

Startled out of my reverie, I look up to spot my TA staring down at me. She's only a few years older than me as a grad student, but she's got her shiny blonde hair pulled back in a tidy bun, and she's wearing a button up blue blouse. It's probably an attempt to deter her students from asking her out because she would be considered a hottie. And some of the college guys are pretty gross. Being last named by someone so close to my age is weird, though.

"Yes." There's a nervous lump forming in my throat. The look in her eyes tells me she feels bad for me, which means this isn't a pleasure visit.

"We need to talk about your grade on the last assignment."

Right, I was so busy with Dev, and all the drama I didn't have as much time to spend on it as I should have. It wasn't my best work, but I didn't think it was an F or anything. The look on her face tells me otherwise.

"What about it?"

Her eyes shift away from mine. "It would be better for you to come to my office. I've got office hours from one to three today. Can you stop by then?"

Great. Now I'm going to be stressed about this all through lunch.

"Sure. Can I ask..."

She nods. "We'll talk later."

Awesome. If I fail this class, I might not be able to graduate at the end of the year. That's unacceptable. I can't be the one member of the Whitaker family that doesn't finish college. What a nightmare.

The front door slams behind me as I rush in, carrying a heap of books in my arms.

"You got time to work on our little project tonight?"

I stumble, and the stack slips out of my arms, tumbling to the floor. "Fuck!" I screech, hopping on one foot. The corner of one particularly thick monster smashed my toes, and now there's intense pain radiating down my foot.

I grab the injured foot, trying to rub the pain away while continuing my little hopping dance around our hallway.

"Sorry. I didn't mean to scare you. What are all these books for?"

"I can't work on our project. I have to do an extra assignment for management to make up for bombing the last one."

"Oh, that sucks. I've been messing around with some of the ideas for outfit designs, and I was hoping you could make them shine for me."

Anna's shouldering more of the writing side, while I'm carrying the heavier load on the drawing aspect of our book, so it's turning out to be a fantastic partnership.

"I really can't." I hate talking about this stuff. Getting a B is considered failing in my family. Actually failing my last assignment with an overall grade hovering in the low Ds would be a complete disgrace. But Anna is not my dad or mom. She's not my perfect brother. Because as much as he wouldn't judge me for the grade, he's never failed a class in his life.

"I'm going to fail this course if I don't ace this assignment. I can't even pull it up with the end-of-year exam."

Some of the tension I've been carrying in my back eases up as I make my confession.

There's sympathy and understanding on my friend's face. Something I'm not so used to seeing. "That sucks. I flunked math in grade ten and had to go to summer school. It was the worst. I would totally help you if I could, but I've got zero knowledge of businessy things. Maybe you should get a tutor? I could help you find one."

The offer leaves a warm glow in my chest. "Thanks. I appreciate it, but I can do this. I just have to dig in deep and ace this thing. I can do it, but I'm probably going to be a nonparticipating member of the house for the next week or so. Other than Halloween. Of course I'm in for that."

"Okay. I'll leave you alone, but let me know if you need anything. The three Cs. Caffeine, cookies, or chips."

"I'm probably going to consume way too many of those this week, but I'm good for the moment. Thanks again."

She smiles, heading off to the kitchen. There is a delicious warm curry smell emanating from that direction, so I imagine Blake is working on some masterpiece or other. He keeps us well fed. Zero regrets on my part about sneaking him past my dad's radar.

The leather chair dips under the weight of my flop after I drop the books and my bag on my desk. I pull out my phone to check if there's any sign of Dev. After he left me all hot and needy and then turned over and started snoring like a middle-aged man in a bad marriage, I haven't been able to pin him down for a repeat hang. I miss his body, and his dick, but even more I miss his face and the way he looks at me. Like I'm not on a one-way trip on board the fuckup express.

I scroll through his texts instead of starting work on my assignment. There's a lot of dopamine in his sweet messages. But the excitement bubbling inside when a new one pops up can't be healthy.

> **Will Loki wear a costume?**

>> **Maybe for five secs**

> **How about this?**

The pic that shows up has me melting. Glittery red horns protrude from the hood attached to a long black shirt with bat-like wings. It's got a devilish tail to match the horns.

>> **ALL OF THE YES**

All caps are essential to get my point across. That might be the cutest thing I've ever seen.

> **Good I bought it. We match.**

And no, I was wrong. This is the cutest thing I've ever seen. A selfie appears of Dev's growly face with a halo of red, sequined devil horns. And I'm now officially dead. Goodbye cruel world.

I send him a skull emoji.

> **You still coming to the party?**

Now I'm breathing a sigh of relief. I was worried after that night. Maybe he's not into me anymore. Maybe he realized that I'm a mess he doesn't need in his life. None of the daily texts were enough to reassure me that things were still good. But this.

The fact that he went out of his way to buy a costume for my furry friend, who he's still afraid of. And he bought himself something to match? That's love. Maybe not love. Too soon for the L word, no matter how much my heart is screaming to jump all in. Jumping all in and regretting it later is one of my special skills, after all.

But no. I've been letting my insecurities get to me. He wants me at his party, even though we can't showcase our relationship.

I send him back a hundred percent emoji, along with a pumpkin and a vampire for good measure.

Good

There's a heart emoji next to the last word he texted me for the evening, and it fills me up. Almost enough to get me through the night of reading the same paragraphs three times, while I try to focus on the supremely uninteresting textbook.

Chapter Twenty-Two

Misdirection

Dev

"Cece is coming to the party tonight. Mind your manners, assholes," Beau is pacing the living room, picking random things up as he goes and stashing them away in drawers or the cupboards.

He does this before every party. At this point, I have no idea why he keeps anything valuable in the shared space. But it's his house. He can do whatever he wants.

I've been mulling it over in my head since I last saw Cece. We haven't been able to spend enough time together, but if Beau knew we were together, maybe that could change? Maybe I should at least feel him out before she gets here. Before he notices my feelings for her displayed on my face. "Hey, Beau."

"What's up, Lucy?" Beau turns to me at the same time Grant wanders up with a super sized bag of cheezies hugged to his chest.

"The elusive twin is coming to the party?" He asks around a mouthful of Cheetos.

JJ is trying to help, but his help already ended up in an extra round with the broom when he knocked over a bowl full of mixed nuts in the kitchen. He comes wandering back in after finishing his clean-up job. "Cece's coming? The hot one with the curves and the angel hair? Man, I'd bend her over the couch any day. That ass?" He whistles.

I've never felt a rage as strong as the one gripping me right now. But before I can push off the wall to mess up his face, he pales. I settle back into my position, watching Beau as he tears across the room toward our goalie.

"What the fuck did you just say about my sister, ass-hole?"

He grabs JJ by the collar, yanking him off his feet.

JJ looks like he's about to shit his pants as he dangles. Beau is extra intimidating in his Negan costume. Hopefully, he doesn't actually have to use the bat, though. A goalie is kind of important to the team. It would be good if he had a couple of brain cells left, but I guess you can't expect too much.

"I'm sorry, captain. I was just joking. I would never touch your sister. I swear."

Cole catches the show, walking in with his arms weighed down by bins, his new girlfriend at his side.

Jazz wanders over to Grant and steals a handful of the popcorn he's munching on. Where did he even get that?

JJ squeaks, scuttling backward like a threatened crab as soon as his feet touch carpet.

Beau swipes a shaky hand through his hair, walking back over to me. "I know he did that to wind me up, but I can't help it. She got fucked over by one of my former teammates, and I can't let it happen again. It tore our team up, and I can't bear to see her hurt like that again."

I nod at him. Right. I don't know what I was thinking. There's too much on the line right now. My career, our championship, and most important, his friendship.

Once things have settled a little, she steps in, taking control of the situation to assign us all tasks.

After she assigns me to kitchen duty, I grab the food bin and lug it in to start putting things away. See, they know I'm the best one in the kitchen here. Not like at Cece's house.

I'm glad this was the chore I landed. I've got the room to myself. There might even be a smile on my face, still thinking of Cece. But then I think of JJ hanging from Beau's hand. And what he said? Fuck.

This entire thing might be a terrible idea. Why did Beau tell his sister she could come? Not that she needs his permission. And why did I think it would be a good idea to have her here? Maybe dancing with other guys. Even if she's not dancing with them, they'll be ogling her, flirting with her. I'm getting all tense again.

My anger level rises again when JJ swaggers in.

"Did I do good?"

"What are you talking about, asshole?"

"I was taking the attention off you and Cece." How is he back to smiling like a cheerleader from the football team? Does he have no sense of self preservation?

"It's okay. I know, but I won't tell anyone."

"You know what, exactly?"

He takes a step backward when I advance on him again. "About you and Cece."

My heart picks up. He can't. "You don't know shit."

"Yes, I do. I saw you with her after the game last week. But don't worry, I won't tell."

I may be in panic mode, but my brain is still trying to rationalize. He saw us, but he has managed to keep his mouth hole shut for a week now. That's a good sign, right? We might all make it through this.

"You're right, you won't. Because if you do, I'll borrow that bat off Beau, and you won't be telling anybody anything for the next few months."

"That's not funny. I actually had to have my jaw wired shut when I was in the eleventh grade," he says. I have no clue if he's telling the truth or if this is some wild story his chaotic brain made up.

"Then you know what you have to look forward to if you say a word about that."

"It is true! I knew it."

Great. He had suspicions before, but now he knows for sure. I'm dating Beau's sister. Behind our captain's back. Behind my best friend's back.

The room has gotten progressively louder as people get drunker. I keep a watchful on everyone because drunk people are unpredictable, and I hate surprises. But my main focus has been watching Cece flit all over the house. She wiggles her hips, dancing with Georgia, then she's in the kitchen. She flits out back and then in. She's like a bee, bouncing from flower to flower to fill up her hive. The complete opposite of me. I'm usually happy to sit back and watch things unfold at these kinds of parties. But tonight, I've been gravitating to whatever room she ends up in.

The only time I step away is to hit the bathroom and when I get back, she's on the dance floor again, arms twined around some skinny dude's neck.

A dark haze clouds my vision, and I lock on them, about to head over there to tell him to remove his hands before I do it for him when Cole appears behind her. He taps her shoulder, and she immediately forgets about the guy, spinning around and clapping her hands. She cranes her neck to peer over Cole's shoulder at Jazz.

Cece is fanning her neck as the three of them make their way through the crowd and out the front door. I take a sip of my coke, letting the bubbles burn the back of my throat, and glance around the room. It's packed with sweaty bodies, and I spot a handful of my teammates, but they all seem to be occupied.

I find myself pushing away from my spot planted against the wall and drift over by the front window. Cool air sneaks through the cracked window washing over my heated skin, and I glance out toward the porch.

Cece is talking animatedly with Jazz, hands flying. The bottle she's holding in her hand slops over the edge a little and she giggles. She looks so hot in the Spider Gwen jumpsuit that hugs every curve of her delicious body. Her eyes are shining and there's a huge smile on her face. I take advantage of the moment to observe her unnoticed. Tracing her features, learning each line.

"What's up?" The loud voice in my ear is accompanied by a rough slap on my back.

I turn toward JJ, irritated at the interruption. He's grinning and bobbing his eyebrows. "See I knew it." He turns his head to follow my gaze, and my stomach dips again. If I'm being so obvious that JJ notices, it's possible some of the other guys have noticed as well. And that would be bad.

"What the fuck was that comment about earlier?" I glare at him.

He throws his hands up in the air. "I did that for you. Misdirection. You ever watch Penn and Teller? Beau got all angry at me. Hopefully, it kept his attention on me tonight, so you could ogle his sister to your heart's content."

My mouth drops open. Fucker is way more devious than I thought. "Don't talk about her like that again. I could punch you, or I could let her do it herself." The color leeches from his face. "But thanks."

"You're welcome. Haven't seen Beau around for the last hour. I think maybe he's tapped out and gone to hibernate in his room."

With that, he smiles and wanders off to find a new adventure. Would not have thought about him as that observant, but he is a goalie, and they've got to be aware of the puck every single moment of the game. I'm impressed, and a little curious why he's got so much invested in my love life.

When I turn back to the window, Cece is gone. Now I'm just being a creeper, spying on an intimate moment between Cole and his girl.

"What are you looking at?" That's the voice I've missed all night.

She presses up behind me, looking over my shoulder to see what's got my attention. "You were spying on me."

"There's a nice breeze here." It's not a lie.

"And a great view?" She's agonizingly close. The heat from her body warming my back, but not in the icky way of the rest of the crowd. Her warmth is welcome.

"Not anymore." The admission slides out easily.

"I knew it. I've barely seen you all night."

"Is that why you were dancing with that asshole?" There's more anger in my tone than I intend. But I can't help getting heated again at the thought of her dancing with another guy.

"Smoke screen. Dancing with other guys to keep Beau's attention off us." She's in on the conspiracy too.

"You and JJ been plotting together?"

"JJ? No. That's your goalie, right? Barely know the guy." She tugs on my arm, trying to spin me around, but I resist. Because if I turn around and see her standing so close,

I'm not sure I'll be able to stop myself from kissing her right here.

"He knows."

"He knows what?"

"About us."

I can't resist her tugs anymore, spinning around to see her wide eyes.

"Did you tell him?"

"No. Remember he saw us after the game? I guess you weren't hidden as well as we thought. But he's cool. He promised he'd keep it to himself. And while I wouldn't have trusted him before this, he's kept his mouth shut this long, so I think we might be safe."

"Oh, okay." Does she sound disappointed?

"You've got your own bathroom in your room, right?" My head spins with how fast she flips to a new thought.

"Yeah."

"Do you think maybe I could use it? I was in the other one earlier and it's kind of a hot mess right now."

"Cupcake, are you trying to get in my room?" A shock runs up my arm as I brush her hand with mine.

"Maybe." She drags her lower lip through her teeth in a studied move, eyes locked on mine. "It's been too long, and you got me all hot and bothered with all that stalkery energy, watching me from the window."

"We can't here. Down the hall from your brother."

"I won't tell if you don't. I'll leave before he gets up in the morning. But I need this. Don't make me go home to my vibrator. There are other things I'd much rather have in me." She leans in, breath tickling my neck she's so close.

My cock was already waking up. Now it's straining the denim at my crotch. Good thing my costume includes a fanny pack.

"Please."

I can't say no when she asks like that. Begs. All I can picture now is her begging on her knees for me to wreck her.

"Fine. But we'll go separate. You go first. If no one is in the hall, you can go in. Turn right at the top of the stairs. My room is first on the left. I'll join you in a few."

She bounces on her toes, leaning in and I think she's going to lay a kiss on me, but she pulls back at the last minute as if she remembers why she shouldn't. Her smiles dips a little, but she turns around.

"Wait." I swipe my key out of my pocket, slipping it into her palm, then giving it a squeeze. "You're going to need that."

She vanishes into the crowd while I move away from the window, circling the room, taking in the crowd. I search for Beau. He's not on the dance floor, the TV room, the kitchen.

JJ notices me making my pass through the kitchen. "I told you, Beau retired for the night."

I shake my head, turning my back on him. He must have noticed me scanning the crowd.

"Have fun. Be safe," he says to my back.

"Shut up."

Looks like he's right. He might be annoying, but the place is a Beau free zone. I take a chance. Make my way upstairs. There are a couple of strangers waiting outside the bathroom, but that's it. My door handle twists under my hand, and I push it open. The first thing my eyes land on when I walk inside is Cece lounging on my bed. She's still got on her bodysuit, and I can't wait to peel it off her.

"Hey, Lucy." The familiar voice sends me into panic mode, and I slam my door shut, turning around.

Beau's brow is scrunched together, his hair mussed, and he's got his headphones around his neck. He's changed out of the intimidating costume into some grey sweatpants, but none of that eases my fear.

"Have you got a private function going on?"

"What? No. What are you talking about?"

He eyes me up and down. "You look like a bouncer, dude."

"I'm not." I try to relax, dropping my arms to my sides, but they're stiff and awkward. At least they feel that way to me.

"I know. I was wondering if you have that accounting textbook you borrowed from me? I can't sleep, so I thought I'd finish up that work for DeAngelo's class."

Doing accounting homework on a party night. Sure. But how do I get the book out without him seeing his sister literally in my bed?

"I think I left in my bag downstairs."

Beau's mouth stretches into a yawn. "Nah, I saw you grab it from the kitchen and bring it up before the party."

Shit. "Oh, yeah. Forgot. I'll grab it for you." I don't move a muscle, as he stands there eyebrows raised in question.

Understanding dawns on his face. "You got someone in there. Sorry, man. I'll..." He swoops his finger in a U turn and slips back in his room.

I don't move an inch until his door clicks shut, then I whip my own door open far enough to slide through it, shutting it behind me immediately.

Cece is sitting up, wide eyed. "Was that Beau?" she whispers.

"Yes," I say through my teeth. "I'm grabbing one thing for him. Maybe hide in my bathroom until I'm back."

She shakes her head. Fine. I knew it was an asshole thing to ask as soon as the request departed my lips. I dart over to my desk, grab the textbook and knock on Beau's door. He answers with another yawn, so I shove the textbook at him and back away.

"Have a good night?" He wouldn't be using that singsong tone if he knew who was in my room and why.

I click the lock as soon as the door shuts behind me. "You should have locked the door."

"I knew you'd be here in a minute."

"But what if some other rando had wandered in?"

"Then I would have chased them away."

"Yes, but..."

"But nothing. Nothing happened. We're all good. But if you still feel like you need to punish me." She rolls over, exposing her ass to me. "Go ahead."

I exhale a long breath through my teeth. "Fuck, Cece."

"Yes, please."

I'm dragging my shirt over my head as I walk over to her, eager to feel her skin against mine, but I'm still trying to get my breathing under control. She wiggles that ass at me again, so I grab two handfuls of it. Squeezing the soft flesh. She's already squirming under my touch. This is so wrong, but it feels so good. I can't quit her, and I don't want to.

"This costume is hot, but it needs to come off."

"I'm going to need your help with that. Zipper is in the back. My short arms don't stretch that far."

She gasps when I lean down, brushing her hair aside to kiss the back of her neck.

"What were you planning on doing if I wasn't here with you?"

"I dunno. Cut it off." She's mumbling into the covers.

"That would be a shame. You look so hot in it. But then I'd rather keep the view to myself."

My fingers fumble with the tiny zipper. "Fuck."

"What's wrong?"

"This thing is too small."

It slips out of my grasp again and she giggles.

"Your hands are too big."

"It's not the only thing. I reach down to palm my length." She can't see me, but she still groans at the innuendo.

When I'm about to give up and cut the damn thing off, my thick fingers finally get a grip on the tiny thing, and I drag it down her back. Inch by inch of tantalizing skin is revealed as it goes. I reach up with my other palm to run it down the exposed skin. She shivers under my touch.

"Sit up."

She rolls over, grabbing my hands to pull herself up. I grab the costume by shoulders and peel it down her body. It's a little damp with sweat, sticking to her, but I finally get it off, tossing the fabric across the room.

"That's what I wanted to see."

She's got another one of those corset things on underneath, and it's white. Holy fuck. I've always thought black or red lingerie was the sexiest, but there's something about the white that hits me in the gut. Pure and innocent white cloth draped over the body I'm about to do dirty things to.

"I've been thinking about your punishment, dirty girl, and I think more than a spanking is in order. I think I need you to get on your knees and take my cock down your throat. I'm going to use that pretty mouth of yours until I clean it out with my cum. And you're going to swallow down every drop like the good girl you are."

She moans. "Okay."

I'd like her to leave the corset on, but it looks uncomfortable. "Let me get you out of this thing." She twists around so I can get at the hooks tracing up the back. I run my hands down the smooth satin, pulling her in tight. How does she breathe in that?

I'm reaching above my head in a deep stretch when her eyes land on my left side, and I can almost feel them burning a hole through my skin.

"Is that?" She reaches out, hand hovering near my newest tattoo.

I nod, stepping closer to her. "You can touch it." She traces the outline of the skating bear. Her light touch sends a shiver up my spine.

"I'm... I don't know what to say." She's staring at it, but I can't decipher the emotion in her eyes.

I swallow. "I hope that's ok. Getting your art traced by someone else. I should have asked, but I didn't..."

She looks up, blinking away tears. "When did you get this?"

She's going to think I'm a stalker. "Right after that weekend."

Her mouth pops open into a surprised oh. "You didn't..."

I shut my eyes, letting out a deep breath. "I didn't think I'd see you again, and it was the best weekend of my life." It hurts to admit that. I'm sure she's had so many more good experiences in her life, she can't understand why I cherish each one. "I'm sorry. I shouldn't have." She follows me, so I can't pull away, shaking her head.

"No. It's amazing. But, why?"

"All of my tattoos have meaning, you know. I had a lot of bad things happen in my life, before Lakeview. So, every time something good happens, I get a tattoo to remember it. That probably sounds crazy to you."

"No. Never. I'm honored you put me there. It's incredible. It's so much, but good."

She's on her feet, arms wrapped around me in a tight hug, head leaning on me. "Thank you."

"No. Thank you."

We hold each other for a while, just existing together, but then her hands slowly slide up my sides, up my back to my head. She pulls me into her for a kiss that starts out soft and sweet, escalating fast into something more urgent, desperate.

"Get this off me," she begs. "I need you."

The corset is almost as difficult to get off as the jumpsuit, but it's worth the reward when she breathes a sigh of relief as it drops off. I can't help reaching around to palm her heavy breasts. My cock jumps again at the feel of her in my hands.

"On your knees." I tug on her hips, pulling her off the bed. She falls to her knees for me and it's the most beautiful thing I've ever seen. She tilts her eyes up to me. There's so much trust in them. It makes me want to earn it. To be worthy of it.

"Let me know if it's too much."

"I will."

I unsnap the button of my jeans, dragging the zipper down, and her small hands hook the waistband to drag the pants down. She eyes my cock with hunger as it pops out of my boxers. Once my clothes have joined hers on the floor, she reaches out a hand to stroke me. I gasp, bucking my hips into her touch, but tonight I want her mouth.

"Open up, Cupcake."

Her tongue darts out to lick her lips, and then she obeys me.

I nudge in closer until the tip is resting on her lower lip. Her tongue is hot and wet and perfect, licking a circle around me.

"You ready?" I need this to be hot and rough tonight. To take out all the pent-up need and guilt. It is a punishment, after all.

I thrust hard, punching the back of her throat. She gags, and I pull back.

"Too much."

She shakes her head, but I move a little slower this time, giving her a minute to adjust to my size, filling her throat. I grab the back of her head, controlling her movements as I slide home again and again. Her throat wrapped around me is like nothing else. I don't deserve the trust she has in me.

Pressure is building in my back already, but I don't want it to end too soon, so I back off, taking a few breaths. I look down at her. Glassy eyes look up at me and I spot her hand between her legs, rubbing away at her clit. Her breath is coming in quick gasps. She looks so good. The tingle is increasing even when I'm not in her mouth, but that's not what I want. I want to come down her throat. Fill her up with my essence, so I push back in. Her tongue is tracing patterns with each pass of my hips, and I know I'm not going to be able to hold it much longer.

My balls lift and tighten, and I hold on tight to her cheeks. Her moans vibrate up my length, and the heat builds to an impossible height. But when she cries out, body convulsing, I lose it. Pleasure rips through me, tearing me apart from the inside as my hips jolt, my dick pulsing and sending hot streams of cum down her throat. Just like I promised.

I groan, easing in and back out in small quick pulses.

She goes limp in my hold, and I finally pull out of her mouth, sliding down to scoop her up in my arms.

I wipe some cum off her mouth, feeding it back to her on my thumb, and she licks it off.

"Good girl. Now it's your turn."

I slide down her body, peeling off her soaked panties to return the favor.

Chapter Twenty-Three

Evil Alliance

Cece

"What are you doing for Thanksgiving, Anna?" I look up from the panel I was sketching out on my tablet.

Our story is almost perfect, so we're drilling down on the details and laying everything out now. The submission deadline for Inx is December first, just after Thanksgiving. I might be biased, but I think our novel is perfect for what they're looking for.

Yesterday, I worked my ass off to get the bonus project finished for my management class yesterday. I've still got other assignments on the go so I can hopefully get through this semester with decent grades. That's all I need. To get through. Get my degree and move on with my life.

I've been so busy I haven't seen Dev since I laid one last kiss on his forehead and snuck out in the middle of the night after the Halloween party. It's been a long two weeks, but I've been thinking maybe we can hang out over Thanksgiving weekend. I wasn't planning on going home and I know he doesn't have anywhere to go, so I thought we might snag some alone time. That would be incredible. A few days to ourselves. No worries about Beau catching us. That's what I want. To be able to call him mine in public. To tell my brother about him. But he's not ready. I'm not sure if he ever will be. He values his friendship with Beau so much.

"I've gotta go home to Maine. Blake is coming with me. Should be fun."

"Too bad. I was thinking maybe some sort of Friends-giving thing, but I know Georgia is going home too." It tracks. Just because I don't have any desire to spend the holiday with my family doesn't mean everyone feels that way.

"Yeah. But Dev is going to be around, right?"

"Yes." I can't help the smile that pops up whenever I think of him.

"How's that going for you?" She slides a note over to me with a slight adjustment to the dialogue for the scene I've been working on. I nod.

"Fantastic. We haven't been seeing each other enough, but he's got hockey. I've got school, and this. We still text.""Do you think you could see him more if you weren't keeping it a secret?"

I pause my work, looking up to see her giving me a concerned look. "Maybe, but we can't. Not yet."

"Okay. But think about it. Do you really think your brother would be that upset if he found out? Dev is his best friend. He must trust him on some level. And you're a grown ass woman. You get to make your own decisions. This isn't the medieval ages. Your family isn't going to sell you off for an advantageous marriage. You get to choose."

"I know, but things are a little complicated right now. Beau is the only person on my side. It's us against the rest of the family. There's something up with him, too. He always puts a lot of pressure on himself, but something's off. And then there's Dev. What if Beau turns on him? I don't think he could handle it. I couldn't make him choose."

She lays a hand on my arm. "You know what's best for you. But you know. You wouldn't be alone. You've got us now."

Maybe she's right. Maybe I should tell Beau?

And for the rest of our marathon work session, my phone eyes me from the corner of the desk, and not in the usual everyday addicted to my screen sort of way. More in an I'm-silently-judging-you sort of way.

It's almost eight by the time I'm walking into my room with a lion-worthy yawn stretching my jaw. Feels more like midnight to me. My eyes hurt from staring at textbooks and screens. Loki, on the other hand, has reached crazy hour. He's darting around his cage, climbing the walls and begging me to let him run free.

"What do you think, Loki? Should I talk to Beau?"

"You can probably get an answer from my magic eight ball that would be as accurate as asking that furry little thief."

I spin around to see Georgia leaning against my door frame. That's what happens when you leave your door hanging open in a houseful of nosy busybodies."Well, what do you think, G? Should I tell my brother?"

Her perfectly plucked brows arch up to her hairline. "The only one that can answer that is you."

Of course she has to go all mysterious psych major on me now. She's got an opinion about everything. Except this one teeny tiny life changing thing.

"So helpful."

The smooth weight of my phone is weighing me down. I slipped it out of my pocket without even realizing it while we were talking.

"I think you have your answer."

Right. I guess I do.

I tap out a quick message.

> **Sibs coffee date tomorrow?**

His response pops up seconds later.

> **Sure. All Capps? 10?**

> **Done**

And that's the way it is between us. The way it's always been. When one of us needs the other, we're there. No questions asked. No hesitation. All in.

It doesn't alleviate the butterflies rioting in my belly, but it does ease my mind a little. We love each other. We're there for each other. End of story.

My stomach was all tied up in knots while I got ready for school, so I put on a dress and did my makeup. To see my brother. What is wrong with me?

There's some regret now for sure. November is no time to be exposing your knees around here. The short black dress is dancing in the breeze, and I have to keep slapping my hands on my thighs to avoid flashing the entire campus. Been there. Done that. Did not like the results.

The butterflies have been attacking in waves. This morning, I was so nervous I thought I was going to throw up my breakfast, but then I was fine for my first class of the day. They're back in full force now, twisting my guts around.

8:30 classes are the worst, and management is my least favorite, so there was nothing to distract me from the thoughts chasing each other around in my brain. Beau's going to kill me. Worse, he's going to kill Dev. He'll tell our dad, and I'll get pulled out of Lakeview. I know logically these are all crazy ideas. He loves me, and he loves Dev. We've always been a team against our parents. It's not his fault he can do no wrong and I'm the perpetual fuck up.

Doesn't change anything. No matter how many times I try to convince myself. There's this deep sense of unease chilling my skin. I pick up my phone for the twenty-seventh time to cancel, only to slide it away with a sigh. Chimes ring out, ending the class, and I realize I didn't take in a single word of the lecture. Luckily, Professor Douglas records all his lectures, so I can rewatch this one later. He likes the sound of his own voice way more than any of his students.

A hand lands on my head, but the fear quickly turns to annoyance when he rubs his knuckles in my hair. "Hey, Sissy. What are doing out here?"

I shove my brother away. "Enjoying the lovely weather, obviously." A drop of rain calls out my lie as the sky finally lives up the gloomy promise it's been threatening all morning. It's the worst kind of fall day. Damp and windy.

He loops an arm over my shoulder in a bro hug. "Let's get inside before you melt?"

"Are you calling me a witch?"

"If I did. You'd be a good witch. You know, one of the ones that collects every flavor of animal and then goes home to curse her enemies in secret."

"Uh huh. You're such an ass."

"Yeah, but you love me."

"Sure. Keep telling yourself that, little brother." The face he gives me would look better on an ogre than a witch. He loves to pretend he's the older sibling.

"Jazz!" My smile really spreads when I see my new friend behind the cash register.

There was already a big smile on her face when we stepped up to the counter, but when she spots us, it creeps up the side of her face, crinkling the corners of her eyes. She looks so different from when I met her at the Halloween party. I'm surprised I even recognized her without the massive wig and intricate makeup.

"Cece. Beau. What can I get for you two?" She ducks her head at Beau.

"She'll have a kid's hot chocolate, and I'll have an Americano black."

I appreciate the eye roll she gives my brother. "Not that there is anything thing wrong with a hot chocolate, but what would you actually like, Cece?""I'll have a London Fog, please." I don't think my stomach can handle coffee right now.

"Got it." Her brown eyes flick up past my shoulder to check the line. "I'd love to chat, but we're kind of swamped right now."

"No worries. We should catch up later." We tapped our contact info at the party, but I've been so busy with my school catch up, and my side project I haven't had time to reach out.

"For sure. Have a good one. Both of you."

Beau drops a ten in the tip jar. "I'll wait for the drinks. Why don't you grab us seats?"

I keep my eyes on the exterior door, watching students come and go. I'm half tempted to slip out with the crowd. Forget all about this crazy idea.

"What's wrong?" Beau asks, slipping into the seat across from me before I can make my escape. A floral aroma wafts up from the red mug he places in front of me.

"What?"

"You're chewing on your nails."

Right. Drawbacks of knowing someone literally your entire life are they know all your tells. We never were any good at playing poker against one another. Forming evil alliances? That we excelled at.

"Nothing. I've got a lot going on. School. This graphic novel I've been working on with Anna. Just busy."

"Sure. Tell me about the graphic novel? How's that going?"

"Great." This I can talk about.

I've been keeping my eyes locked on my hands and then my drink since he sat down across from me. Afraid the twin intuition would give me away, and he'd guess my secret. But now that I'm looking up at him, he's the one who looks off. His usually perfect hair is a little off kilter. Not enough for most people to notice, but I'm not most people. There are small lines of strain around his eyes that I've seen before. Whenever he's been under a lot of pressure, they appear. Trying out for a new competitive team. Applying for colleges. Dealing with our father.

"What about you? Are you doing okay?" I reach over to place a hand on his.

"I'm fine."

All I need to do is lift a brow at me, and he knows I can see right through his lie.

"No, you're not. Don't lie to me. What's going on?"

He takes a sip of his drink, cursing. It spills over the sides of his mug when he slams it on the table. "That was fucking... I mean, freaking hot."

"Beau. You can swear in front of me. Also, I'm kind of disappointed you're the reason they put those warning labels on hot drinks. I thought better of you.""Shut up."

"Never. Now tell me what's going on? Is it the team? Girl problems. I don't need details. Just the basics."

"It's not girl problems. I don't have time for girl problems. And even if I did, you're the last person I'd tell."

"That's because you know I'd side with the girl. Us women have to stick together."

"Thanks."

"You're welcome. But you know I'm on your side if it's anything else. Now spill."

"It's just team stuff. You wouldn't be interested."

"Come on. I've been listening to you talk about boring hockey stuff for decades now. I'm something of an expert. What's going on?"

He sighs, fingers tapping out a familiar rhythm on the table, and I keep quiet, letting him get himself together.

"There's been a lot of pressure this year after losing some of our best players to graduation. It's something of a rebuilding year. And even though we have some amazing players, they're not working together as well as they should be. There's a lot of friction and issues. And it's all on me."

The reason his hair is less than perfect becomes obvious when he runs a hand through it, then smooths it down on repeat.

"You're a team, right? It's not all on you."

"Yes, but I'm the captain this year. I've got to pull them together. It's my last chance at this." The creases around his eyes have deepened, and the look in his eyes is wistful, almost haunted.

"It's not your last chance. You've got years to play hockey." I try to activate a little twin mind reading power, but he's not giving anything away. At least not anything specific.

"Sure."

"I'm sure you'll get a contract. You're an incredible athlete." We might tease and torment each other, but when it comes down to the important stuff, I support him a hundred percent.

"Anyway, at least I've got Dev."

He's still visibly tense, but there's a visible softening of his shoulders, as if his best friend helps ease the burden of leadership for him. My stomach drops, leaving me breathless. I can't take that away from him. It sounds like Dev is the one thing holding him together right now. If I mess that up, it's on me.

"Right. Yeah. It's good to have friends." I nod at him, but it's an unhappy smile that pulls my lips up.

"He's not just a friend. He's like family. I don't know what I'd do without the guy."

My mouth has gone dry, and the London Fog tastes like dishwater when I take a swallow. "Well, let me know if you need anything else from me. I'm always here for you."

"I know. Thanks, Sissy. It was great talking about this with you. But you're the one who invited me. I know there must be a reason. What's going on with you?"

The tea goes down the wrong way until I'm coughing and sputtering in the most embarrassing way.

He leans in. "Everything okay?"

I nod, clearing my throat. "Just went down the wrong way. My voice is raspy, dragging on each word."

"I'm sorry for monopolizing your time. What's going on with you?"

Umm. Think brain think. "My graphic novel." That's exciting news. "Anna and I are putting the final touches on it. We're going to enter it in a publishing contest. It's really good. I like to think my characters were solid before I started working with her, but now, together. We're leveling up. It's an amazing collaboration."

"Good for you. That's amazing. I've always been jealous of your artistic abilities."

"Have you?" I'm surprised. He's always been consumed by sports. Especially hockey. Not much time for anything else. Other than when Dad drags him in on some work nonsense.

"Yes. Creating something out of nothing. That's amazing. Just like you. You're fantastic. I can't wait to read your comic."

My neck feels hot. I love compliments, but they also make me weirdly uncomfortable. But I also feel even guiltier. It's going to swallow me whole if I don't get it under control.

He glances at the gold watch on his wrist. What other college kid wears a fancy watch? Not many. "I've got to get going. I have a class. Don't wanna be late. Thanks for listening."

I'm not saying you're welcome. I don't deserve the praise.

"Right. Me too."

I push up from my chair, and he reaches out to put a hand on my arm.

"Listen. You are coming home for thanksgiving, right?"

I'm studying my shoes again "I wasn't planning on it."

"Cece. Please. I need you there. I can't handle dad on my own. Please tell me you'll come home."

I sigh, knowing I owe him after what I'm doing, or rather, who I'm doing, behind his back.

"Fine."

"Great. We'll take soon. Love you."

"Love you too."

And then he's off, leaving me behind with my over-packed suitcase of lies and deceptions weighing me down.

Chapter Twenty-Four

Perfect Line

Dev

The swishing of skates close behind pushes me to my limits. Blood rushing through my ears, I channel my inner speed skater, bending low and pushing hard to gain momentum and keep my advantage.

"Fuck yes!" I throw my hands in the air to celebrate my victory as Beau slides up beside me.

His face is red with exertion and the look of shock would be insulting if it wasn't well earned. I've never beaten him in a sprint before, but after upping my training regime this summer, and putting extra emphasis on speed training, I finally did it.

"I can't believe you fucking beat me. You beast." He eyes me up and down.

"Maybe it's not me," I say, still smirking. "Maybe you've let yourself get soft. Don't worry, it happens."

I slide back as he shoves me, and then grab him in a headlock. "This may be the first time I've beaten you in the speed department, but I've always been able to take you in a fight. Don't push me."

"I'm not fucking soft, asshole!"

I shrug. "Want another round? Or maybe we should try a shootout. I'm pretty sure I could hit the back of the net more times than you, too. Make it a trifecta."

His face hardens, and I can tell he's thinking it over even if we're getting low on time.

"We should really get back to the house. Do you really trust JJ to finish your dinner?"

"He's got Grant to keep him in line. And Grant's girl-friend is over too. She can handle a roast. But if you're chicken, just say so."

What's the point of having a best friend if you don't know all his buttons? A couple of cracks sound out as he stretches his neck from side to side.

"You're on."

This is my favorite time on the ice, and the best part of my job at the local public rink. It reminds me of all the time I spent at the one back home after I got into hockey. I'd sit in the stands to do my homework, work at the concession stand or the skate rental counter, but then I'd get the privilege of a gorgeous sheet of ice all to myself. The perfect deal. Sometimes I invite Beau or some of the other guys to join me. Sometimes I work my ass off on drills by myself.

"First to twenty."

"Done."

We skate around, dropping small cones all over the rink. Each shot will be progressively more difficult until we hit unhinged territory. We probably won't even make it to try those impossible shots out, but we still set them up as usual. This is a game we've played before. The highest I've gotten before he hits twenty is fourteen. But this is another skill I've been practicing while he was busy working in some stuffy office over the summer break. "Heads or tails?" I hold out my lucky puck. It's a Steelers puck I won when I was a kid, and it's one of the things that I keep on myself at all times. Hidden away in my backpack. A perpetual reminder of what I'm working toward.

"Heads," he calls as I flip it in the air.

The worn black object hits the ice with a soft thump logo side up.

"Go for it."

He's all cocky attitude as he lines up the first easy shot, drilling it in.

"It's looking good for our next game." We're moving up the standings, but we've got two games coming up next week after the holiday. Anything could happen, and we really need these wins to guarantee our spot in the playoffs.

"Yeah. I'm happy with the dynamic. It's improved so much since I got Hail and Cole working together. I'm impressed even with myself. There's still a lot to work on, though."

We're neck and neck after the fifth shot, and he's lining up for his sixth.

"Always," I agree, eyeing the angle I'm at now. I'll need to hit the perfect line to sink this one. I point my stick, squinting, and line up the shot. Bam. The net flies back with the force of the puck.

"Nice one."

We're tied twelve all when Beau flubs his next shot. "Fuck!"

I'm screaming on the inside when I nail mine.

"How's next year looking for you?" I ask him. "Planning on entering the draft after graduation?"

He misses the mark and has to skate back to the cone to line up.

Now he looks a little shaken. A look I'm seeing on his face more and more frequently this year. Like he's unraveling at his seams. He misses the next one, slamming his puck into the ground. Maybe I should have let that one be.

"Not sure."

I miss the next one, but he makes his, catching up.

"If you need any help with the team or anything, let me know."

"Will do."

I'm not sure he's telling me the truth, but then I'm hiding things from him, too. And whatever secret he's got, it can't be anywhere near as bad as mine. Fuck. What am I going to do? I'm falling for his sister, but there's no way I can tell him. He'll murder me. As he should. I don't have any sisters, but if I did, I wouldn't want a guy like me near them.

His twentieth shot pings off the top bar but drops in, and he's got it. But I was at nineteen. If it wasn't a first to twenty situation, I might even have tied him.

We're both sweaty from the effort and concentration when we wrap it up.

"You're killing it out there. Good for you."

The hand he claps on my back is a little shaky.

"Thanks. I don't want to be just the enforcer. I want to be a well-rounded D-man. But I feel like I got targeted as a brute early on. So, I'm trying to prove I can do more than that."

"Well, you're doing it. We should get back now. I don't want to get home to find my house on fire."

"Right."

We pack up our shit. Showers can happen at home. The facilities here are basic, not like the ones at the college. They've got all the amenities courtesy of the program's wealthy donors.

"We're out, Syd. See you on Saturday." I duck into the office to let the rink owner know we're leaving.

His white hair is bent over a document, and he's got a phone pressed up to his ear, but he holds out his hand to stop me, gesturing the seat across from him.

I shrug, looking back at Beau. We take up a lot of space in the tiny office, settling into the two small plastic chairs. I can almost see my friend's brain overheating at the piles of paper on the desk, cardboard boxes piled in the corners, and overflowing trash cans. Syd does a lot of work for this place with not enough funding, which is one of the reasons I help out wherever I can, even when I'm off the clock. These places are so important to people in the community. Kids like me.

"Fine. Got it. It'll be ready. I've gotta go." Syd pauses, drumming his fingers on the cheap pine desk as he listens.

"I told you I've got it. Now I've got to go. I've got someone waiting to talk to me."

"Will do. Bye."

He smacks his phone on the desk a little too hard.

"Sup? Need some help?"

He shakes his head, locking his faded blue eyes on me.

"I'm glad I snagged you before you headed off for the day. We've actually got to close the rink over the holiday weekend. We've got the go ahead on the repairs the city has been promising for the last couple of years, but we're going to be shut down until the new year. So that means. You're free for Thanksgiving."

I can feel Beau's eyes on me, and I know what he's thinking.

"Are you sure? There's nothing you need from me to prep the place? Clean up? I'm not going to leave you stranded by yourself here. I was planning on being here, anyway."

"No. I don't even have to be here. My daughter invited me to her place in Boston, and I can actually go. You enjoy yourself."

I nod, swallowing hard.

"That's awesome, dude. You can come home with me for the holiday. That will be great. I could use you at my back."

A smile deepens the creases on Syd's worn face. "You've got somewhere to go? That's great." He nods at Beau. Syd is one of the few people who knows a little of my back story. He knows I work all the holidays because I haven't got any family to visit.

"I'm glad you've got a place to go."

"Come on, let's get home. You can pack up your stuff after dinner. We'll leave first thing Thursday morning."

All of the fucks. I can't get out of this. Working at the rink was my excuse. It's always my excuse. I've never been able to take Beau up on any of his offers. In the past, it was more about not accepting charity and inviting myself over to my wealthy friend's house. But now. Now there's Cece. I can't stay in the same house with her all weekend and not give myself away.

"It's okay. Your family already has plans. I can't insert myself in there at the last minute." I protest, shaking my head as we leave the office.

"Nah, it's all good." He's tapping away on his phone. "Sent my mother a text. She can make an extra reservation at the club and get an extra room ready. She's always telling me to invite my friends home. She enjoys showing off for as many people as possible."

"But."

"No, buts. You're coming. It's done. You'll be helping me out, too. My father will keep some of the asshole contained if we have company."

I can hardly say no to that.

They managed not to burn the dinner or the house, but my stomach was in knots, so it was hard to enjoy dinner. I slammed it back, rushed through the cleanup, and raced up to my room. Now I'm sitting on my bed, eyeing my cell. I have to call Cece. I have to at least give her a warning that I'll be there. Beau roped her into the trip home, too. It's like he's setting up an intricate trap even he doesn't know about.

"Dev?" She's all smiles when her face pops up on the video call. She's got on some sort of white sheet on her face, and her hair is piled on her head.

"I thought we already did Halloween," I say.

"What? Oh, this? This is a face mask. Moisturizing, you know. Maybe I'll pick you one up. It's good for your skin."

"I'll pass."

"As you wish. What's up? Is everything all right?"

"No."

Her eyes fly open. "What? What's..."

Shit. I should have been a little more verbose. "Nothing. Everyone is fine, healthy. It's this weekend."

"Yeah, I'm sorry I have to go home. I promised Beau, and then Dad called me to drive in the screws. I'm totally committed now. I couldn't get out of it if I got hit by a train. They'd just send a wheelchair to roll me in."

"That's the thing. I did too."

"You did what? Got hit by a train?"

"No, I got roped in to coming home with Beau for Thanksgiving. The rink is shutting down and Beau just happened to be with me when I found out, so he insisted. I couldn't say no. I'm so sorry."

"Oh." She shakes her head so vigorously her face mask flaps off her face. "That's not what I expected."

"Me either. I'm so sorry. Maybe I'll pretend to be sick in the morning?"

"No, no. It'll be fine. I have to stay in the guest house, anyway. My animals are not welcome in the main house. It might actually be nice to have you there for emotional support. Although I can't say it will be fun for you. My family is a lot."

I nod, as if I know anything about what it will be like. My experience with family holiday meals is limited. A couple of my foster families prepared meals or brought me to family events. But some of them left me at home since I wasn't a permanent fixture. So mostly I've always picked up shifts at whatever job I was currently working.

"But it'll be fine. We can keep our raging hormones under control for one weekend."

"Yeah."

"Okay then. I guess I'll see you Thursday."

"See you then."

It'll be great to see her, but I'm not so confident I can keep my hands off her if we're sharing space for that long. But I have to. It's even more important now that I can see Beau is under some pressure. I don't need to add to that.

CHAPTER TWENTY-FIVE

HOT AND BOTHERED

CECE

"Okay, I'm off, but you should really stop pacing. You're going to make yourself dizzy. I'd hate for you to pass out and hit your head on the coffee table with no one here to rescue you."

I've been nervously pacing circles with my suitcase in tow while I wait for Beau to show up, but I stop in my tracks. "Morbid much? You're hoping I'll hit my head and come to an untimely death, so you can tell stories of my tragic ghost haunting you."

Her laugh is bright. "No. I much prefer your living company, but feel free to haunt me after your death. I'll make sure you're seen."

"Thanks. I was going to wish you a happy Thanksgiving, but now I'm not so sure."

"Happy Thanksgiving to you too. Have a great weekend and try to keep your hands off your man."

"Yeah. I can handle it. Probably better than I can handle my family."

"Feel that. At least we have tolerable siblings."

"Yeah."

"Okay, I'm off. See you Sunday night. Ta ta."

And she's out the door in a cloud of floral perfume and hairspray, leaving me waiting by the door anxiously.

The street is pretty quiet, so it's obvious when Beau's SUV rolls into the driveway. I stall for a minute.

I jump back when I swing open the door to find Beau and Dev both standing there. And the smile I force my lips into is probably a little unhinged.

"What can we grab?"

"The beasties are all ready to go. Be careful, please."

The cages are sitting on the floor. Loki slept through the entire process of getting him moved, but Rogue and Gambit are more active than usual, pink noses twitching as they scuttle around their cage.

Beau scoops up Loki's cage. "I can't believe you're making me take these creatures in my car. I'm going to need to get it detailed and it was just done last month."

"They're family. I can't leave them here by themselves."

"I'm your family. Not these rodents."

He grumbles the entire time he's carrying him out to the car.

I pull Dev over to the side of the door, so Beau can't see us, dropping a quick kiss on his lips.

"How are they doing?" He bends down, checking out the piggies he helped save.

"Great. Back to normal. All healthy."

"Good. I'm glad."

He still looks a little freaked out as he hefts the cage up, but he does it, lugging the heavy thing up and out the front door. I follow along behind with all their supplies in a tote bag, rolling my suitcase behind me.

"Stinks already." Beau's nose is wrinkled in disgust when he turns to give me a dirty look.

Dev offered me the front seat, but I can keep a better eye on my beasties back here, so I refuse.

My hand creeps up to touch my lips. They're still tingling even after the brief contact. It's not at all awkward being here in the car with my brother and his best friend who I'm sneaking around with. I really hope I can keep the polite charade up.

The car rolls smoothly down the driveway and out into the street, and there's no turning back now.

They're chatting away about hockey, so I shut my eyes, trying to get some sleep on the ride home. I'll need all the rest I can get to deal with our parents.

The car pulling into our long driveway pulls me out of the sleep I fell into. I'm surprised I fell asleep. I must have been more tired than I thought.

"We're here. Time to wake up, passenger princess."

I yawn, drag my eyes open, and the anxiety comes rushing back at the sigh of the big white house looming over us at the end of the tree-lined drive.

"Wow," Dev says.

"Welcome to our loving home." Beau's words are leaking sarcasm.

Beau pulls up around the back of the house in front of the smaller matching guest house.

"Pets first," I say as we come to a stop.

"I know. Can't wait to get these little monsters out of my car."

"Whatever. You love your niece and nephews."

"Sure I do."

But he's careful when he lifts Loki again, making sure not to bump his cage against the door.

I spin my keys around with a jingle until I find the one that opens the guest house, swinging the door open. It's toasty and warm, with the gas fireplace flickering away in a warm welcome. It's all for show. Like everything else in this house. There is nothing genuinely welcoming here.

"You can put them over there." I point toward the sideboard in the small dining room area. It's not like we ever eat there. Even if I can get away with breakfast or lunch in here, I'll just veg out on the couch with a plate.

I drag my suitcase into the bedroom, lugging it up on the soft green bedspread and head back out.

"See you at lunch?" It's more of a hopeful question than a statement.

"No way. You're getting changed and coming into the main house to suffer like the rest of us."

"What's wrong with what I'm wearing?"

"Oh nothing. I'm sure Mom will love the sweatpants."

Our mother might just have a heart attack if she sees me looking like this. But I kind of want to test it out.

But that's not part of the plan. It's better to concede the little things and then defend yourself on the big points. I brought one conservative mother approved outfit in my suitcase, and I'll snag some more items from the overstuffed closet in my former bedroom. I'm sure I've got something else in there she'll deem appropriate for dinner tonight.

"Fine. I'll change. See you in a bit."

I'm still stalling, scrolling videos when I get another text from my brother.

> **Help me.**

> Be there in a few

Fine. I drag myself off the bed, slipping into some slate grey dress pants and a coral blouse. I throw on some basic neutral eye shadow and lipstick before heading for the house.

I'm surprised to see my brother behind the big door as it swings open rather than Eddings. He's probably got a lot going on to get ready for the party tomorrow. No casual, cozy turkey dinner for the family. It's the club tonight and then a fancy cocktail party full of people trying to kiss my father's ass or gossiping with my mother.

The planning for the event is already well under way, with a couple of white vans parked to the side of the house unloading decorations and glassware.

"Hey, Sissy." He pulls me in for a quick hug as if he needs the reassurance. Very unusual for Beau. Time with Dad must already be taking its toll on him.

He swipes at his hair, smooths his collar and cranes his neck behind him.

"Where's Dev? He get scared off already?" I wouldn't blame him if he did.

"I told him he could stay up in his assigned room for now. Catch a shower. Prepare himself. I knew Dad wanted to talk to me about some business deal, and he wanted to brief me on a couple major players that will be at the club tonight. It looks like my time is spoken for. You'll have to keep Dev entertained so he doesn't get accosted by scary debutantes or Dad's cronies."

Oh, I can think of many ways to keep him entertained in the club. Years of suffering through stuffy events have taught me all the secret places you can hide out in. Heat rises up the back of my neck.

"That okay?" I must have paused for too long.

"Yeah, totally. No problem. It will be nice to have someone normal to talk to."

"Cool."

"I'm going to grab some suitable clothes from my closet to drop back at the guest house. Which room is Dev in? I can check on him. See if he needs anything."

"He's in the cherry room. That would be great. Thanks. He should probably come down soon, anyway. His presence will be expected at lunch."

"No problem." He looks so grateful. I'm trying not to feel guilty about all the impure thoughts.

I take the back stairwell to avoid all the extra people buzzing around the main floor, setting up tasteful fall themed decor, and standing tables.

The cherry room is to the left, so I head that way first. I don't want to show up with an armload of clothes. My knock is tentative and there's no answer at first.

"It's Cece. Can I come in?" My eyes are flicking up and down the empty hall. Paranoid that someone will see me. Which is ridiculous. I'm just stopping by for a friendly visit.

"Yeah, give me a sec." His voice rumbles through me, and a moment later, the door swings open.

Lust punches through me, my insides liquefying. A white towel rides low on his lean hips, leaving an obscene amount of abs on display. His biceps flex when he swipes away the droplets clinging to his dark beard.

"You look nice." I follow the trail of his eyes as they slide down my body.

I laugh. "Um no. I look like I'm on my way to drop the kids off at private school. You look nice."

It's way too tempting. I check my peripherals again. The way seems clear, so I give myself permission, reaching out to run my palm down his gloriously bare chest.

His eyelids drop to half mast, while another part of him twitches to life under the towel.

"Did you want to come in for a sec? Is that okay?"

"Yes, please." I dart under the arm he's got outstretched, holding onto the frame. "It's fine. No one else is up here. But maybe close the door."

The door clicks shut behind me, and then my feet leave the ground as strong arms spin me around, lifting me up for a kiss. His body is heated and still a little damp from the shower. It's fine. It will steam out the wrinkles.

His lips find mine, hands sliding under my ass to get a good grip.

"Cupcake, I've missed this."

"Me too."

He backs up to the bed, dropping down, and my legs fall to the side, straddling his muscled thighs. I press myself closer to explore his mouth. Desperate for the taste of his lips. His tongue sends shivers down my spine, and I reach up to cup his cheeks.

His hands trail a tingly line up my sides, and he hovers near the sides of my breasts, not quite making contact.

Then he pulls away eons before I'm ready. My breath is coming in rapid pants, and I'm all hot and squirmy everywhere.

"We can't do this." He's even raspier than before.

"I know. I know. Sorry."

He chuckles. "What are you sorry for? I'm the one who started this."

"Yeah, but I shouldn't have come in here. I know how dangerous it is. I always want my hands on you. Especially when you're naked. What are you doing answering the door in a towel? That part is on you."

"See. I told you it's my fault."

"I came up here to grab some clothes, and I told Beau I'd fetch you. He's busy with our father."

"Don't say stuff like that. Makes me think we've got time for more."

"Maybe... no. We don't have time for that. A little? No. Terrible idea. Get dressed before I lose control again."

"You're going to have to get up."

Right, he can't go too many places with my ass planted in his lap. He helps lift me off with a groan and places me gently on my feet.

"Let me throw some clothes on. Then I can help you carry stuff downstairs."

"Cool." I swallow hard, debating whether I should watch the show or shut my eyes. I'm already hot and bothered, but if I catch a glimpse of the full package, I might lose any last grasp of my self control. He just does that to me.

I squeeze my eyes shut, listening to him pad around the room and the rustle of clothes. When I sneak a peek, he's got on dress slacks and a button-up shirt.

"You came prepared for every Whitaker family occasion I see." I love him in his hockey gear, or sweatpants, but there's something about a suit clinging to the beast of a man that gets me going. A sense of barely contained civility.

"Beau told me what to pack. I'd rather be wearing my jeans, but I guess the place we're going to is fancy."

I snort. "You could say that. Still, I'm not complaining. You look hot like that. Let me help you." My fingers work away at the buttons on his shirt, taking their time to slip them home. Every inch of skin covered is a shameful waste.

"Want me to help with your tie?"

He growls in complaint. "I have to wear a tie?"

"Yup. Sorry. The elite white dude energy is powerful at the club." He reaches down to snag a silky blue striped tie from his bag, and I slide it around his neck.

"I can do it," he says, stilling my hands.

"I know you can, but I want to."

"Fine. Let me just..." His thumb swipes around the edges of my lips. "You've got some lipstick."

I laugh, looking up to spot a coral stain around his mouth, too. "You too." I return the favor, and his tongue darts out to lick my finger as I'm cleaning him up.

"Stop it." My nipples are like glass at this point, so I lean in a little closer until we're chest to chest to ease some of the pressure.

A knock at the door sends a jolt of adrenaline racing through me, and I glance back at Dev. He looks fine. No smeared lipstick. No signs of the illicit kiss we shared.

"Who is it?" Now he sounds irritated, and I don't blame him one bit. Whoever is at the door can fuck right off.

"It's Beau. I'm coming in. You decent?"

I stumble back a few steps, while Dev clears the gravel from his throat. He raises a dark brow at me, and I give him a shaky little nod, heart pounding.

"Cece?" Beaus says as he pushes through the door.

"I was just... I told you I'd talk to him."

"She was helping me with my tie." Dev slides in with a smooth save.

"Was she? Cool. Did you get your clothes, Sis?"

"Not yet. I was heading there next. I'll just go. Leave you two."

Beau snags my arm as I'm trying to hustle off. "Wait a minute."

"What?" How can he not hear my heart trying to leap out of my chest?

"You've got a little something. Under your eye." He points to my right eye, and I swipe my thumb over the spot, pulling it away to spot some mascara clinging to my digit.

"Thanks. Okay, I'll just get my stuff."

"You need help carrying it?" my brother asks.

"Nah, it's fine. I'm good. Meet you downstairs."

I rush out of there like I'm being chased and bolt for the protection of my childhood bedroom.

Chapter Twenty-Six

In The Club

Dev

I could see Beau's shoulders get more and more tense the closer we got to his family home, and I can't say I blame him. The place is cold and imposing. It looks more like a fancy old house you'd visit on a museum tour than a place real people actually live in. Warmth is not a feeling I associate with a family home. Although a couple of my foster places had a comfortable vibe. Maybe I've watched too many sitcoms. I'm expecting some ideal family situation. And maybe it's just a fantasy. Something that only exists on TV screens. It's what I've always yearned for. A permanent home. The hockey house is the closest I've gotten.

At least the Whitakers let us drive to the club together, so I don't have to deal with that awkward meeting yet. It was weird. Neither of their parents ventured out to greet us as we walked in. Some glorious homecoming. Probably better in a public setting.

If it's possible, I've been even more uncomfortable than Beau since we started our journey. Between worrying about the proximity with Cece, and the feeling of being dropped in a world I don't belong in like a time traveler from the 1800s showing up in the 2000s. My suit feels snugger than usual, and I keep reaching up to adjust the collar trying to choke me out.

The feeling only intensifies as we turn up the driveway. Massive trees crowd the massive black gate at the turnoff. It's as if they're on a mission to keep out the tired and weary masses. This is not the place for you, it practically screams.

The gates swing open to admit us after Beau greets the guy at the gate. I'd call him a guard, but if he is, it's more of an undercover sort of thing. He's got on a crimson vest over a crisp white shirt, and his hair is slicked back in a tidy sweep.

He looks down his nose at us but gives Beau a huge smile.

"Mr. Whitaker, so nice to have you back."

"Thanks. Good to see you, Jerome."

"And Miss Cecelia. You look lovely."

I glance back at her to see her nod with a tentative smile. I don't like the condescending way he uses her first name or the judgment that's heavy in his tone.

He glances at me. "You've got a guest? Name please."

"Dev," I reply, but his stare keeps burning into me as a small smirk twitches at the corners of his mouth.

"This is Devlin Connell. My mother should have added him to the reservation."

"Hmm." The man looks even more weaselly, frowning at the tablet in his hand. "I don't see him here."

Fuck. I know I don't belong here, but now my skin is getting all hot, and I reach up to tug at my tie. I didn't even want to come here, but knowing how unwelcome I am is still an awful feeling.

Beau glances at his watch, then straightens his back and zeros in the employee. There are now a couple of cars behind us waiting to enter the hallowed ground. "Add him to the list. My father is waiting for us, and I don't have all day. He'll be pissed if I tell him why we're late."

"Right. Of course, Mr. Whitaker. How do you spell it?"

Beau spells out my name, and the gate finally swings open slowly, as if it's reluctant to let me in too.

"Jerome thinks he's the shit. Sorry about that ass." Cece reaches out to pat my arm, pulling it back quickly when she realizes what she did.

Beau doesn't seem to notice. "I hate throwing the family name around, but he was just being difficult. Sorry."

"It's fine."

The trees lining the way are mostly bare, but the ground underneath them is immaculate. As if they send someone out every day to sweep and rake away the fallen ones. I'm sure they do.

A large stone building comes into view. It resembles a castle without the turrets, and it almost looks like it grew up out of the hill it sits on. It watches our approach, casting a shadow over the parking lot filled with shiny cars that cost more than my entire college education.

Beau eschews the valet parking, but he swings into the curve by the front door to let Cece out.

"See you in a minute."

"You bet I'll be waiting for you. No need to breach the walls on my own."

She's changed into a dress for the evening. Much more subdued and fancier than her usual attire. But it looks good on her. I'm pretty sure she could give the paper bag princess a run for her money if she wanted to. The navy dress has a flowy chiffon skirt that covers her knees, and a tight satiny top with an embroidered pattern of vines stitched on it. I'd love to run my hand over the little detail before I ripped it off her. Little fluttery sleeves cover her shoulders, but she threw on a long red wool coat to keep the cold air off her bare skin. She looks like she's accustomed to wearing the three-inch heels, but also like she'd toss them in a bush to dance barefoot on the grass if she could. I don't really like how this place seems to drain her exuberance away. I love that about her.

She's still standing outside the massive front door when we've made our way across the parking lot. Her arms are wrapped around herself in a hug to stave off the cold.

I have to resist the urge to pull her into my arms for warmth.

"You should have gone in, Cece." Beau scolds his sister.

"I would have, but Trent showed up, and I couldn't do it."

"Who's Trent?" I ask, the skin at the back of my neck prickling to attention.

"Cece's on-again, off-again boyfriend." Beau informs me. "He's a dick. I have no idea why you keep going back to that ass."

"Thanks for the plentiful helping of condescension, brother. It's off. Forever. Don't worry. I'm never touching that guy again. Not even if we were the last two people on the planet. Screw repopulating Earth. If that's how I had to do it. Better the human race dies out."

"Did he do something to you?" My fingers are twitching into fists at my sides. If he treated my girl badly. If he did anything to her, I will be happy to smash his face in. I'm sure Beau would help me. Just like that asshole mouthing off at our game.

"He did lots of things to me, but as my brother so kindly pointed out, I went back to him, but it was always more of a casual thing on both our parts. Don't get all worked up. Are you really cheating if neither of you has much emotional investment in the relationship?"

I still don't love hearing about her getting treated like that, but at least she wasn't super into the guy. Now I feel worse about what I'm doing to her. Forcing her to keep our relationship secret is keeping her at a distance that I'm not comfortable with, because I really care about her.

A guy about our age dressed in the same outfit as the keeper of the gate holds the door open as we pass through, and it's like stepping into another world. The dark wooden floors have an aged shine to them. The ceiling in the foyer stretches all the way to the second floor. Beau leads us to the left, where we hand our coats off to another smiling staff member.

I reach for my backpack, twitching a little when I remember I left it in the trunk of Beau's car. He convinced me it wouldn't be the best idea to bring it along, and even though it caused me physical pain to leave it behind, Cece gave my hand a secret squeeze and I knew I could handle it. As long as she's here next to me.

Vases filled with flowers in every color of fall grace every table we pass. An expensive-looking garland drapes the railing of the massive staircase leading to the second floor. We bypass that, following the small stream of expensive looking people talking and laughing as they walk through the foyer into the next room.

A gorgeous blonde woman stands behind a wooden podium, greeting Beau and Cece with a smile. "Welcome, Mr. and Miss Whitaker." At least she shows Cece the respect she deserves, but her blue eyes are locked on Beau's with a hungry look in them.

"I'll take you to your table. I see you brought a guest with you this evening." She turns to me, and I can see the dismissal in her eyes as they give me a cursory sweep, taking in the too short sleeves of my only suit.

Another subtle reminder that I don't belong in this world. Beau, on the other hand, he was born for this. He strides across the room with an effortless grace, nodding his head, and saying hello as he passes other tables.

We're led to a table by a window overlooking the green. It's not so green at the moment, but it still looks beautiful even during the barren time of year.

The gentleman that stands up when we stop is an older version of his son.

Except the hair. It's a deep brown shade but shot through with distinguished silver streaks at the temples.

Their mother has a big smile on her face, but it's strained around the edges and doesn't reach her eyes. Not like Cece's wide-open smile. I've never understood what people meant when they said someone's teeth were blindingly white. Until now. They're as perfect as the smooth skin stretched over her face. She's got to be at least ten years younger than their father, but it's hard to tell under the coat of makeup and likely cosmetic surgery. Nothing that makes her look weird, but there's a glossy smoothness to her that she didn't come by naturally.

"Beau, Cecelia. Good to see you." He pulls out Cece's chair for her but doesn't offer any affection to either of his children. This is probably the first time he's seen them in a couple of months, and nothing. Not even a handshake.

He offers one to me. Stretching his hand out. "You must be Devlin. Pleasure to meet you. I hear you've been an excellent partner for Beau on the ice." His voice is as smooth and polished as the rest of him.

"Yes, sir. Beau is an excellent captain. Nice to meet you."

"You can call me John." He squeezes my hand in a tight hold, giving it a brief but firm shake, and holding on a little too long until I let go first.

Meeting new people always stirs up my anxiety. I used to go into new families, confused and scared, but hopeful.

But after one too many experiences being rejected or disappointed, I started to dread it. This is no different. They
might not be my family, but if there's any hope of making
this thing with Cece last, I'm going to have to get to know
them. Try to fit in, which seems like an insurmountable
obstacle now that I'm here. In their territory.

"Hello. Nice to meet you. I'm Joanne." She holds out a
limp hand, her long pink nails digging into my palm when
I go in for a shake.

"My pleasure." I don't even know where that came from.
I don't think I've said anything like that in my entire life.

"Beau, Cecelia." They get the barest of acknowledg-
ment.

"Hi, Dad, Joanne," Cece says, polite and subdued. Not a
trace of her usual exuberance.

I'm about to sit next to Cece when John waves to
the chair next to him, and I carefully ease myself down,
conscious of every move I make.

He doesn't waste any time. "So, where are you from,
son?"

"Detroit."

"Not so far away, then. And what do your parents do?"

A server stops by to take drink orders, saving me from
answering the awkward question. "I'll have a cola."

Beau orders a beer, and Cece accepts a pour from the
bottle of red wine sitting in the middle of the table.

"You can have a proper drink. It's all on me tonight.
Don't worry about the cost."

I shake my head. "No, thanks."

"Dev doesn't drink, Dad. Lay off." Beau shoots a glare at his father that has me recoiling even though it's not directed at me. Why did I agree to this?

"I see. Are planning on going pro?" He turns back to me.

"Yes. I've been drafted by Vancouver."

"Excellent. Good for you. Playing professionally isn't the right choice for everyone." Now he's directing a pointed look across me at his son. "But for someone like you, I'm sure it's a tremendous boost for you and your family."

What does that even mean? I kind of expected Beau's dad to be a bit of a dick, but I didn't really grasp the breadth of it.

"Dad, what are you even talking about?" Surprisingly, it's Cece who jumps into the conversation. I do not want to cause any division in their family. No matter how dysfunctional they clearly are.

"I just mean, his family would benefit from a professional hockey salary."

"Have you ever thought about the fact that he might not have any?"

All chatter and movement at the table comes to an awkward halt.

"Even more so then."

No apology, no backtracking. Just leaves it at that.

"Why don't I show you the buffet, Dev?"

She stands up, gesturing for me to come with her.

"Remember, plate only half full, Cecelia." Her mother calls after her retreating back. The little dig hurts me more than anything Mr. Whitaker said to me.

"I'm sorry about them," she whispers as we make our way around the tables.

The next room over is some kind of massive hall. Those polished wood floors fill the entire space, and buffet tables are lined up along the walls. This isn't some five-dollar buffet, though. There is every kind of meat and seafood imaginable. A table full of salads. Chefs in white hats carving slices off roasts and serving up hot items out of those fancy silver serving dishes. One wall is all desserts. There is so much I can't even take it all in.

"Holy shit."

Cece giggles next to me, and it's the first time she's sounded like herself since she came into the house wearing that dress. Like she slipped into another personality as soon as she put it on. I'm glad it's just a mask and the real her is still in there.

"At least the food is good. At Christmas they serve the dinner in another room, and Santa comes out here to deliver presents to all the younger kids. Then, after dinner, we'd all come out here to play with our toys. Run rampant around the hall. Take off our shoes and skid around the floors. The adults were too hammered to care. It's the only time I've ever liked this place."

It's hard to stop myself from overflowing my plate, but I can come back for seconds. The urge to stock up on food when it's available never really goes away.

Cece barely puts anything on her plate and doesn't take one of the rolls that she was eyeing. They smell delicious, so I grab an extra, slipping it onto her plate on the way back to the table.

"Oh, I shouldn't."

"Why not?"

"I don't know. Carbs are evil?"

"Carbs are the energy that keeps our bodies running." I've taught myself a lot about nutrition over my years playing hockey. Trying to achieve peak physical condition, and one thing I know is that the no carb craze is a load of bullshit.

"Can I quote you to my mom?"

"Please don't."

"I'm fucking with you." She says it a little too loud and earns a glare from a silver-haired lady in a powder blue dress. That just makes her giggle even louder.

The rest of dinner passes in much the same way, although John seems to have lost interest in me, and Beau looks even paler and more strained than before.

"I'm sorry about that nightmare. I shouldn't have made you come with us."

Beau finally relaxes, apologizing to me as we're getting into his car.

"It's fine."

"It's not. But you did well. I think Dad actually likes you."

I turn back to give Cece an incredulous look. "I'm pretty sure that's not even close to the truth."

"No, really. He would have kept hammering at you all through dinner if he didn't like you. Or at least respect you."

If that's what admiration and respect look like to him, I don't want to know what he does to his enemies.

CHAPTER TWENTY-SEVEN

GAME MISCONDUCT

CECE

I f my father doesn't scare Dev off, he's unshakable. Even Beau looks more thrown off by our dad than usual tonight, and he's the clear favorite.

"How did you know about Dev's family?"

Beau's question leaves me cold again. Does he suspect? "Oh, I don't know. You must have told me."

"I wouldn't do that."

"We talked about it at the vet. It was a long night." Dev is making a habit of saving me when my mouth gets me in trouble.

"Oh, yeah." He still sounds a bit distant, but I think that's more a reflection of everything else tonight rather than suspicion.

"Why is spending a single day with them so..." I'm yawning around the last word.

"Because they're terrible."

That wakes me up. Beau knows, but he usually doesn't talk about it so bluntly. Maybe it was all the talk of going pro. Dad was really driving the nails home on that one.

There's nothing I want more than to spend the night in Dev's arms, but I'm not sure how to make that work. Asking him to sneak out of the house in the middle of the night is probably a terrible idea. He'll set off the alarm and the police will show up or something. I could sneak into his room, but that's risky.

By the time I get home, I have the perfect solution. Beau drops me at the guest house, and I slip in, checking on my pets. Everyone looks good, although Loki is awake and annoyed that he can't come out to play. I slip him a couple of extra treats along with his food as an apology.

Then I gather up a few things, stuffing them in a big tote bag before I slip across to the main house. I type in the code, resetting it after I get inside, and slip up the back stairs. The good thing about a house this large is it's easier to avoid people when you want to.

I tiptoe up the stairs, checking the hall, and then sneak into my old bedroom. No one can get mad at me for sleeping in here. It is my room, after all. It's only my pets that aren't welcome in the house.

I shoot Dev a quick text, leave my door unlocked and hit the bathroom to brush my teeth and get changed. Disappointment sinks when he hasn't replied by the time I've finished my routine.

I slide under the thick comforter, sinking into the pillow-top mattress when I hear a soft knock.

The covers go flying when I leap out of bed and over to the door. I pull it open, yanking him through, and shutting the door behind him.

"Did anyone see you?" I ask.

"No. That's why it took so long. Beau was out in the hall the first time I tried to come. He came in and we chatted for a bit before he went to his own room. Then I waited a bit and tried again. All clear this time."

"It was a tough night. I needed you." It makes me realize how much I've started relying on him. For comfort. For confessions. When I see something funny, he's the first one I tell. When I'm feeling upset, he's the one I want to reassure me. It's so much more than a fling, but can it really be anything meaningful when we can't even tell the one person closest to both of us?

"I needed you too, Cupcake."

He settles beside me on the bed, and I wrap myself up in his arms, inhaling the comforting smell clinging to him.

"I'm glad you're here," I mumble into his chest.

"Me too."

He pulls back the blanket for me to get settled, then slides beside me, dragging the thick blanket over us both and rolling over to pull me tight against him. His lips land on my head.

I snuggle back, content to be in his arms. In this moment I don't need anything else. Just him.

"Cecelia!"

My mother's shrill screech rips me out of the deep sleep I was enjoying.

I jerk upright, my heart pounding so hard I can feel it thumping against the wall of my chest.

"What are you doing with that boy in your bed?"

No, no, no, no. This can't be happening. I could have sworn I locked the door last night. I did, right? Or maybe not. It doesn't matter. I've got to stop her before she brings the whole house in here.

My feet stumble under my frantic attempt to get up, but I pull myself back up, racing for the door.

"Joanne. Could you not."

"What's going on?" My father's voice booms down the hall as he comes racing up the stairs.

"She has that boy in her bed. Under our roof. It's disgraceful."

"What?"

He storms over to the door to my room, jerking it open. Dev is yanking a pair of sweats over his boxer briefs, but he's still all shirtless and ruffled. It's obvious he just climbed out of bed. My bed.

My father's face deepens from a blotchy red color to a purple shade that I've never seen before. The vein in his neck is pulsing.

"We didn't do anything." The defense sounds weak, even to me.

"Cece? Are you okay? What's wrong?" Beau comes tearing in wearing a similar outfit as his friend. His eyes narrow when they land on Dev. "Lucy? What are you doing in here?"

"He was in your sister's bed, Beau. What do you think of that?"

"This is why playing hockey is no good for you. Puts you in the path of unsuitable people. And your sister too. Did you know about this?" Dad steps toward my brother.

Unsuitable. What a bowl of crap. What a complete asshole.

"I'm a twenty-one-year-old woman. What I choose to do is nobody else's business. Get out of here. All of you."

"This is my house, Cecelia. You don't get to tell me to leave this or any other room."

"Fine then. I'll leave." The righteous anger pushes me toward the door. "Dev?" I turn back to him, hoping he'll follow, but he's standing there frozen in place, looking at my horrified brother.

"You're not going anywhere, Cecelia, but you. You can leave, Mr. Connell. I didn't invite you into my house to take advantage of my daughter."

Dev nods, trying to step around my brother to make his escape, but Beau won't allow it. He yanks his arm back, winding up to send his fist crashing into Dev's nose.

It's like it happens in slow motion. There's a thumping noise. I scream at my brother. Dev's hands whip up to cover his face, while bright red blood oozes between his fingers.

Tears well up in his eyes, and he backs away, hands held out in front of him. Beau steps toward him again and my body finally unfreezes. I leap in front of Dev.

"Beau. Stop it. Leave him alone. We weren't doing anything last night. I was upset. I asked him to come."

My brother doesn't even turn to look at me, eyes still locked on his friend. "Last night? How long has this been going on? How long have you been sneaking around behind my back?"

I shake my head. This is not the time or place for this conversation. I'm standing here all vulnerable, with my legs exposed beneath my short PJs. The entire family invading my room, and my boyfriend bleeding behind me. That's right. He's my boyfriend. Not some fling.

"Beau don't. Please. We can talk about this later."

"What's there to talk about?"

My fingers are going numb, and my legs are turning to jelly, but I stand my ground. Beau will regret hurting his best friend. I know he will. I'm not going to let him make it worse.

"Cece. I can't believe I have to do this again, but that's it. You're leaving that school. You can stay until the end of the semester, and then you can finish your education elsewhere. I thought I could trust Beau to keep you safe, but I was wrong."

"What exactly did I do?" I'm swiping at the angry tears streaking down my face. "Have a mature, consensual relationship with a fellow adult?"

"You call it mature to sneak around with your brother's teammate behind his back? Sleep with some nobody. He's only in it for your money and status."

"Why? Because nobody would be into me for my personality or my looks? Am I that unappealing? Gee, Dad. Thanks."

"That's not what I was saying. You just have to be careful, Cece. With our family name, you can't be spending time with just anybody. Especially after what you did last summer." And there it is. Another reminder that underneath it all, I'm an embarrassment to the family.

"Is this how you feel about it, Beau? I'm too good for your best friend? Or do you think he's too good for me?"

Beau moves in closer to me, but I shake my head at him. "Neither. But I trusted you both, and you've been lying to me. I can't believe either of you would do that. I asked him to look out for you. Not fuck you."

"Beauregard! Language."

My brother winces at his full name.

"News flash. I'm capable of making my own decisions. This isn't the nineteenth century. I'm not some heiress you can sell off to the highest bidder."

"But I'm still your brother and I still have to look out for you."

"Honey. Let's let these two figure this out. I need to look after the party details." I'd almost forgotten my mother was in the room's been so quiet since she started this mess with her screams.

"Fine. But this isn't over. I mean it, Cecelia. You're done with that school."

Dev. I've been so wrapped up in this argument I forgot to check on him. He's bleeding. In pain. I spin around to find he's vanished and rush out of the room ahead of my parents.

"Dev!" I call out, racing into the hall. He's not there. I take the stairs two at a time, but there's no sign of him. The house is as empty as my heart.

Thundering footsteps echo through the foyer, and Beau skids to a halt beside me.

"He's gone, Cece."

My knees give out and I sink to the floor. I can feel his presence when he joins me, but I refuse to look at him. My chest heaves with silent sobs.

"I'm sure we can figure this out. You don't have to leave Lakeview if you don't want to."

"What's the point?" I sniff, dragging a hand across my face.

"You've got friends there. You don't want to start over at another school for your last semester." He drops a hand on my shoulder, but I shrug it off. The sight of his fist connecting with Dev's nose is still replaying in my head.

"Yeah, but I can't have Dev, so what's the point?"

The only sound in the large room is him clearing his throat, and when he talks again, it's in a low tone as if he's scared of frightening me away.

"He means that much to you?"

"Yes." I hiccup. "I... I... love him." It fills me up, and I know the words are true. I don't want this to be temporary. I want him by my side, but why would he want to be with me? My family is so unbearably fucked up. They'll never accept him. Beau hates him now. I've screwed that up too.

"Wait... you love him?" I'm too tired to shrug off the hand that lands on my shoulder this time. "Does he love you back?"

I shake my head. "I don't know. We've never talked about it. We spent so much energy keeping it a secret from you."

"I'm sorry, Cece."

"It's fine." I sniff, leaning into his comfort. My heart is in a million painful pieces, but I'm sure they'll mend. Eventually. One day.

CHAPTER TWENTY-EIGHT

ONE OF A KIND

DEV

I have to steel myself to walk through that glass door. It takes everything in me, but I think of Cece standing in front of me, defending me from her family, and I know I have to do this.

The place has seen better days. Cracked red vinyl benches and scratched tables sit on the black-and-white checkered floor. I shake my head at the bored-looking woman in the blue diner-style dress that walks up to me. "Meeting someone."

"Sounds good. Coffee?"

I shake my head. Caffeine will only make me more jittery than I already am. Don't think I can handle that right now.

"I'll bring you some water." She must be bored. Only two tables are occupied and one lone guy at the counter. The chef is leaning over the counter to chat with him.

"Thanks."

I head for the booth in the far corner where he's sitting. His eyes were locked on the door as the door chimes announced my entrance and he gestured me to join him. As if I wouldn't recognize him or something.

He pushes up from his seat as I approach, reaching out to shake my hand. Disappointment sags his features when I ignore the offer, sinking with a creak onto the bench. I'm not ready for that yet.

"Hi, son," he says. "I'm so glad you came."

"I'm not doing this for you."

"I know. That's fine. It's good to see you. You look so good. How's everything going?"

A bitter laugh slips through my laughs. "You want a rundown of the last fifteen years?"

"No. Yes. I just needed to know you're okay."

I sigh, running a hand through my beard. I came here for a reason. Closure. Information. Healing. Something. I'm going to have to give a little if I want this to work.

"Hockey season has been pretty good. We won champs last year."

"I know. As soon as I found out where you were, I started keeping track of your progress. You play defense, right?"

"Yup."

The waitress stops by with a glass of water and two menus. "I'll be back," she says when we barely glance at her.

"I'm glad to see things are working out well for you. How were things, after...."

"After you abandoned me for your addictions?" It comes out sharper than I intended, but there's a lot of hurt and resentment buried inside.

"Yes. I know words can't make up for what I put you through, but I am sorry. I always struggled, but after your mother died, I couldn't handle it. I let it take over. And I will always be sorry for that. I know I don't deserve your forgiveness. You probably never want to see me again after this, but I still needed to tell you."

"Did you need to tell me for me, or for you?" I'm still tempted to get up and walk away, but I think I need this too.

"For myself. I've always been selfish, but I'm trying to learn. To be better. I told you I've got a job, and a new fiancée. I'm trying to be the best I can for them, after I failed you so hard."

The pain is always there, usually a dull ache, but it ramps up to a throbbing intensity. Why couldn't he have been there for me?

"What did I do?" This is it. The question that's been nagging at me. What did I do to him? Why did I lose his love? Why did he abandon me?

"Oh, Devlin. It was never you. It's never been on you. I was sick. I couldn't look after myself, much less you. I'll always regret I wasn't strong enough to put you first."

"Me too." I tell him. "Can I see some pictures?"

"Of my fiancée?"

"Yes." I need to see them. Make sure she looks good, healthy. The kids are okay. Not like me. No one deserves that kind of life as a kid.

"Of course." He taps on his phone, sliding it across the table to me.

The woman in the picture is probably in her forties. Her dark blonde hair frames her face in a shoulder-length bob. The kids at her side are glowing with health, the girl has a big gap-toothed grin, and the boy is sticking his tongue out at the camera. They've both got plump, rosy cheeks and nice clothes on.

My heart hurts for the boy I was. It could have been me. If my mother hadn't died. If he hadn't fallen into a dark hole. If anyone had ever wanted me enough.

I think that's why I needed to come here. After seeing Cece with her family, I needed something. The thing is, they've got money, but they're just as fucked up as the rest of us. She's suffered a different kind of neglect and control. But deep down, we're the same. Two hurt people trying to connect.

That's all gone to shit now. My best friend in the entire world hates me, and I've lost the girl I'm in love with. I never even got to tell her.

"I think I'm going to go now."

He reaches out a work-worn hand again, and this time I don't reject the advance. His palm is coarse, but warm when it closes over mine. There's no instant connection or healing, but it's a small step.

"Do you think I might be able to see you again? Some-time."

"Maybe." I nod. "Not right away. But eventually, maybe."

"Good. At least I can keep an eye on the stats. See how you're doing. I have been coming to your games. I hope that's okay. After you spotted me that one game, I've started sitting near the back. I'd never bother you while you're out on the ice. But I'm there. I'll stop if you want me to."

I shake my head. "No, it's fine."

I've never had someone in the crowd at every game. Rarely had someone to watch me. He can do that.

"Good. Okay, and you don't have to say it back, but... I love you. You look so much like your mother. Her eyes." His face softens, and my eyes burn. Not for him. For her. The one I never got to know.

"I'll let you know if I want to see you again."

"Good, good. Let me walk out with you. Can I give you a ride somewhere?"

"No. I'm good, thanks." I'm not accepting anything from him, except his apology.

The sun has broken through the clouds by the time we make it back outside. It suffuses me with warmth. The ache is still there, but it's a little less sharp. It's Cece I miss the most. She's come to mean so much to me, and if I can't get her back, I don't know what I'll do. And Beau? I don't know how I'll make it up to him or if there's any chance we can still be friends. But now I know it's possible. If I can see my father after everything he did. If he's capable of healing and moving on from his pain and loss, there's hope for me.

There's a knock on my door, and Beau calls out my name, but my light is off and it's late. I feign sleep until he moves on.

The next morning, I slip out of the house before he's up for the day. There aren't too many places to go this early in the morning, so I hit the smaller coffee shop on the west side of campus. Everyone goes to All Capps. I can hide away here until class and hopefully avoid Beau for another day.

I need to talk to him, but I also need to figure out what I'm going to say. What I'm going to ask him. What is it I want? Forgiveness? Permission? I'm not sure.

Somehow the fates are on my side, and I don't cross paths with him anywhere he can corner me alone. Until I get home. I skipped my last class, hoping I could sneak up to my room and hide out some more until tomorrow. Tomorrow we have practice, so there won't be any way to avoid him. But at least he can take his anger out on me on the ice. I'll let him. I'll welcome it. The ache in my nose is a reminder of what I did to him.

"Hey."

My head jerks up, startled to hear him as I'm stepping through our front door.

"Hi. I can go. I'm looking for a new place. I'm sure I can get something for next semester."

"Why would you do that?"

"Because. Because." I take a step back through the door. "You don't want me here."

"Dev, come back."

I swallow past the growing lump in my throat.

"It doesn't matter. Dad is going to make Cece leave Lakeview. None of it matters."

I thought the ache in my heart was bad before, but this takes it to the next level. I reach up to rub at my chest, hoping to ease the pain, but it's no good. It's still there. I don't know if it will ever go away.

"She's leaving? She can't leave."

"Why? Will you miss your fuck buddy?"

His eyes are narrowed, fists clenching and unclenching at his side, and my arm flies up to block my already tender nose, but he doesn't advance on me.

Maybe I don't have a right to the anger, but it still steams me up hearing him refer to her with the crude term. "She's not a fuck buddy. Why would you even say that about your sister?"

"You've been hiding this from me for how long? Days, weeks? You don't get to be angry with me."

"Yes, I do. Cece is special. You can't talk about her like that." Now I'm stepping forward, ready to challenge him.

"Special in what way?" He tilts his head, studying me.

"She's special. One of a kind. One of the best people I've ever met. She's so kind and generous. She's always smiling, even when she grew up with that. Now that I've seen it, I'm sorry for her and for you. But I don't want her to feel that way ever again. I want her to know she's loved and cared for. Appreciated for every unique thing about her." It's a relief to get the feelings out. She should be the one I'm telling, but it's still helpful to say them. To let her brother know how much she means to me.

His tight fists are easing up, knuckles returning to their regular color. "If she's so special, why were you sneaking around with her like you were ashamed of her? If you value her like that, you should have been shouting it to the world."

"Because. Because I love you too, man. You're the best friend I've ever had. The closest thing to a real family. And I didn't want to ruin that. You threatened us all to back off. Stay away from your sister. I couldn't tell you." I was weak. I should have stood up for her. He's right.

"You love me too? Does that mean..."

He's staring me down while I puzzle out the question. I love him, yes, but also... "I love her. I love Cece, and I don't want to lose her. But I don't want to lose you either. And I'm sorry, but if I had to choose. I'd choose her. If I have to follow her to her new school or wait for her to graduate, I will. Even if you hate me. I don't think I can stay away from her."

I shut my eyes, bracing for the blow. It doesn't happen.

After an agonizing wait, he steps in, slapping me on the back.

"That's all I needed to hear. And you were probably right not to tell me. At least in the beginning. If I found out you were fucking around with my sister, I would have gotten you kicked off the team, or maybe myself. But if you love her. That's different."

"But I'll only drag her down. She's too good for me. It's probably better she's moving away."

"If you're looking to get punched in the face again, that's a good way to go about it. Of course, she's too good for you. There is no one on the planet that's good enough for my sister. But if she has to be with someone. Anyone. I'm glad it's you. You've been through so much and yet you keep learning. You read all those shitty self-help books. You don't drink. You work harder at this sport than anyone I've ever met. And I know you'll work harder to keep her happy than anyone else. Now that you've dragged your head out of your ass."

I can't believe it. This can't be real. I'm not going to be able to keep both of them, am I?

"Now. We have to figure out what to do to make sure she doesn't have to leave."

CHAPTER TWENTY-NINE

NEW FAVORITES

CECE

Working with Anna for the last couple of days kept my mind off everything, but as soon as we hit submit, sending our work to Inx, I drop my head on my hands.

Anna screeches, jumping up and clapping her hands, but I can't drag myself up. There's this hollowness in my soul swallowing all the emotions. Because if I let myself feel them, I'm afraid I'll get pulled under. It's better to be numb.

"Cece. We did it. This is amazing. We need to celebrate."

"I can't. I've got too much to figure out." Where I'm going to go when my father kicks me out of this house. What school I'll end up at next year.

"Cece. I know you're upset about Dev, and I know you've got some things to work out, but I think you should come out with me. Get a coffee or go for a walk to clear our heads. We can brainstorm this together."

I don't even lift my head off my arms, just rock it back and forth in a negative.

"Please. If we're going to have to leave too, I'd like to spend some time with you before we all lose each other."

Her words are blanketed in guilt, but I'm not sure I even care. May as well go with her. I'm sure she'll get sick of my moping ass soon enough. "Fine."

"At least change your clothes. You've been wearing those for three days. What if someone takes your picture?"

Another harsh reminder that I don't get to live my life like other college students. Someone could take a random photo of me and sell it to the highest bidder. Cecelia Whitaker drunk again. I can't even just be a heartbroken college student who just lost the two people who mean the most to her in this world.

"Fine."

I drag myself upstairs to slip into something clean. My arms ache when I reach back to pull my hair into a ponytail. I slap on a pink ball cap as a final measure. The blonde locks have gotten a little greasy.

She drags me out of the house for a walk. The air is chilly, but there's not a cloud in the sky. It almost matches my insides. But I'm filled with thunderclouds to match the icy air.

She takes me on the long route in spite of my protest, so I'm a little winded by the time we're walking back down our street.

The sun is glinting off something shiny and silver in the driveway. Is that my...

A hint of excitement rises, then explodes into pain again. If my father decided to give me my car back, it's because he knows I'll need it to move away.

The roof is smooth under my hand.

"My car?"

"Come on," Anna says, dragging me away from the vehicle.

"What's going on?"

Anna fumbles with her key, finally sliding it home and throwing the door open.

My brother is standing in our living room, and... "Dev!" I cry out, racing over to him, but then I stop myself, looking to my brother. What's going on here?

"I don't understand."

I want nothing more than to jump into Dev's arms. My heart is begging for it, but my mind is telling me to be cautious.

"I hate that I did this to you. I know you don't need my permission, Cece, but I need you to know that you're both my family. And if you two want to be together, I'm not going to fight it. I'll even try to embrace it."

"Really?"

I take a cautious step toward Dev. He reaches behind his back, pulling out a bouquet. It's not an ordinary one, though. Yes, there are flowers. But there are also...

"Is that a comic book bouquet?"

"So they say." He's looking a little uncomfortable holding it out for me, so I take another few steps to grab it from him.

I stick my nose in the purple and yellow flowers, eyeing the plastic-wrapped comic books. It doesn't matter if I already own them. They're going into plastic sleeves and getting put on display. They're my new favorites. Just like Dev.

Georgia squeals from the kitchen doorway, startling me. I didn't even realize she was here. But she's standing next to Blake, and they're both smiling.

Dev holds out his arms, and I step into them, crushing the bouquet between us.

"Let me take that," Anna says, pulling it away from me and moving off to join our other friends.

"Hi," I say to him, tilting my head up. I hope he can't hear the uncertainty in my voice. It feels like this can't be real. "Am I dreaming?"

His hands swallow up my face. "I hope not."

"Dev, I need you to know..."

"Cece, I love you."

My heart bursts, flooding my body with warmth. My numb limbs tingle back to life, and my heart knits itself back together, stronger than before.

"I love you too, but."

He places a finger over my mouth. "No buts."

"I have to leave. I'm going to be gone. Who knows where. How is that going to work?"

"You're not going anywhere. And even if you did, it wouldn't matter. I already told your brother I would follow you anywhere. I would wait for you as long as it took. Even if it was years. I've never felt this kind of love in my life, so at first, I didn't understand it, but now. Now I know. It means my heart is yours now. It beats for you and only you."

Beau clears his throat. "Luckily, you don't have to go anywhere."

"What are you talking about?" I turn to him, confused.

"I talked to Dad. Worked things out. He's going to let you stay."

"Even if I'm dating Dev? Because that's not negotiable." This man has shown me more love and kindness in spite of everything he's been through than my father ever could. I'd choose him every time.

"Yes."

"What did you do, Beau?" I pin him under my gaze, trying out the twin ESP again, and failing. "Dad wouldn't just let all this slide."

"I told him I'd pay for you to stay here. To stay in school. I'd buy you another house if I had to. I would have. I've got access to grandfather's trust now. I would have blown it all for you. But he said no. He said he'd let you stay."

Those shadows under his eyes have deepened. Dealing with our father must have taken its toll on him.

"Thank you."

I shift out of Dev's arms to wrap mine around my brother. "Thank you so much."

"Always. Anything for my twin. After all, we did share a womb. Even though I'm pretty sure you were hogging your side."

I laugh around the warm tears leaking on his shirt. They're happy ones now.

"I don't think so. Now go back to your man. All I ask is you keep the PDA to a minimum around me. Because you're still my little sister and I can't handle seeing that."

"I'll try." I'm not making any promises, because when I'm near Dev, I crave his touch more than anything else in the world. And now that we've got each other, I'm never letting him go.

Beau gathers up my roommates, dragging them out of the house.

A comforting silence wraps around us after their voices disappear and the front door clicks shut.

"Hi again."

"Cece. I need you to know that I never should have hid you like that. You deserve to shine. I've never been that great with words, but the way you make me feel. It makes my heart ache in the best possible way. When you're not around, I can't stop thinking about you. And I want the entire world to know you're mine."

"Same. Don't worry, I'll tell them for you. I know you don't do social media."

His rare smile appears, and he leans down, cupping my cheeks between his.

Our lips meet in a kiss that promises a long future together. Full of love and comics. Hockey, and conventions.

I want him by my side through every second of it, because we both deserve this. This consuming love.

Chapter Thirty

Epilogue

Dev 1.5 Years Later

The sun hardly ever shines in Vancouver. But today, I had to put on shades to drive to Stanley Park. Driving always seems like a good idea until you have to find parking.

"A picnic in the park was a fantastic idea. I think this is the nicest day we've had since we moved here." She squeezes my hand, which eases the shaking a little.

I need her closer, so I slide my hand out of hers, pulling her in tight to my side. It's not easy to walk this way, but so worth it to feel her comforting weight pressed against my side. Knowing she's here with me makes me feel safer than I ever have.

This past year has been a wild ride. We made it to the second round of the playoffs before losing our spot to Edmonton. That hurt, but they've got a mature, well-balanced team, and we're in a rebuilding year. Everything about my first pro season was intense. The competition, the uncertainty, the travel. It's so much better with Cece able to come along for a lot of the away games. She's been doing freelance graphic design work while working on her graphic novel series with Anna. I couldn't be luckier to have a girlfriend with such a flexible job. I've seen how hard it is on some of the guys who have to constantly leave their wives, girlfriends, and children behind. I don't know if I could handle that.

But she's my home now. My constant. And she has been since the day we graduated. College already seems like a distant dream, but I'm thrilled that Beau's in town. He's only staying for a couple days before he has to head back for training camp, but what's the off season for if you can't spend it visiting old friends?

The closer we get to the picnic site, the faster my heart is pounding. Spots blur my vision, and my head gets fuzzy. I drag in a few deep breaths, trying to calm myself down.

She tilts her head up, catching my gaze. "What's up? You're quieter than usual. Is something wrong?"

My smiles come easier now. Especially when she's around. "No. Everything is perfect. You're perfect."

She giggles. "I'm not perfect."

"You're perfect to me."

She leans into me in a gentle shove.

I slip my hand into my pocket for maybe the hundredth time today.

The sun glinting off Beau's dark blond hair is the first hint that this isn't one of the quiet picnics for two we love to share.

"Is that?" She holds her hand up to shield her eyes from the sun, squinting. "Beau?"

And she's off, breaking into a sprint and hurling her arms around her brother.

She's talking at the speed of light, getting him all caught up on her graphic novel sales and asking him how he's been.

I catch up to them, tapping her on the shoulder. "Cece, look over there."

She follows the finger I'm pointing at the shoulder, falling silent.

There's a balloon arch leading into the shelter in every shade of pink and gold. And through it, her friends start emerging. Anna and Blake showed up, along with Georgia, all the way from her new home in New York City. Some of my current teammates and their significant others she's gotten friendly with. And a few more former members of the Lightning showed up. JJ's got a huge grin on his face, and his hair has gotten unruly since I last saw him.

Fear hits me when I turn to see tears chasing each other down her cheeks.

I lean down to whisper in her ear. "Cupcake. You okay?"

"Yes. They're happy tears. It's a lot though. I wasn't expecting this. It's not my birthday or anything."

As we've been chatting, I slowly shifted her toward the balloon arch until we're standing directly under it.

"No. It's not your birthday, but I hope you'll remember this day for the rest of your life."

Her eyes widen to impossible pools of deep blue, and her mouth drops open. "Dev?"

I drop to one knee in front of her, and all the chatter of our friends stops. Now the only sound are the birds singing to each other from the trees, and the wind rustling through the leaves.

"Cecelia Whitaker, will you marry me?"

Laughter wars with her tears, and she wipes them away with a shaky hand. "Yes. A million times, yes."

The ring is extravagant, but elegant. The large round stone in the center is set into a double band of tiny diamonds. As soon as I saw it, I knew it was the one. Its sparkle matches hers.

"Can I have your hand?"

"Right. Sounds important."

Everyone laughs. Then they start clapping and stomping as I slide the ring onto her finger. Her hands are soft and freshly painted with a coat of lilac polish.

"Now you need to kiss me," she says.

I brush her pale hair behind her little shell of an ear, and whisper for her alone. "Pushy, aren't you?"

"Yup. And that's why you love me."

"That is one of approximately a million reasons I love you. Give or take."

But I do need to seal the deal, and her rosy, pink lips are tempting me to do indecent things to them.

When our lips finally crash together, the noise from the small crowd swells. I'm second guessing my decision to invite everyone. I want her all to myself now.

My arms wrap around her waist, pulling her in close.

We explore each other's mouths like it's the first time. Every kiss between us feels like this, though. I never knew love could be like this.

We're both breathless when we break apart to join our friends.

Everyone wants a piece of us. Hugs and backslaps. Congratulations and suggestions. I'm here for it.

This is what a family is supposed to be like. Even my dad showed up. He brought along Meredith and her kids. It's still a work in progress. My relationship with them, but little by little they've snuck into my life. And it's been healing. Because when it comes right down to it. Your parents are just people, too. People who make mistakes and suffer losses. And sometimes they get past their own shit and learn to be better people. And sometimes they don't.

But when you have friends like ours, you're never alone. And together we're so much more than we were alone.

I finally catch back up to my love after we're both a little overwhelmed by all the affection.

"Cece. I will never stop loving you. You know that, right?" My hand finds its way to her back, rubbing small circles. I can't seem to stop touching her.

"I know. I love you too, Dev."

"Forever."

"Forever and a day."

"You're not going to let me win this one, are you?"

"Nope," she says.

"That's fine. I don't need to win. I already won the best prize of all."

And I dip down for one more kiss that tilts my world on its axis.

Need more hot hockey book boyfriend's in your life? It's finally time for Beau's story. If you love an enemies to lovers where both main characters are athletes, you're going to love **The Opposition**. Preorder now to be one of the first to read.

Two Friends, Two Days, One Bed. What could possibly go wrong? – If you haven't read Aspen and Jordan's story yet you can get it for free when you sign up for my newsletter. Author Nikki Jewell.

ALSO BY NIKKI JEWELL

The Lakeview Lightning Series

The Breakout: Book 0.5

Three days. Two best friends. One Bed. What could possibly go wrong? When Aspen drives his best friend Jordan to a romance book convention, he's not expecting the storm of the century to trap them in a bed and breakfast on the way home. But what happens when the chill of the snow can't cool the fiery heat between them? Available free when you sign up for my newsletter.

The Comeback: Book 1

In the game of love and hockey, second chances are rare, but Abby and Sebastian are about to get theirs. From childhood friends to heartbreak, their story is a testament to the power of forgiveness, and the courage to face one's fears. Available in ebook and discreet paperback.

The Red Line: Book 2

The Red Line takes you on a wild ride where hearts and skates collide. Natasha and Jackson's tale is a fiery mix of passion, and ice, challenging the rules of the game and love. Will they be able to keep things hot when their no-strings fling grows into something more? Available in ebook and discreet paperback.

The Game: Book 3

These two college seniors have some serious ex problems. And fake dating is the perfect solution. But when the steam between them gets too hot, they both might end up getting burned. Available in ebook and discreet paperback.

The Penalty: Book 4

Don't date his teammates. Cece had no intention of breaking her brother's one rule. Until the weekend that changed everything... This grumpy sunshine brother's best friend story is available in ebook and discreet paperback.

The Opposition: Book 5

Beau's story, coming 2025.

Acknowledgements

Dev has my entire heart. There are some characters that grow on you through a series, and he is one of them. Plus, Cece with all her chaotic vibes. I feel her in my soul. I'm so happy I was able to get their story out in the world and I hope you love them both as much as I do.

As always I must thank my supportive husband. From giving me time and space to hole up on a book deadline, to looking after our family and the house when I flit off to Vegas for an author conference, he's always there for me. I love you always and forever. Even when you leave me in my dreams. To my twins. Choose love and never stop dreaming. That's the best advice I can give you. I love you so much.

Steph always gets a shoutout. You're my bestie, and I love you always. From our amazing weekends, to hearing about your kickass plans you inspire me. Thanks for putting up with my brand of crazy.

Thanks to my editor Susan. It's important to find an editor that gets you and you fit the bill. From the nerd culture to the love for my characters, you're always there with insights and comments that make me laugh out loud. I can't wait to share Beau's story with you.

My cover designers knocked it out of the park once again. Taylor at Sweet 15 Designs LLC brought it with the hot manchests, and Hope Brown of Nerd Sisters Designs gave me some beautiful discreet covers.

And to Meg, my PA at Literary Inspired. You've helped me keep myself together over the last few releases and I appreciate you. I'm looking forward to foisting off more tasks on you in the year ahead, so be prepared.

To my ARC team. I can't express how much I love you guys. From the love for my Lakeview boys to the reviews that make me smile every time. You're the best, and I can't wait for more opportunities to connect with you.

Author Nation. What an experience. The connections were amazing. The insights were incredible, and the Thunder show was a highlight. Got to get in that spicy romance author "research". And to Alby. You're the bestest author friend I could have. It was so great to be able to reconnect with you at conference, and I can't wait to enjoy our dinner under the mushroom next year.

Nick at Alexxa's I promised you a shout out. Sorry I couldn't fit the helicopter down there joke in my book, but thanks for the laugh. And Daniel, hope you make it out of Vegas by next year.

ABOUT THE AUTHOR

Nikki Jewell is the queen of steamy romance and sipping coffee like it's her lifeblood, and she's always up for a new book boyfriend. Whether it's one she wrote or someone else's creation. She has a coffee addiction so legendary that she's even convinced her coffee beans to write her a thank-you note.

When she's not mainlining caffeine, Nikki is busy crafting tales of passion, love, and swoon-worthy heroes. She's especially fond of athletes, celebrities, and rock stars, so you'll find lots of those in her books. Her steamy romance books have been known to raise temperatures, set hearts aflutter, and make readers swoon in public.

When she's not writing, she escapes the confines of her writing cave to wander the great outdoors, communing with trees, birds, and squirrels that judge her for drinking coffee in the wilderness.

Nikki's secret identity as a romance writer is so well-guarded that her twin children don't know about her double life. But let's face it, what kid wants to read about their mom's romantic escapades? Probably none. Her husband is in on the secret and he's the real-life hero who keeps the inspiration flowing, even when her characters refuse to cooperate.

So, if you're in need of a fictional escape filled with passion, laughter, and maybe a few coffee stains, Nikki Jewell is your go-to romance guru. Just be sure to have a fresh brew on hand and monitor your heart rate—her stories have a tendency to make it race!

The Game is the third book in the five book Lakeview Lightning College Hockey Romance series. You can follow Nikki on Instagram, Threads, and TikTok @nikkijewell_books to keep up with her latest shenanigans. She's got a new Facebook page that she doesn't know what to do with as well.

instagram.com/nikkijewell_books

tiktok.com/@nikkijewell_books

Made in the USA
Coppell, TX
11 April 2025

48173109R00204